Shannon Hardsma

Here's to the UNDERDOGS!

Here's to the Underdogs! © 2019 Shannon Aardsma

All Rights Reserved

This is a work of fiction. While the settings may be based on real locations, the author has taken the liberty of making changes when necessary to fit the story. The characters are either entirely fictitious or loosely based on real people the author has encountered in her life, though names and other changes have been made.

The characters Luca and Joanna belong to writer Saige Ross. She was gracious enough to loan them to Shannon Aardsma for use in this book.

While several song artists are mentioned within the book, no specific titles or lyrics are directly referenced.

Cover Design by Megan McCullough

Formatting by Kozakura (www.fiverr.com/kozakura)

Sold and Distributed through Amazon

*Dedicated to Mark Hodgson
and Saige Ross*

Chapter 1: Ben

    The cacophony of voices and feet was lost to me as I traversed the crowded hallway, stopping at my locker. All I wanted was to get away from here, from this whole town, from everyone. Since that wouldn't be possible until after graduation, I simply shut out the noise around me.

    I mindlessly put in my locker combination, the shock of something cold hitting my face bringing me back to reality and making me aware of the laughter around me. My glasses shielded my eyes from most of the green substance that sprayed at me, but the paint that made its way past the barrier stung and clouded my vision.

    As my vision cleared, I saw who the culprit was. Darren and his companions stood around me, laughing at my planned misfortune. A glance at my locker made it clear what they'd done to cause my humiliation. The outside of my locker was lined with a thin tube of paint, rigged so that when the door opened, thus breaking the seal, it would spray the unsuspecting victim-- me.

    "Real mature, Darren," I said as I wiped the paint from my stinging eyes. I slammed my locker shut and hurried to the desolate bathroom.

Much scrubbing ensued before I managed to get the paint off and even then, it left patches of my face tinted green. The paint staining my shirt was more stubborn, unfortunately. I heaved a sigh, gripping the sides of the sink and glared at the empty, green eyes that stared back, hating who I saw. So many times, over the past several weeks and months I had thought about ending it all. Maybe I would finally work up the nerve to end my suffering.

As I gritted my teeth, the door opened and someone walked in.

"Ben? You ok?" Her soft voice calmed me. She placed her hand on my shoulder and looked at me in the mirror. As always, her auburn-orange hair was perfect.

Colette and I had known each other since I pulled her hair in Kindergarten. She got back at me by cutting off my ponytail (yes, I had a ponytail at the age of five), and we had been best friends ever since.

"You're going to be late to class," she continued.

"What are you doing in here? You're going to get in trouble."

Her beauty was out of place, surrounded by not-so-pristine urinals and stained sinks. As she was standing just behind me, her flowery perfume greeted my nose and was a welcome difference from the usual stink of the bathroom.

"Who, me? Nah." She smiled, then her smile quirked into a smirk. "Hey, I like the green hair look."

"What?" I looked in the mirror once more and now noticed the green in my dark hair.

Colette chuckled. "Let's go, hmm?"

Still discouraged, I nodded and followed her. She easily rested her arm on my shoulder as her combat boots made her only about an inch shorter than my height of five-nine. Around most people, I was self-conscious about my height, but Colette and I had been friends for so long that I didn't even think about it.

Colette walked with me until we came to her classroom, then I continued on alone. Although I walked into class a few minutes late, Mr. Furges didn't say anything. He simply nodded toward my empty seat in the back of the classroom. Ignoring the looks from my classmates as I weaved through the rows, I took my seat quickly, and class resumed.

Finally, the morning was over, and it was time for lunch-- the best part of the day aside from Physics class. I found Colette's table and sat across from her. She dipped her spoon into the goop they told us was food, then tipped her spoon to let it slowly drop off.

She expressed her distaste for the school's lunch option with an unemotional, "Yum". Then she spotted my lunch and promptly stole the apple from my tray, taking a large bite.

"Would you like a bite?"

Colette gave me a look that made it clear my sarcasm had not been appreciated. Taking another bite of the apple before returning it to my tray, she asked, "So. Any plans for after school?"

"Working on the Physics project."

"What project?"

"You know. The big one?" I stared at her intensely for emphasis.

"The one due at the end of the year? Ben, you could do that in a day easily."

"Well, of course. You're looking at pure genius here," I smirked. *If only*, I thought.

"Then why work on it now?"

I shrugged, finishing our shared apple. "I wanna get it over with."

Her long, orange curls bouncing as she shook her head, Colette replied, "If you put half the energy into history that you put into Physics, Ms. Bobbin would like you a whole lot more.

"History is dumb."

If looks could kill, this moment in the lunchroom would have been my last as Colette glared at me. Unfortunately, looks *don't* kill, and we presently moved onto a new topic as we ate.

Too soon, the bell rang. I took both of our trays and disposed of them, then caught up with Colette. We had history together, so we got our books from our lockers and hurried to our class. This was one class I didn't want to be late for since the teacher, Ms. Bobbin, already did not like me.

Colette and I sat in the back of the classroom, but Ms. Bobbin still found me, and her eyes bored into my skull. I stared at my paper and pretended to be working. History class couldn't end soon enough.

Yet, it eventually did. Time for the final class of the day: Gym. If there was any class I hated more than history, it was gym class. I was rubbish at both. Alas, both were required. So, I headed to the locker room to change. Guess who I ran into.

"Sup, Connley. Dodgeball today. Ready to get pounded?" Darren and his minions cornered me at my gym locker.

I was late enough to have avoided everyone else, but Darren had waited.

"Do you ever use sentences longer than five words?"

"Don't get smart." He shoved a massive finger in my face. "Your girlfriend won't be saving you this time."

"What are you talking about?"

Darren shrugged. "Didn't see her in the gym, and you're the last one Coach is waiting for."

Thoughts were running through my mind, but I pushed them aside. I had my own troubles to worry about -- Darren for one -- without clouding my mind with where Colette could be.

"She's not my girlfriend."

"Whatever. See you in the gym where you better be prepared to go home on a stretcher."

"If I were on a stretcher, wouldn't I be going to the hospital?"

"Save it, Connley. The point is, you'll be hurting."

With that amazing comeback, he tromped out of the locker room, his buddies high-fiving him as they followed.

"Idiots," I mumbled. There was no way I could get out of this useless class and escape my impending doom, so I changed into shorts and entered the gymnasium.

Coach spotted me immediately. "It's about time, Connley. Hurry up and join the others on the baseline," he bellowed. "Now that everyone has arrived, we can get started."

I loped over and lined up next to my classmates, none of whom seemed exceedingly glad to see me or even gave any sign that they noticed me. Coach counted us off, and we jogged to our respective sides of the gym. Darren, on the other team, of course, eyed me hungrily. A wicked grin spread across his face, making his otherwise pleasing features appear ugly. I gulped, my heart pounding in my chest though I was standing perfectly still. Coach blew the whistle, and, as the other kids ran to the middle line to snatch a ball, I backed near the wall and kept my eye on Darren.

HERE'S TO THE UNDERDOGS!

I may not have been any good at running or making baskets or throwing a dodgeball accurately, but I could dodge-- and that's what I did. Dodgeball after dodgeball whizzed past my head and slammed into the plywood wall behind me, but not a single one touched me. My task of dodging became even easier once I'd acquired a stray ball with which to deflect those aimed at me.

One by one, the other kids were gotten out until it was just me and Darren. My defensive ball had been knocked out of my hands by an impressively forceful shot, and I was left without a weapon to use against my nemesis. Eyes fixed on Darren, I slowly crouched down and picked up a dodgeball. Today was the day I was going to win. I was finally going to be more than an outcast nerd. I would be the one to beat Darren.

Darren put his ball under his arm and cracked his knuckles. Holding it once more, he turned the sphere over in his giant hands. He took aim and hurled the ball at my face. I knew I had to act fast before he grabbed another ball and threw it. Time seemed to slow down as I jumped backward out of the way of the red blur barreling toward me and threw my own blue projectile. I felt my dodgeball roll off of my fingers and closed my eyes as his ball flew past my head. There was dead silence as I landed on the ground on my back, and I figured I must have missed him. Then again, I wasn't being pummeled by dodgeballs. Slowly, I opened my eyes and looked over to where Darren had been standing when he threw his ball at me. To my surprise, he wasn't standing there. He was crumpled on the ground, his hand over his eye. An unbelieving grin spread across my face as Coach rushed over to Darren and looked at his eye, blocking my view of Darren's face. The rest of the kids stared in silence, looking from Darren to me and back to Darren. I was still finding it hard to believe that I had actually hit Darren when Coach ruined my happy moment.

"Connley! You're benched for the rest of the period!"

"For what? Actually participating in gym class for once?"

"No, for the headshot."

I looked at Darren. The left half of his face was beet red, a bruise just forming on his cheekbone. I suppressed a smile and looked back at Coach. "You can't be serious! If I hadn't dodged every one of *his* shots, my head would have been knocked clean off! And it's not like I *tried* to hit him in the eye. I just threw the ball!"

"That's it, Connley! You have detention for arguing!"

When I stopped to think about what I was saying, I could generally reason myself out of predicaments that arose in gym class. Coach wasn't unreasonable when you respected him, but give him an ounce of undeserved trouble, and you were done for.

Coach took a breath to calm down, eyes softening.

"Just get cleaned up and make your way to detention, Connley. The day's over anyway."

Begrudgingly, I obeyed. When I got to detention, three other students were already there. I didn't recognize any of them, but a few minutes later the door opened and a fourth walked in.

"Great. What are *you* doing here?" I asked.

"I should ask you the same question. You never get in trouble." Tony took the seat next to me.

"I hit Darren in the eye."

Tony threw his head back and laughed. "Yeah, right! That's a good one. What did you really do?"

"Just what I said. We played dodgeball for gym class, and I hit Darren in the eye with the ball."

"Respect, little brother. But you know he'll get you back for that. Probably today."

"And I suppose you aren't going to be around to help."

"No way. Josh and I are going to the arcade." He leaned back, arms behind his head as though he hadn't a care in the world.

"Did Josh get his car fixed?"

"Nope."

When he didn't continue, I prodded, "So, how are you going to get there?"

"We're borrowing your jeep."

"Tony! You can't do that!" I pinched the bridge of my nose in frustration as my face flushed with anger. Before I could tear Tony's head off, the detention manager arrived, and I was relieved to find that it was Mr. Furges. He sat down at the desk and took out a book. Without looking at any of us, he began speaking.

"Alright, I want a nice, quiet detention. Get out your homework or a book. I would suggest homework, Mr. Connley."

Mr. Furges looked right at Tony over the wire rim of his glasses, then noticed me.

"Ben? Why are you here?"

"Because of an accident in gym class."

"Oh." Mr. Furges' eyes widened. "Don't tell me *you* did that to Darren?"

"Yes, sir." I was aware of the eyes of the other students on me as Mr. Furges pointed this out.

He laughed. "My, my, good job, Connley." Continuing to chuckle, he turned back to his book, then addressed all of us. "Oh, and don't forget to turn in your phones."

HERE'S TO THE UNDERDOGS!

A collective groan went out. We each placed our phones on his desk, then returned to our seats. Two of the other students got out their homework, one got out a book, and Tony, still leaning carelessly back in his seat, ignored Mr. Furges' suggestion and closed his eyes. It appeared that his plan was to sleep through detention. Tony got held back last year because of his slacking off on his schoolwork, and so far this year, the trend had continued. If he failed again, that failure would probably end his school career.

I pulled my Rubik's Cube out of my backpack, solving it three different ways before boredom set in, and I gazed out the window at the clear blue sky instead. A tiny figure flew in front of the window and looked at me as it hovered. In the afternoon sunlight, the small creature's ruby breast glinted iridescently, colors changing with every sudden, jerky movement. Hummingbirds had always fascinated me. They were tiny, yet incredibly complex. Such complexity made macroevolution questionable to me at times.

Tony smacked me in the back of the head, interrupting my thoughts.

"Ow! What the heck, man!"

I rubbed the aching spot on my head as Tony pointed to the clock. The half-hour detention was over, and the other students were hurriedly retrieving their phones and exiting the classroom. Tony followed them, leaving only me and Mr. Furges. Leisurely, I walked up to his desk to take my phone.

"Is everything alright, Ben?"

"Of course, Mr. Furges."

"Do you want me to drive you home?"

It sounded like an innocent question, but I knew the reasoning behind it: Darren.

"That would just be putting off the inevitable, Sir."

Mr. Furges frowned. "I suppose you're right. I'd like to see Darren get just retribution for his actions." He paused. "You could always learn to fight."

"That'll be the day," I scoffed. "Have you seen me? No way could I ever take on Darren and his cronies."

"You might surprise yourself. I believe in you, Benjamin. You can do anything you set your mind to."

"Anything academic maybe. But when it comes to anything physical, I'm just not cut out for that kind of thing."

Mr. Furges shook his head. "Good luck, Connley." He handed me my phone, grabbed his book, and walked out of the classroom.

Chapter 2: Colette

"I can't believe I had to pick you up from school. What were you thinking?" I reprimanded my sister.

Morgan sat in the passenger's seat, staring out the window and silently mocking me.

"Morgan! This is serious! What are Mom and Dad going to say? You got suspended!"

"It's not that big of a deal."

"Really? Because to me, blowing up a classroom is a pretty big deal."

"I didn't blow up a classroom. My experiment exploded. There's a difference."

"A difference that doesn't matter because you still got suspended, and you are going to be in big trouble when we get home." Glancing over at Morgan, I saw her wipe a tear off her cheek. I sighed, collecting myself. "I'm sorry. I'll talk to Mom and Dad and try to calm them down. I know the experiment was an accident."

We rode in silence the rest of the way home. I had never seen Morgan this upset over anything. She was only thirteen years old, and yet I had not seen her cry in six years, though there must have been times that she had. I knew she wasn't as tough as she tried to appear, yet it still surprised me that she was this distressed. Hoping that I could convince our parents to go easy on her, I pulled into the driveway. Morgan ran up to her room immediately. Our parents weren't home yet, but I expected our mother to be in about ten minutes, and I worked on homework until I heard a car door shut outside, and my youngest sisters ran into the kitchen.

"Hi, Colette!" Ruby yelled.

"Why are you home so early?" Sapphire asked as she hopped into my lap.

"I got out of school early," I answered, running my fingers through her curly, blonde hair.

"Ok." Sapphire climbed off my lap, and she and Ruby ran to the living room.

I shook my head at the twins. They always had so much energy and were the craziest five-year-oldsold's I knew. They were identical except for their hair-- Sapphire's was blonde while Ruby's was even redder than mine. Both had blue eyes like our dad.

As I turned back to my homework, Mom walked into the kitchen, laden with groceries. I hopped up and helped her put them away.

"Thank you, Colette. What are you doing home so early?"

I played with a curl, then turned to her and answered, "I had to pick Morgan up from school."

Searching my mother's calm face for any signs of anger proved fruitless. She was always so hard to read-- not like Dad. I always knew what my dad was thinking by his expression and his deep blue eyes, but with my mother, it was impossible to tell. Not even her soft, brown eyes held any clues.

"Why did she get sent home?" Her voice was even but stern.

"A science experiment gone wrong." I looked down at the counter.

"Colette. What are you not telling me?"

"Morgan got suspended," I mumbled.

"What?" She moved toward the stairs, but I stopped her.

"Mom! Please go easy on her. She's really upset about this," I pleaded.

She pressed her lips in a flat line and nodded understandingly. "Alright. I'll hear what she has to say." Then she turned and walked up the stairs.

I tried to do my homework, but I couldn't concentrate. Dad wouldn't be home for another few hours, and I wanted to talk to him. Deciding that I wouldn't have any luck getting my homework done before then, I put my books back in my backpack and headed out the door to walk to Ben's house.

Chapter 3: Ben

Slowly, I made my way home. Unfortunately, I was almost to the alley where my fate awaited me. Why didn't I go home a different way to avoid this place of shattered dreams and bones, you ask? I couldn't. Normally, I would have taken the long way home-- a route that added an hour to my journey, but Aunt Michelle was used to my arriving home late. Unfortunately, for the past week that route had been closed off due to road work. So, the only way home was past the alley. A small glimmer of hope glowed in my heart. Maybe Darren wasn't *that* mad and would leave me alone. But I knew that was wishful thinking. I took a deep breath and headed straight toward my doom. I was almost past the alley and was beginning to think that maybe my hope wasn't purely wishful thinking when a rough hand grabbed my backpack and pulled me into the alley, throwing me against the brickwork of the apartment building that made up one of the alley's walls. I dropped my backpack and looked past the goon at Darren.

"Whatever you're selling, I'm not interested," I quipped. My joke was rewarded with a punch to the stomach. I doubled over, folding my arms across my stomach in an attempt to stop the pain. When I was able to breathe again, I stood back up slowly, an arm still wrapped around my middle and gripping my side. I held out my other hand toward Darren.

"What happened in gym class was an accident, I swear."

Darren snorted at my pathetic attempt to avoid any more violence and nodded to his buddies. I closed my eyes, ready for what was to come. After taking a few more hits to the gut and a solid punch to the eye, I fell to the ground. I put my arms over my face and tucked my knees up as well as I could despite the pain. Darren's companions didn't let up. As their sneakers met my ribs, it took all my concentration to not blackout. Finally, they stopped, and I felt Darren's breath on my ear as he knelt next to me and whispered, "Think twice before you mess with me next time." To help the warning set in, he kicked me in the ribs one last time.

I sat up against the alley wall and spat out some blood. "Why don't you finish me off?"

That got Darren's attention. He loomed over me. "What are you talking about?"

"Just end it. A couple good hits to the head should do it. Better yet, have that one stab me." I gestured to a red-haired goon who had a Bowie knife strapped to his hip.

Darren snorted. "Why would I help you do what you've been too chicken to do yourself?"

With that, he and his crew left the alley, snickering.

I sat up against the wall until the pain subsided a little, then grabbed my backpack and pushed myself to my feet. The movement sending a new wave of nausea over me, I leaned against the wall for a moment. My right side was scratched up and bleeding from scraping against the pavement with each kick. Each breath I took racked my body with pain.

Ok, I thought. *I just won't breathe.*

In no hurry, I walked out of the alley and limped home, hunched to ease the pain. I had never been more thankful that I could sneak into my room unseen by climbing the oak tree, stepping onto the roof, and then stealing in through my bedroom window. Climbing the oak tree had never been this difficult though: my footing slipped several times, the bark scratched my hands, and every move I made caused searing pain to shoot through my gut, compounded by the throbbing in my head.

I collapsed on my bed as soon as I had made it through the window, careful not to glance in the mirror hanging from my open closet door. I didn't want to know how terrible I looked; I just wanted to sleep the pain away.

My room was small and cozy. I left my window unencumbered so as to allow easy access to my room from the outside on just such occasions as this. The bareness of the window was accentuated by the clutter along the rest of the wall, my dresser taking up the entire left section from the window to the corner, and my nightstand and bunk bed sufficiently filling up the rest of the wall on the right. My closet, stuffed full of what was mostly "junk", opened up just off the end of my bed on the adjacent wall. The third wall housed the door to my room, as well as a movie and game shelf; and the fourth wall was plastered, floor to ceiling, with posters.

A knock at the door interrupted my sleep. I knew it was either Colette or my aunt, and either knowing the condition I was in would cause me unwanted hassle at the moment.

Maybe if she thinks I'm asleep she'll go away, I thought as I turned my head to face the wall. Somehow, lying on my stomach caused the least amount of pain.

HERE'S TO THE UNDERDOGS!

I heard the door open and the sound of Colette's boots as she walked over to my bed. She probably would have left, except I forgot that the right side of my shirt, the side facing away from the wall, was blood-stained.

"Benjamin, I know you're awake. What happened to you?" she asked, calm as ever as she sat on the edge of my bed.

I sighed and rolled over to reveal my black eye.

Colette's eyes widened, a gasp escaping her lips. She gently touched my cheekbone just under my eye.

"Who did this? It was Darren, wasn't it? Just wait till I get my hands on him." She started to get up, but I grabbed her hand.

"Please, don't do anything. I'm ok. Honest." I tried for a smile but probably failed miserably.

Colette studied me. "Stand up."

I complied, guessing at what was coming.

"Take your shirt off. I know you have more than a black eye."

I winced in pain as I pulled my shirt over my head to reveal what I had been too scared to look at myself. Colette gasped again and covered her mouth.

"Stay here."

Unsure of why Colette was so surprised and worried, I looked down at my torso and then in the mirror. Out of three years of getting into quarrels and fights with Darren, I had never looked this bad. Blood had crusted over the scratches on my right side, and my stomach was covered in black and purple splotches. I was almost more black and blue than tan.

I sat on my bed as I waited for Colette to return. I'd been harassed by Darren and his crew many times before, both in and out of school; I'd even been given a few black eyes by Darren, but never had I been beaten to this extent. Whether I managed to avoid such a fate because I had

Colette with me or because I had outsmarted my nemesis, I'd always had a way out.

A few minutes later, Colette returned with a first aid kit and closed the door behind her. Silently, she cleaned my scraped-up side and bandaged it, then sat on the bed next to me. She looked over at me for a moment, lips pursed, then wrapped me in a hug. I held back tears as I wrapped my arms around her.

"Thank you," I whispered.

"Always."

I pulled out of the hug and looked away.

"Something has to be done about this. Maybe my dad-"

"Colette. It's ok. I'm used to it." We both knew I was referring to more than Darren. I hadn't had the best father-figure growing up either.

"But you shouldn't have to be!" Trying to calm down after her outburst, she let out a breath, her green eyes studying me, traces of sadness in them, yet clearly looking for a way to cheer us both up. "Want to come over for dinner?"

"Yeah. That'd be nice."

I grabbed a clean shirt and headed to her house, ignoring the pain that remained despite her doctoring.

* * *

"Thanks for letting me stay for dinner."

"Of course, Benjamin. It's always a pleasure to have you," Colette's mom smiled at me.

Ruby laid her head on my arm. "Can he live here?"

Colette's mom reasoned, "Ruby, don't you think Ben should stay at his own house?"

"Nope! He should stay with us."

Sapphire laid her head on my other arm and nodded in agreement, the movement against my arm snarling her hair.

I looked to Colette for help, and she laughed then told the girls to pick their heads up and finish their dinner if they wanted dessert.

"Why do you *always* sit between them? This ends up happening every time," Colette reminded me.

"I know… I just can't say no to them when they look at me with their big, blue eyes."

Colette shook her head. "I feel sorry for your future wife if you ever have a daughter. She is going to be spoiled rotten."

"I'm going to marry Ben!" Sapphire proclaimed.

"No, I am!" Ruby shouted.

The two got into an argument over who was *really* going to marry me, and I was stuck in the middle of it with no idea what to do. Their argument was interrupted when we heard the front door open.

"Daddy!" they squealed in unison, running from the table.

Mr. Tance walked into the dining room a minute later, a twin in each arm.

"Benjamin. Good to see you again." Mr. Tance put the girls down and shook my hand, that inviting smile of his creating wrinkles around his eyes. But then the smile faded and was replaced by worry. "What happened to your eye, son?"

I was taken aback by the word. *Son.* It had been a while since anyone had called me that.

"I, uh, tripped."

He raised his eyebrows and stared down at me, though not harshly. The look in his eyes was kind and concerned, the way Colette's eyes got when she was worried about me.

"That is the worst lie I have ever heard. I expect more from you, being the smart kid that you are."

Mrs. Tance cleared her throat and looked at her husband then at Colette's four younger siblings: the twins plus Morgan, and the other "man" of the house, Marcus. Mr. Tance nodded in understanding, smiling as he sat down to eat his dinner.

After dinner, Morgan helped Mrs. Tance clear the table, and Mr. Tance led me to his office and closed the door.

"Now. Who did this?"

"Who? I don't know what you mean."

"Benjamin." He rubbed his forehead. "I know some bully is behind this, I just don't know who. Tell me. And don't even think about lying. I'm a lawyer, remember? I know how to catch a lie."

I looked away but knew that denying the truth any longer was pointless. "Yes, Sir. I don't know the names of the kids who did the physical beating-up, but Darren was behind it."

"Darren? I thought he graduated."

"He was held back along with Tony."

"Of course, he was. He's a fool who thinks grinding others into the ground and becoming more dominant will make up for his lack of brains. Are you hurt anywhere other than your eye?"

I thought about lying and saying 'no', but I couldn't lie to him again after everything he'd done for me and my family this past month: pulling strings so my adoptive siblings stayed in the family, helping Aunt Michelle get settled, and he'd always been a better father to me than my own.

"Yes, Sir." I pulled up my shirt to reveal the worst of what was unbandaged.

"Oh, my."

"It looks worse than it feels," I said as I let my shirt fall, recovering my marred stomach.

"I don't believe that for a second. I'm going to see what I can do about Darren."

"Please don't, Mr. T," I protested. "I can avoid him for the rest of the school year, and then he'll be out of school and unable to bother anyone else."

It took some convincing, but Mr. Tance finally agreed to at least wait. If no more problems were caused, there would be no reason to press the matter.

When we were agreed, Mr. Tance and I exited his study and rejoined everyone else in the living room where we found Mrs. Tance and Colette trying to contain the twins while Marcus and Morgan sabotaged their efforts. As soon as she saw me, Colette ran over to me and grabbed my arm.

"We need your help getting them to bed. Please, you're always able to get them to bed when you're here!"

"Alright," I chuckled. "I'll help."

I ran to Sapphire and picked her up upside down– a mistake as it caused a surge of pain through my abdomen. Disregarding the throbbing in my side, I continued the bedtime procedure, avoiding Marcus as he grabbed at my ankle from his hideout behind the couch.

"Marcus! I thought we were a team!"

"But I fear Morgan more than I fear you!"

At the age of fifteen, Marcus was two years older than Morgan and a good bit taller than her, but she scared him to death. She scared me a little, too, for that matter. She scared just about everyone except her mom.

Sapphire giggled and squirmed, but I held onto her and cornered Ruby, aware that Morgan was sneaking up on me from behind. I threw

Ruby over my shoulder (gently, of course, though it caused another spike in the pain I was feeling) and dodged Morgan as she leaped for my back. I managed to flip Sapphire so she was right-side-up and tickled the girls as I carried them over to their father. Everyone had enjoyed the show except for Morgan who was dismayed that her plot had been foiled. Mr. Tance gladly took the girls from me.

"No! We want Ben to tuck us in!" Ruby complained.

Sapphire stretched her arms out to me, and I looked back at Mrs. Tance, then to Mr. Tance towering in front of me. Mr. Tance laughed.

"Alright, girls. If Ben is willing, he can tuck you in. But you have to promise to go right to sleep."

"We promise!" they cried in unison, and Sapphire jumped into my arms.

I succeeded in carrying both girls to their room, and, as I was tucking them in, Sapphire reached up and gently touched my black eye. I took her hand and kissed it, then pulled the covers up to her chin.

"I love you, Ben."

"I love both of you." I kissed each girl's forehead then turned off the light and went back downstairs to rejoin the others. Mr. Tance met me at the bottom of the stairs.

"How do you do it, Benjamin?"

"I have eight younger siblings, Sir. If you lived in my house, you had to learn to put them to bed if you wanted to survive," I smiled.

Mr. Tance chuckled. "I suppose that would be necessary."

"Well, it's been a great evening, but I should get home." *Not to mention, my ribs are killing me after all of that.*

"I'll drive you," Colette offered, and I was happy to accept.

Chapter 4: Ben

Saturday. Every sane student's favorite day of the week. Since Aunt Michelle had taken Alice, Garrett, and Joey — my only younger siblings still living at the house — out shopping today, I was able to sleep in until ten o'clock. Still in my pajama pants, I went downstairs into the kitchen to make myself pancakes. I looked out the window over the sink at the garage to see if my car that Tony had stolen was back. It wasn't. At least I wouldn't have to make that bone-head any pancakes.

As I rounded the counter, the corner caught me in the stomach, and I folded over in pain.

"Stupid counter," I mumbled.

"Talking to yourself?" Colette asked through the screen door. "That's never a good sign."

The door squeaked as she swung it open, then closed with a crash.

"I was actually talking to the counter."

"That's not really better. How you doin' today?"

"A bit better. Want a pancake?"

I lit the burner on the stove and scooped some batter into the pan.

HERE'S TO THE UNDERDOGS!

"Do you even have to ask?"

"You're right. And I'll put chocolate chips in as well."

"My favorite."

I handed Colette a plate with a single pancake and was getting the syrup out of the fridge when the screen door squeaked and crashed again.

"Morgan! Marcus! What are you two doing here?" Colette demanded.

"We hid in your backseat," Morgan explained. "Hi, Ben. Whoa, what happened to you?" Morgan tactfully asked, noting the bruises on my exposed torso.

Before I had a chance to answer, Marcus burst out, unphased by my bruises, "Pancakes! I love pancakes!"

"Would you like some, Marcus?" I asked begrudgingly.

Marcus nodded vigorously while Morgan shrugged indifferently.

"I guess I'm making pancakes for everyone. Marcus, would you like to help me make more?"

Marcus gladly agreed to help, and soon we had a stack of pancakes, loads of bacon, and a pan full of cheesy scrambled eggs. We devoured our feast faster than we had prepared it, then sat around the table wondering what to do with our school-free day.

"Beach?" Marcus suggested, wanting to take advantage of the oddly warm weather this week.

I looked down at my bruises, then up at Marcus. "Really?"

"Why not? Just wear a shirt."

"Like a normal person does," Morgan mumbled.

Slowly, I turned to face her. "At the beach? Guys don't normally wear shirts at the beach!"

I hadn't noticed that Colette had left the kitchen, but now she came downstairs with one of my muscle-tanks.

"Just wear this. It's beachy enough." She tossed it to me.

"Fine," I surrendered with a huff. "Just give me a minute to change."

After changing into some shorts as well as the shirt Colette had picked out, I hurried to the Tance's house. Colette and her siblings had left beforehand to change, and we now piled into her lavender Corvette Convertible that she had gotten for her sixteenth birthday last year— *stupid rich parents.* Apparently, Morgan's grounding for getting suspended didn't start until Monday as she accompanied us.

We split up upon arriving at the beach, Colette taking Marcus and Morgan to find a suitable spot on the sand to set up while I sneaked off to get ice cream for everyone from the ice cream truck. I retrieved the cool snacks, then scanned the beach for my motley crew and quickly spotted Marcus chasing seagulls. Shaking my head, I walked towards him and was glad to locate Colette not far off.

"What is he doing?" I asked Colette as I jerked my thumb toward Marcus after distributing the ice cream.

"I don't even question it anymore. Morgan and I found a good spot over there to set up." Colette pointed to a sunny area that was relatively vacant of people where she and Morgan had already laid out their towels and propped up a colorful beach umbrella. Morgan was lying on her towel, her nose stuck in a book. Leaving Marcus behind, Colette and I joined her.

"Morgan, you're not going to swim?"

Without looking up from her book, she replied, "The water is too cold, and there are people." Her long chocolate hair was pulled back from her slightly-chubby face into a ponytail, and large sunglasses hid her dark brown eyes. She had positioned her towel so as to be under the protection of the umbrella as much as possible.

I shrugged and laid out my towel in the sun. "What about you, Colette?"

"I want to soak up the sun first." After pulling her sheer bathing suit cover-up off and stuffing it in her beach-bag, she stretched out on her towel and dug her toes into the burning sand. As always, she was modestly dressed, her high-waisted bottoms nearly reaching the red tankini top to cover her middle.

"You two are officially boring. I think I'll join Marcus in tormenting innocent seagulls."

"Have fun, Sweetie, and play nice with the other kids," Colette said without cracking a smile. I contemplated kicking sand at her, but there was the possibility that I might get Morgan by mistake, and I didn't feel like dying at her hands.

Marcus practically inhaled his ice cream, and then he and I resumed running through the small flocks of seagulls. After chasing seagulls for a few minutes, I decided to take a walk along the beach. The water was refreshing as it wrapped around my feet, then got pulled back out into the ocean. As a child, I was always fascinated by the ocean. My mom used to bring me, and as the water receded, we would look for the best shells we could find for her to use in her jewelry-making business. Tony had somehow convinced me that the water was a giant hand coming to grab my feet, and, as the water crept farther up the beach, I would run screaming to my mom who would scoop me up in her arms. She would then run to the edge of the water and scold it, sending it back to the sea where it belonged. It always obeyed her. Once it was safe, I would squirm out of her arms to find the perfect shell before the evil hand returned. I grew out of that eventually, but every time I came to the beach, I thought about her and those happy times.

HERE'S TO THE UNDERDOGS!

I was so lost in thought that I wasn't paying any attention to where I was walking until it was too late.

"Oof!" I ran into something, then heard a small splash. I looked down, and the girl was staring back up at me.

"I am so sorry. Let me help you." I grabbed her hands and helped her stand, her hazel eyes staring directly into mine.

"Thanks. Even though it was you who knocked me over in the first place."

"Sorry about that. I was…distracted. Are you ok?"

She nodded, tossing her long, dark, and now wet braid over her shoulder. I wanted to say something, but the words all caught in my throat, and before I got the chance, she smiled and walked past me. As I looked back at her, she quickly turned her head away, making her braid swing to reveal a star tattoo at the base of her neck with two of the points fading out to become wings. I watched her walk away and rejoin her friends, laughing and splashing in the water together.

"Earth to Ben."

I spun around and was facing Colette. "What?"

"What are you staring at?"

"Nothing," I blurted out.

Colette scanned my face skeptically, then shrugged. "What are you doing?"

"Just thinking." I knelt down and picked up a smooth, perfect shell, turning it over between my fingers as I thought of my mother. Colette crouched next to me.

"She'd like that one." After a pause, "Have you heard from your dad recently?" I shook my head as I washed the shell. We stood and kept walking.

HERE'S TO THE UNDERDOGS!

"Where do you think he is this time?"

"Who knows. A rainforest in South America. A jungle in Africa. Mountains in Europe," I answered, a bitter sarcasm present in my words. "The point is, he could be anywhere."

"Wherever he is, I'm sure he'll be back soon."

"Mhmm."

"You know what? Forget about him. Let's enjoy this weekend." She slipped her arm through mine, and we joined Marcus and Morgan in building a sandcastle. All day as we gathered sand and mud for the castle then for burying Colette up to her neck, and we even survived an incident with Jeremy, Colette's ex, a thought tugged at the back of my mind. A picture, really. The girl with the hazel eyes and star tattoo.

* * *

All weekend I was haunted by the unnamed girl. I felt like I knew her, but couldn't figure out why. On Monday, I drove my Wrangler to school rather than walking, and at every stoplight I scoured the cars next to me, hoping to see her seated in one of them. At school, I scanned the crowded hallways looking for her. By lunchtime, I had had no luck.

"Hey, Ben. I have hardly seen you all day," Colette said as she sat across from me. "Sorry. I've been...preoccupied."

I had also forgotten to bring my own lunch. I stared down at my bowl of mush and could almost swear it looked back up at me.

Pushing the tray away from me, I stated, "I'm not that hungry today."

"Yeah." Colette put her fork down and stacked out trays. "Me neither. School lunch is never very appetizing. Although… I think you may have a different reason for not being hungry." A sly smile spread across her face.

"What are you talking about?"

"Are you still thinking about that girl?"

"What girl?" I knew I must be blushing by now.

"Oh, come on. You know who. The girl at the beach." She wiggled her eyebrows.

Knowing there was no point in denying it, I answered, "I feel like I know her. Or at least should. I don't know why though. I haven't been able to stop thinking about her all weekend."

Colette made some sort of squealing sound that I guess sounded relatively human. "My little Benny has a crush!"

"Shh! And no, I don't. This is different. It's— I don't know what it is, but—"

"I don't care what you say, you at least have a small crush on this girl."

I shook my head in resignation. There was no point in arguing with Colette about this so I gave up, disposing of our trays before walking with Colette to history class.

Chapter 5: Colette

Every Monday, Ben and I went to his house after school to study. His rambunctious younger siblings were gone to the park with Michelle by the time we arrived, so the house was quiet. It was almost eerie. After Ben's mom died, his dad took off and had not been heard from since. Six of the seven children that Ben's mom had adopted — Chase was old enough to live on his own — were adopted by relatives to save them from going back into foster care, and Michelle had come to Westbrooke to look after Ben and his four siblings who still lived at home: Tony, Alice, Garrett, and baby Joey. His mom had died nearly three months ago giving birth to little Joey, yet I still hated going to his house when it was empty and silent. The gray exterior and hollow interior were haunting and unnaturally quiet. When the house was filled with noisy children, it seemed happy; now that they were gone, it was like a graveyard.

After making popcorn as a snack, we sat on the couch and laid out our history notes first. "Why do we have to take history?"

"Do we have to go over this every week, Benjamin? History is important. It connects us to our nation's past, and, if we pay attention to it, we can avoid making mistakes that have already been made."

"But no one ever learns from the mistakes. Besides, history books are biased and never tell the whole truth."

"Oh, no. We are not getting into that. Just open your notebook."

He sighed, but flipped through his notebook to the previous week's notes. Ben was smart, but he hated history and thought of it as a waste of time and, therefore, didn't study it unless I made him. When it came to Chemistry though, he was a whiz; and for me, that was a very good thing since I didn't understand a word of it.

We studied for about half an hour, Ben being uncharacteristically quiet, before we heard a car drive up the long, shaded driveway.

Ben looked up and processed audibly, "No one should be home. Aunt Michelle has the littles, and Tony is at basketball practice."

He got up from the couch and walked into the kitchen which was out of my line of sight— something I'd always disliked about the layout of his house. The screen door slammed shut, and there was silence for a long time. When I could stand it no longer, I strode into the kitchen but stopped in my tracks when I saw who it was. Finally, Ben spoke.

"Dad? What are you doing here?"

There was anger in his voice, but his face was riddled with sadness and pain.

"I thought no one would be home."

"What was your plan? To slip in and out without being seen so no one would even know you were here?" As he spoke, the pitch of Ben's voice rose, his anger increasing. "Where have you been? We haven't heard from you in weeks! Not since…" Ben's voice trailed off, and his father completed the sentence.

"Since the funeral. Have you ever considered that maybe it's better that way?"

Ben's dad kept his tone even, free from anger. *Could he possibly feel guilty for leaving?* I thought, waiting for Ben's response. If that were true, he would never admit to it.

"Abandoning us was never the better choice."

"Benjamin, you have to understand. After your mother died-"

"Save it," Ben cut him off. "You're no longer welcome here. Get. Out."

Ben's voice was so steely, it sent shivers down my spine. I couldn't believe that my light-hearted, optimistic friend could be this cold.

"I am still your father, and-"

"How can you even say that?" Ben yelled. "When was the last time you acted like my father? When was the last time you were a father to any of us!"

Mr. Connley took a step back and looked at Ben with what appeared to me to be anger. Ben seemed on the verge of tears. Then Mr. Connley got right in Ben's face and shook his finger at him.

"You listen here! I *am* still your father whether you like it or not!"

"Keep telling yourself that." Ben pushed past his father and ran out the door, letting it slam behind him.

Mr. Connley ran his hand over his face. "He doesn't understand-"

I was already on my way out the door as I held up a hand to silence him.

It didn't take much searching to find Ben. I knew where he would be: the bridge— or rather, *under* the bridge. A short walk from his house was an unused covered bridge where a lot of teens hung out, but only a few knew about the hide-away *under* the bridge. In between the abutment and deck was a four-foot gap that was easily accessible from one end of the bridge to those who knew about it. When Ben wanted to get away from the house and hide for a while, he always went there.

"Ben?" I crawled under the bridge and sat next to him, swinging my legs out over the edge. There was about a twenty-foot drop to the shallow river below. Looking to the left, the rapids could be seen. They weren't terribly turbulent unless there had been a lot of rain recently. During the summer, many people swam above the rapids and scampered across the rocks of the fast-flowing river. To the right, the river continued calmly on.

When Ben didn't say anything or even acknowledge my presence, I placed a hand on his shoulder.

"How are you doing?" I spoke softly, and when he again didn't reply for a few minutes, I wondered if he had heard me. Just as I was about to speak again, he drew a shaky breath and answered.

"I guess I'm ok. I just can't believe that, after everything, he'd sneak back hoping to come and go unseen. He's never been around much, but after my mom died, everyone thought that maybe that would be the turning point in his life. I tried to tell everyone that nothing would be different, but, as always, no one listened. The whole family was so surprised when he took off."

"I know. I remember."

"It's no wonder all of my older siblings are so screwed up. You know, Tony is just like him. They're both lazy and selfish, and yet somehow my mom fell in love with my dad. I think she regretted marrying him, although she'd never admit it. She was faithful to him to the last."

HERE'S TO THE UNDERDOGS!

"Ben...do you want your dad to stay?"

Again, he was quiet, staring blankly at the rushing water that filled the silence between us.

"I don't know. I doubt he's ever going to change."

I finished the thought for him as he didn't continue, "But you would still like to have a father."

He started to speak, but his voice was too shaky. I wrapped my arms around him, and he gladly returned the hug and hid his face against my shoulder.

"I can't promise that things will magically get better or that your dad will ever be the father he should be. Of course, that's what we all hope for, not only for you, but for your siblings as well, especially the younger ones. But life isn't always fair. It isn't always *right*. Yet even though I can't tell you that someday things will be perfect, I can promise that you'll never be alone through this. I will *always* be here for you."

* * *

Ben wouldn't allow me to walk home with him that night. I considered following him anyway, but ultimately decided to respect his wishes. Tuesday morning couldn't come soon enough. In between every class throughout the day, I hunted for Ben, anxious to ask him about the previous night. Finally, after English class, I spotted him at his locker and rushed over.

"Where have you been all morning? I've been waiting to talk to you!"

He shut his locker and turned to me, a smile plastered on his face. Despite his happy appearance, his eyes betrayed him. There was no joy in them, and he looked like he hadn't slept at all.

"Was he still there when you got back?"

"Nah. Aunt Michelle said he had gotten a motel room at Brookeside."

He started walking toward his next class which was in the opposite direction of mine. I followed him anyway.

"So he's staying in town for a while?"

Ben shrugged. "I guess so."

"Ben! Talk to me!"

"I have to get to class. Catch you after school."

With that, he slipped into his class and left me standing in the hallway, alone. Part of me wanted to stroll into his classroom, grab him by the ear, and drag him out to talk to me. The sensible part of me was convinced that that was a terrible idea. Still determined that, eventually, I would get him to tell me everything, I temporarily abandoned my cause and ran to my class.

Chapter 6: Colette

"The little rat. He is so dead."

I was standing at Ben's open locker. After searching the school for him, I had put in his combination to see if his books were still in his messy locker. They weren't. He had left without me. He was avoiding me.

As I fed my anger thinking of how I was going to wring his scrawny neck the next time I saw him, a hand reached out and rested against the locker next to Ben's. I turned and was face to face with Jeremy leaning over me.

"How's it going?"

"Get lost, Jeremy. I feel like strangling someone in particular, and, seeing as I can't find him, I'll settle for you." I slammed Ben's locker shut and started walking away, listening for Jeremy's footsteps behind me. As I suspected, he quickly fell in step with me.

Jeremy was over half a foot taller than me, making his strides longer than mine, but as I was in a hurry, he was able to keep in perfect step with me. His eyes were honey brown, lighter than his hair, and he had a scar just below his left eye that he'd gotten skateboarding.

HERE'S TO THE UNDERDOGS!

"Ah, come on. Can't I at least walk you home?"

"No. Now scram."

He ran his fingers through his short brown hair, then stepped in front of me and walked backward, keeping eye contact.

"You can't avoid me forever, you know."

"I don't see why not."

Not realizing how close we were to the exit, Jeremy bumped into the doors, allowing me to walk around him and step into the sunlight. That didn't stop him for long though.

"Why won't you give me a chance? What do you have against me?"

"My dad doesn't like you."

"That's a lie. Your whole family loves me! Well, except for Morgan."

It's true that my family *did* like him when we were dating, but he apparently hadn't gotten the memo that that was no longer the case. I stopped and turned to him. "The truth is, I don't have anything against *you* in particular, just guys in general." Hoping that partial lie would satisfy him, I kept walking.

"What about Benjamin?"

"I couldn't get rid of him even if I wanted to. Besides, we are friends and only friends. There is no chance of anything romantic ever developing between us."

"I see. So, you're just afraid of romantic involvement."

"Not afraid. Just not interested."

"We'll see about that."

Without replying or giving him a chance to say more, I got in my car and drove away, not intentionally avoiding his toes with my tires. He jumped back and could do nothing more than watch me drive away. Through the rearview mirror, I could see him still standing there, his hands in his pockets and his signature smirk turning up the left corner of his mouth and crinkling his scar. A few of his basketball buddies — Tony included — surrounded him, clapping him on the back and joking. As I turned out of the parking lot, I lost sight of him and his friends, but I assumed they were off to practice basketball.

As I pulled into Ben's shaded driveway, I could hear shouting from inside the house. Quickly, I got out of my car and rushed into the living room to see what the commotion was. I can't say I was surprised by what I saw: Ben and his dad, both red with anger, standing toe-to-toe, arguing. Despite being four inches shorter than his dad, Ben was right in his face and was not about to back down. They were in the middle of the living room, backed by the couch, arguing about Ben's dad coming back and living with the family. It was hard to make out the whole conversation, each yelling over the other's words, but I heard enough to know Ben was strongly against this prospect. I couldn't place his reason though. His dad coming back to finally be a father was a good thing, right? Then it hit me. The unmistakable, sour stench of beer. That's why Ben didn't want him there— he was drunk. It was obvious now: the way his words sometimes slurred together and his unsteady stance. Losing his wife had hit him hard and changed him for the worse. Now the argument seemed different. Ben was angry, but anger was absent from his voice. He spoke with concern and pain. This had probably started out as a simple conversation that blew up into an argument, and Ben was trying to keep as calm as possible.

I was about to step between them when I heard a small whimper from behind me. Spinning around, I looked down at Garrett, Ben's four-year-old brother. Tears were threatening to stream from his brown eyes. I scooped him up and carried him outside. The argument could still be heard, so I kept walking until we were a little way down the driveway and sat under one of the maple trees. It took Garrett a few minutes to settle down and stop clinging tightly to my neck. He looked up at me, his dark locks hiding his eyes, his mouth turned down in a quivering frown.

"Why are they fighting?"

"You know how sometimes you and Luke used to fight over a toy or something? And later you'd realize it was silly to fight, right?" He nodded sternly. "Well, sometimes grownups argue for silly reasons."

"Grownups are loud when the argue." He laid his head back down on my chest. "I know. Do you remember when we talked about thunderstorms?" He nodded. "You said the thunder isn't bad, the lightning is."

I had to stifle a chuckle as he stumbled over the word "lightning". "That's right. And it's the same when grownups argue. They're just loud because they love each other, but the shouting is nothing to be scared of."

"What's the scary part?"

I stared at him, unsure of how I was supposed to answer that. "Does there have to be a scary part?"

He sat back and looked at me, his little brows furrowed. "If there isn't, why won't my heart be quiet?"

"Aww, Garrett." I put my hand over his heart. His big eyes searched mine for the answer to his question. "Your heart doesn't beat faster just when you're scared."

"When else?"

"When I...tickle you!" I held him in the crook of my elbow and tickled him until the tears were gone from his eyes, and he was laughing and screaming with joy. "See?"

With his chubby fingers, he tried to tickle me. To keep him happy, I played along and pretended it tickled. He soon got bored of this though and ran off down the driveway a little farther. After giving him a head-start, I chased after him and swung him around when I caught him, then settled him in my arms.

"Do you think they are done yelling?"

"I don't know, Garrett. You know how stubborn Ben can be," I said with a wink.

Garrett giggled then squirmed out of my arms. I was about to chase him again when someone tackled me to the ground from behind.

"Benjamin! Get your fat self off me!" I would have laughed if I could have even breathed under his weight.

"I thought I was a shrimp. I thought you could beat me at wrestling no matter what."

"You are, and I can, but this isn't wrestling." I tried to roll over so he would slide off, but I couldn't.

"Dogpile!" Garrett shouted as he jumped on top of Ben. Thankfully, Ben got up, Garrett wrapping his arms around Ben's neck so as to not fall. Without wasting a second, I got up and faced Ben. I noticed that his right cheek was a little red, but before I could process this, he grabbed my hand and pulled us out of the driveway as his dad drove through.

"Is he going back to the motel?"

Ben shrugged. "That would be the best case scenario. Unless he left altogether."

Garrett extended a hand toward the house. "That way!"

"Who says you're in charge?" Ben joked.

"You're my horse. Now go!"

We obliged and ran to the house, Garrett tightening his grasp around Ben's neck and laughing.

As soon as we had reached the house, Ben got Garrett off his back.

"Ok, go play now."

Garrett didn't need to be told twice. He scampered through the door and up the stairs. As soon as he was gone, I turned to Ben.

"You. Me. Talk. *Now.*"

"Why did you turn all Neanderthal?"

"I'm emphasizing the importance of this to your life."

"Ok, ok. I don't see why this is so important, but I'll comply."

"Good call."

We strolled to the garage.

"So, what happened to him?"

"He took up drinking after Mom died, and now he wants to move back in. I'm going to do all I can to keep that from happening until he's sober."

"I understand that." I reached up and touched his cheek. "Tell me he didn't do that."

"It's my fault. I should have known better than to try to talk to him when he's like this."

"But he hit you?"

"It's not the first time…" After a short pause, he asked, "What are you thinking?"

"Nothing."

"You are. I can tell. You're thinking of talking to your dad, aren't you? Don't, ok?"

"Why not?"

"Cause everything has already been hard enough on the younger ones. I don't think getting the court involved in this will help."

"Maybe you're right," I sighed.

We were both silent for a long time.

"Wanna come to church with my family tomorrow evening?"

Ben looked up, surprised by the sudden offer. "Yeah. Maybe so." He looked at his watch. "You should probably go home now. It's five-thirty."

"That late? Wow. Are you going to be ok tonight?"

"Of course. Why wouldn't I be? I've got the house to myself since Aunt Michelle has the littles and Tony is staying at Josh's."

"That's what I'm worried about."

He put his hands on my shoulders. "I'll be fine. Honest."

He nodded and dropped his arms. "See you tomorrow at school."

"There's no school tomorrow, remember? Teacher workday."

"Oh, right. Well, I'll see you sometime tomorrow probably. At least for church."

"Ok." I smiled, glad he'd mentioned church, and walked to my car. Casting a final glance back at Ben, I drove away.

Chapter 7: Ben

So, maybe I lied. Maybe I was nowhere near ok. Maybe I should have laid down my pride and let Colette stay. But it's not like I had planned for this to be my last night. I just couldn't stand it any longer after what took place over the evening. Let me back up. Colette drove away, and for a while everything was fine. I made dinner and sat on the couch, planning to end the evening with a good movie. My relaxing was interrupted by a phone call from my older sister, Victoria.

"Tori? What's up? Haven't heard from you in a while."

"Ben? Ugh, of course, you'd be the one to pick up."

Victoria and I used to get along, but that changed after my mom died. I had always been closer to my mom, and Victoria had always been closer to my dad, so when Mom died, we essentially took sides. Victoria closed herself off from the rest of the family except for my dad. It felt like I had lost two people: my mom, and then my sister who had always been like a best friend. Hearing her voice on the phone now only reopened the wound.

HERE'S TO THE UNDERDOGS!

Attempting to smooth the shakiness of my voice, I answered, "I'm the only one home. Who were you expecting?"

"Dad."

My throat went dry. "Why? He's been gone for nearly three months."

"He told me he was going back. Didn't he get there?"

"He did. He's staying at a motel."

"Why not at the house?"

I felt my jaw clench. "Cause I won't let him."

"Benjamin! Why not?" she yelled into the phone.

"He doesn't have the right to stay here anymore. Not after leaving us."

"Oh, you're such an idiot. What motel is he at?"

"Brookeside," I replied flatly.

"Fine. I'm calling there."

Before I could even say goodbye, she hung up. "Love you too, sis," I mumbled to no one but myself.

I returned to my movie but was no longer enjoying it. Then I remembered that I should have gotten replies to all of my emailed college applications. With that glimmer of light at the end of a dreary day, I opened my laptop. Sure enough, I had emails from three of the four colleges I had applied to. I read aloud to myself as I opened the first email.

'Mr. Connley:

Your application was quite impressive. We regret to inform you that at this time we have no openings.'

"Not my first choice anyway," I mumbled. "Next." 'Mr. Connley:

Though a student of your educational caliber would be a benefit to our campus, we cannot grant you a scholarship at this time…'

"No way I can afford to go there. Ok. Third time's the charm, right?"

'Mr. Connley…'

"And three times rejected. Great."

As I was about to close my laptop, an email came in from the final college. I took a deep breath and opened it, dumbfounded by the reply.

'Mr. Connley:

Are you serious? You expect us to accept your so-called application? Your "qualifications" are laughable at best...'

I read the rest silently. It continued to say how unqualified I was, and how they would never even consider accepting me into their college. I couldn't understand it. I had talked to one of the professors at a college fair several months ago, and he said he would pass along a recommendation; that I was the perfect student for the college; that there was hardly any need for an application. Despite his praise, I had put all my effort into that application. This was my college of choice. I was certain they would accept me if they had space. What was even more mind-boggling was the unprofessional way in which they had rejected me. Still unable to wrap my mind around the final email, I closed my laptop and stared at the black screen of the TV.

My aimless gaze was broken when Tony ran into the house and up the stairs. I didn't pay him much attention, but Josh — Tony's best friend and "partner in crime" — came in and plopped on the couch next to me.

"Sup, Ben?"

I avoided the question with a question of my own. "What are you two going to do tonight?"

"There's an epic party at Sarah's house because of the day off tomorrow. Hey! You should come!"

Tony was walking down the stairs at this time. "Yeah, bro. It'd be good for you to hang out with someone other than Colette."

"I have other friends," I muttered, crossing my arms.

"Colette's siblings don't count. Come on, man. You need to get out more."

"I don't know… Parties aren't really my thing."

"Aw, come on. It's gonna be loads of fun!"

With everything that had happened that evening, I figured going to a wild party couldn't hurt so long as Colette didn't find out.

"Sure. Why not?" I wasn't very enthusiastic, but Tony either didn't notice or didn't care.

"Then let's go!" He waved me toward the door.

Depressed, but slightly hopeful, I followed Tony and Josh outside to discover that they expected me to ride in the back seat of my own jeep that they were once again stealing. The way my day had been going, I didn't feel like arguing.

I'd never been to a party like this before. Normally, I probably would have enjoyed it, but tonight the noise, drinking, and excessive glow stick illumination in the dim lighting didn't appeal to me.

"I don't know about this, Tony. Maybe I should just go back home." I started backing toward the jeep, but Tony wrapped his arm around my shoulders and urged me forward.

"Just stick with me. I'll show you what you've been missing hanging out with Colette."

Left with no other choice, I walked into the house with Tony and Josh. Music blared, drunken teenagers ran around, couples hid in dark corners making out— totally where I wanted to be.

A blonde in a pink dress walked up to us.

"Tony! Josh! So glad you could make it. Who's this?" Sarah turned to me and wrinkled her nose, looking me over like I was some dirty stray they'd brought into her ornate home. I took no offense at the fact that she didn't recognize me from school— she wasn't the sort I'd normally want to hang around anyway.

"This is my younger brother Ben. I figured it was about time I introduced him to what normal teenagers do on a non-school night."

I hadn't realized until now because I wasn't really paying attention, but Tony and Sarah had been shouting to be heard above the cacophony of music and yelling. Tony leaned over and whispered something in Sarah's ear in reply to which, she nodded and motioned for us to follow her. Josh had already melted into the mass of gyrating teens, but Tony grabbed my arm and pulled me along to the kitchen which was equally crowded.

"Final step in your initiation, little bro." Tony gestured to the solo cups stacked on the counter next to a large Igloo cooler.

All I could think about was my dad. "I'll pass."

Sarah scoffed. "Figures he'd be too chicken."

"Come on, dude. Just try it," Tony prodded.

By now, Sarah had gathered about a dozen people to watch me chicken out. Although I had no desire to taste a drop of beer ever in my life, I also had no desire to become even more of an underdog than I already was. With a sigh, I gave in and grabbed a red goblet of doom. As I filled my cup with the brown poison, its stench drifted up to my nose and filled my head with images of my father from earlier that same day. I felt the sting of his hand on my cheek, saw his anger-filled eyes. The more I thought about him, the more determined I became that I would never be like him, no matter how much I drank. He was a drunk. He'd walked out on us when we'd needed him most. He didn't care about any of us. It didn't matter if I got drunk tonight, I wasn't planning on giving myself the chance to become like him anyway.

I stared at the liquid in the cup for one last moment, then chugged it and slammed the cup down on the counter. A cheer went up from the onlookers, and Tony clapped me on the back.

"That's the way!"

As I swallowed, the liquid felt like what I'd imagine fire would feel like sliding down your throat if you could liquify it. The bitter taste lingered in my mouth, yet I felt a little better. Not happier, but better, as though I were feeding my pain, but it made everything make more sense and cleared my head. Tony refilled my cup and handed it to me, eyes widening slightly when he looked at me.

"Whoa. Relax, dude. You look like someone just insulted your intelligence."

All the thoughts of my father flooding my mind had twisted my face into an angry scowl. My jaw was clenched so hard that it was beginning to hurt. I forced myself to take a deep breath and relax, the alcohol making it easier to loosen up.

"I'm ok." Putting the cup to my lips, I tipped my head back and took another gulp, getting more used to the taste and feeling already. The second taste was still tart, but warmer.

"Let's get you back into the main party!"

Tony and I pushed our way through the crowded mansion until we were in the living room, the wildest part of the house. There was a game of beer pong taking place on the coffee table, the participants having to kneel to play; a few teens were either passed out on the couch or… involved…with another teen in the same location; and many were talking and dancing on any open floor space. Tony did his best to keep me interacting with the others for a few minutes, but soon got distracted, and I was left on my own.

HERE'S TO THE UNDERDOGS!

The night raced by. All was going well until one of Darren's friends showed up. He zeroed in on me quickly.

"Well, well. Who let you in?"

By this time, I had quite a bit to drink, but I still managed to ignore his comment.

"Hear your dad's back in town *and* a drunk. Haven't seen him since your mom died." The quickening of my breath was just noticeable enough for him to comprehend. In a mock-baby-voice, he said, "Aww. Miss your mommy?"

"Shut up," I growled.

"What are you going to do? Call your daddy cause mommy's not around?"

Before I even knew what I was doing, I punched him hard in the jaw. Had there not been so many people, he would have fallen to the floor, but instead he fell back into the crowd and was pushed back towards me, his fists up and ready for a fight. I obliged. One on one, my odds were actually pretty good. His advantage came from having just arrived and, therefore, being completely sober. I held my own though and dished out as many punches as I took. Had the fight not been broken up by Tony and Josh, I probably would have kept fighting until I dropped. I fought Tony for a moment until I realized it was him.

"Settle down, little bro. What did you do?"

"Me? Nothing! He started it!" I thrust an accusing finger toward the brute.

"Michael would never! It was all your brother's fault, Tony!" Of course, Sarah would take Michael's side.

HERE'S TO THE UNDERDOGS!

"Maybe you should go home, Ben. Get some sleep. You're wasted." He ushered me toward the door.

As we passed Michael, he whispered, "You'll never fit in, loser."

I would have wrenched out of Tony's grasp and gotten in Michael's face for round two, but I had been telling myself the same thing for a long time.

Once Tony had led me out of the house, I pulled away from him and kept walking.

"Ben!" He grabbed my wrist and turned me to face him. "Where are you going?"

"Home. Like you suggested."

"Yeah, but I was going to drive you."

"Don't bother," I grumbled. "I'll walk."

"I'm not even sure you *can* walk."

Exasperated, I snapped, "I can walk, ok? And why would you want to help me? You never have before! Just leave me alone! It's what you're good at."

Tony's features hardened slightly. "Fine. Whatever."

Watching him turn back to the house, I had the urge to hug him, my sudden burst of anger receding. I don't know when the last time was that I had hugged Tony, but seeing as this might be my last chance, I almost ran up to him. Before I had made up my mind, though, another car pulled into the driveway and three guys got out and walked into the house with my brother— I had missed my chance. With a sigh, I turned and walked back to my house, a journey about ten minutes long. Ten minutes isn't a long time, but left only with my thoughts as I walked, it was long enough for me to make my decision.

Chapter 8: Ben

My driveway had never seemed so long; the house had never felt so lonely. With all of the lights off, everything was shrouded in a thick darkness that seemed to mock me. Like a living thing, it jabbed at me with all the hurtful and hateful words that had ever been spoken about me, by others as well as myself. Stumbling up the stairs, only one thought was on my mind. I entered the bathroom and closed the door behind me, sliding to the floor against it. I rummaged around in the cabinet under the sink until I found the small blade I'd been hiding there ever since my mom died. A small part of me knew this was a stupid idea, but I didn't care. As I held the blade, the light caught on it and obstructed my reflection in the small piece of metal. That was probably for the best. Eyes closed, I leaned my head against the door and a single tear ran down my cheek.

"I'm sorry, Colette," I whispered.

I looked at my wrist and touched the cold blade to my skin. A line of red was lifting where the blade passed perpendicular to my arm, and at first I didn't feel the pain. But even with all the alcohol in me lessening my senses, I eventually did feel it as I cut deeper. The pain washed over me bringing tears to my eyes and almost knocking me out. I'd been in pain plenty of times, so I assumed I'd be fine. I had never experienced pain like this. It made me sick to my stomach. I blocked it out though, made myself focus and keep going. By now, my arm was covered in blood, the red substance dripping to the floor like a soft rain. My shirt started clinging to my stomach as the red spot on it grew. As the blade clattered to the floor, I closed my eyes again. I was now becoming numb to the pain—or was I just starting to lose consciousness? I opened my eyes and looked down at my arm. With fuzzy vision, all I could make out was colors, and mostly I saw red. I was vaguely aware of someone pounding on the door and calling my name. Then I fell to the floor and passed out.

* * *

When I woke up, I was very disoriented. The first thing I noticed though, was Colette curled up in a chair in what seemed like a very uncomfortable position, sleeping. She had that ability: to fall asleep anywhere, anytime, no matter how uncomfortable it seemed. I tried to sit up, and my small amount of stirring roused her.

"Benjamin! Oh, thank God. Seriously." She rushed over to the bed and knelt beside it, gripping my hand.

I now took in my surroundings. It appeared that I was in a hospital. My head was pounding and my arm ached. *Why though?* Then it all came back to me. I looked down at my wrist, the cut I had made sewn up with ugly medical thread. My other arm had an IV stuck in it.

"Ben? Are you ok?"

"Yeah. How did I get here?" I croaked, still groggy.

HERE'S TO THE UNDERDOGS!

"I found you and called the police." She paused. "Why? Why would you-" Her voice was too shaky to continue, and tears started streaming down her cheeks.

"I'm sorry. I'm so sorry. I wasn't thinking straight." A tear streaked down my own cheek.

"Don't you ever do anything like that again. When I finally got through the door and saw you lying there...I thought you were already gone."

A nurse walked in and interrupted the scene.

"It's good to see that you're awake, Benjamin. How are you feeling?" The nurse checked my blood pressure and such as she talked.

I wiped the tear off my cheek before answering. "Besides the pounding in my head? Not too bad considering."

"You're lucky your friend found you when she did."

I turned to Colette. "Yeah. I really am."

Colette smiled slightly and wiped away her tears with her sleeve.

"You are a strong young man. Your vitals look like they're where they should be. I'll leave you two." She smiled and left, closing the door on her way out.

"Why were you at my house?"

"I just...had this feeling," Colette answered. "I rushed out of the house in the middle of family devotions and drove to your house. When you didn't answer as I called to you, I knew something was wrong."

"Wow. That's lucky."

"That's one way to think of it."

"Oh. You think it was," I searched for the right way to put it, "a God thing?"

"Maybe."

I simply nodded.

HERE'S TO THE UNDERDOGS!

"If you're out of here by Sunday, you're coming to church with us." Although she stated it as a command, her eyes told me it was a plea. I nodded again. "And maybe you could stay at my house for a while. You could sleep in Marcus's room; Mom and Dad would love it, and the twins would be ecstatic."

"I don't know… What about Michelle?"

"She has a three-month-old to watch. I already talked to her about this, and she said she'd feel better if you stayed with us. Please, Ben…"

I looked into her hopeful green eyes; a few shades lighter than mine. After a long moment of thought, I let out a soft breath.

"Alright. I'll stay with you guys."

A relieved smile created dimples in her cheeks. "Good. Mom and Dad will be thrilled."

She sat on the bed next to me, and we talked for a while before she got out some cards and we played War to pass the time until visiting hours were over. When the nurse came in and told Colette that she had to leave, I thought Colette was going to pop a fuse. She thought it was ridiculous that she had to leave, but the nurse assured her that I would be watched closely and taken care of. Meanwhile, I was lying in bed trying not to be offended by being spoken of almost as a baby, but also smiling because it was fun to see Colette lose a battle for once. Before leaving, she promised me that she would find out how long I was going to be kept here.

After Colette left, the hospital room began to feel very lonely, but it also gave me a chance to think about the night before. I looked down at the stitches in my wrist. *What was I thinking?* The short answer: I wasn't. I was drunk and depressed. I mean, seriously? This wasn't even a good way to commit suicide. I shook my head. Thinking it now would do no good. Sleep was a good idea, so I closed my eyes and tried to ignore the beeping of the machine next to me as I drifted off to sleep.

Chapter 9: Colette

As soon as visiting hours started on Friday, I rushed to Ben's room to check on him. I found him balancing a cup of pills on his nose. "You look well."

As I had suspected would happen, he jumped in surprise, causing the cup to fall off his nose and spill the pills into the bed. Laughing, I walked over to him and helped recover the scattered pills.

"What are all these?"

He dumped them into his hand and, one by one, dropped the pills back into the cup as he identified them.

"Let's see. Anti-depressant, anti*psychotic,* pain med because I need that on top of the morphine, and, oh, look! Anti-depressant." With a sigh, he set the cup on the table next to the bed.

"Aren't you supposed to take those?"

"Yes."

"...And are you going to?"

"No."

"Ben, you have to. Isn't a nurse supposed to stay to make sure you do?"

"Yes, but luckily for me, she got called away."

"But now *I'm* here to make sure you take your meds." I placed my hands on my hips and looked down at him.

"You know I hate medication. Meds are drugs."

"Drugs that help you."

"Listen, I don't need pain killers as I'm already on morphine. And I'm not psychotic."

"What about the anti-depressants?" I asked, folding my arms across my chest.

With a shrug, he answered, "I just don't want those."

"Ben!" I pinched the bridge of my nose in exasperation and pleaded, "Please. Just cooperate."

Glaring at me, Ben picked up the cup of pills. "Fine." One by one, he swallowed the pills, drinking a big gulp of water with each.

"Good. That wasn't so bad."

"It was horrible." Now *he* folded his arms over his chest.

"Oh, don't be such a baby." His answer was silence. "Stop pouting. You're going to be fine."

He glanced at me out of the corner of his eye. "How long are they keeping me here?"

"By tomorrow your wrist should be healed enough for them to send you to the Psych Ward."

"Psych Ward? Why?"

"Because you tried to commit suicide, Ben. They just want to make sure you'll be ok after they release you. If you seem fine, you should be released after twenty-four to thirty-six hours."

Ben groaned and leaned his head back. "That's a long time."

"It's not that long. Only a day or so." When I was again met with silence, I decided to change the subject. "Are you hungry?"

"Of course. Do you have food?"

"I sneaked some in." Digging through my bag, I found the goldfish crackers I had stashed and handed them to Ben. He gladly took them and stuffed a handful in his mouth.

"Careful, Benjamin. You'll make yourself choke." He mumbled something that I couldn't make out in response. "Please swallow, then talk."

He gulped down the mouthful before trying again. "I said, have you ever seen me choke? Ever? Food is too important and precious."

"Whatever you say," I relented as I shook my head.

For the next few hours, I kept Ben company, but he looked tired and started falling asleep as I was talking to him, so I left to let him rest. As I was leaving, a nurse stopped me in the hall to inform me that he would be moved to the Psych Ward the next day and would not be allowed visitors as it could hinder their observation of him.

"How long do you think he will be kept there?"

"If he continues behaving the way he has been, not long. Probably only twenty-four hours if he takes his medication and cooperates."

I thanked her and left, praying all the way home that Ben would be ok.

Chapter 10: Ben

I'm not sure when I fell asleep. I barely remembered Colette leaving, but I woke up refreshed and even more clear headed. As I sat up, my headache gone, I glanced at my arm and saw that the IV was gone. At first I was glad—that meant I'd be getting out of here soon. Then I realized that also meant that I would be moved to the Psych Ward. I considered jumping out the window and making a run for it, but my plotting was interrupted by the nurse.

"Well, Mr. Connley," she smiled. "It's good to see that you are awake."

She made her way to the bedside and handed me a cup of pills and some water. Begrudgingly, I choked down the pills and forced a smile. After all, she was only doing her job. Taking the cup from me, she placed a small pile of clothes at the foot of the bed.

"These should fit you just fine. I'll be back in a few minutes to take you to the Psychiatric division." With that, the soft-spoken nurse exited, closing the door behind her.

I reached forward and grabbed the clothes. I was glad to have something to wear other than the hospital gown I was in, but it would have been nice to have my own clothes. This must have been the required dress code for the Psych Ward.

Not sure of how long I had before the nurse returned, I quickly donned the outfit. Surprisingly, the gray sweatpants and t-shirt were both incredibly soft, though I would have rather had a long sleeve shirt to cover the disgusting stitches in my wrist. The nurse returned to find me glaring at the stitches.

"Here is a splint for your wrist. It's healing quickly, but now that you are going to be up and moving around, this will keep the stitches from coming out."

Carefully, I slid the splint over my hand and secured it around my wrist.

With a smile, the nurse said, "If you're ready, please follow me."

Silently, she lead me down the hall to an elevator. Two floors up, we stopped, and the doors opened to reveal a small waiting room, the doors to the Psych Ward about fifteen feet in front of us. Dragging my feet, I spanned the distance and waited while the nurse swiped her key-card and entered the passcode. The doors unlocked with a piercing buzz, and the nurse hefted one open. I had to sign myself in, then continued following the nurse down a long, cream-colored hall perforated with doorways leading to various resident or activity rooms. We had almost reached the end of the hall before the nurse turned into a cheery cracker-box of a room: a large window opposite the door allowed the afternoon sun to warm the room; a bed was situated along the right wall and took up most of the room, though it was only a single; a dresser stood opposite the bed. Nothing hung on the walls, and no carpet protected the cold floor.

"This will be your room during your short stay. The dining room is at the end of the hall, and the bathrooms are back down the hall on the right. I'll let you explore the rest of the division on your own." Flashing a quick smile, she turned on her heel and left me standing alone at the foot of the bed, staring out the window at the beautiful view of the parking lot.

"Hi!"

I jumped up and spun around. A short kid of about thirteen with huge, round glasses stood in the doorway.

"Uh, hi."

"Just get here? Silly question. Of course, you did. I haven't seen you around before. Why are you here? What's your name? I'm Alfred, but people call me Alfie."

I stood in silence for a moment, unsure of whether he was done speaking or not. I took his expectant expression to mean that he was finished.

"I'm...Ben."

Before I had even quite finished speaking, he started rattling on again. Honestly, I only caught about half of what he said. He grabbed my arm and pulled me down the halls, introducing me to the other residents and poking his head into the various community rooms, explaining every detail of every room. The tour ended with the rec. room. Alfie ran and jumped on one of the couches.

"I love this room."

I looked around and nodded. The couch Alfie sat on was to my right against the wall adjacent to the door. In front of me was a TV, angled towards the couch and various chairs spread around that section of the room. The other side of the room had a couple small tables with matching chairs and a game cabinet. A few residents were playing Sorry around one of the tables.

"It's nice. How long have you been here?"

He stared at the wall for so long I thought I had broken him. Then his eyes snapped back to me, and he replied, "Almost a year."

"Wow." The single word couldn't describe my amazement and horror at the thought of living in this place for so long.

"It's ok though. I have friends here!" He grinned so incredibly wide that I couldn't help but smile.

"That's great, Alfie."

"And now *you* are my friend too." He patted the spot on the couch next to him. I obliged and sat down.

The rest of the day, Alfie followed me around, continually rambling on about something or someone. During group therapy, Alfie spoke a majority of the time and shifted constantly in his seat when he was quiet. His chattering didn't even stop at mealtimes, and yet he managed to finish his food before me. Of course, that could have been in part because I didn't feel like eating anything and mostly picked at my food. After dinner, the nurses made their rounds delivering meds. Alfie greedily swallowed his meds like they were candy.

Apparently, the rec. room was the evening hotspot. Residents filtered in, sitting at a table to play chess or work on a puzzle, reclining on the couch with a book in hand, or standing and staring at the wall like they were studying for a pop quiz on every crack running through it. Alfie poked at my splint, and I quickly drew my arm to my stomach and cradled it.

"What's it for?"

"Um, I hurt my wrist."

The look in his eyes told me he understood. "Oh."

Alfie was quieter after that, which only meant he paused to breathe every once in a while. I eventually got the chance to excuse myself when

HERE'S TO THE UNDERDOGS!

Alfie got involved talking to another resident. I sneaked away back to my room and closed the door behind me, running a hand over my face.

"Made it through one day," I whispered as I sat on the bed. Through the window, I could see the city, lit up and live. I flopped down heavily on the bed. The bed was surprisingly comfortable, and I fell asleep in no time at all.

When I awoke, I nearly screamed. The first thing I saw was round glasses sitting at the end of a little nose, dirty-blond hair brushing the top of them.

"Alfie! What are you doing?"

"You're finally awake! Do you always sleep this late? It's practically nine o'clock!"

With that he dramatically flopped onto the bed on his back.

"Nine o'clock isn't that late," I said as I sat up. "When did *you* wake up?"

Still sprawled across the bed, he replied, "I have been awake since five."

"Five?" I stared in disbelief. "How do you get up that early?"

He shrugged in reply then shot to his feet and grabbed my hand. "Come on! You're going to miss breakfast!"

I had no choice but to follow. For a small person, Alfie was incredibly fast. And he had also lied. Upon arriving at the dining room, I was informed that breakfast went until nine forty-five, so I would have had time to at least wake up a little better before being rushed to eat. But I love food, so I didn't complain. We piled our plates with food — how Alfie was going to manage eating all of his was beyond me — and sat at one of the round tables. I had more of an appetite today than yesterday, and I gratefully dug into my sausage gravy and biscuits. It wasn't as good as what I could make at home, but it was still tasty.

It was during this moment of rambling thoughts that a fight broke out. All eyes turned to the hall where two of the residents were at each other's throats. Orderlies soon arrived and broke up the fight, dragging the residents far away from each other. The scene simply reminded me of why I was here and how much I wanted to leave. If all went well, I would be gone by the end of the day. I hung my head over my plate and picked at my breakfast, no longer hungry but rather meditating on the hopeful thought of leaving soon.

"You're not staying long, are you?" Alfie said, his words traced with sadness.

"How did you know?"

He picked at his food, apparently also having lost his appetite, and shrugged his shoulders. "I can just tell whether someone's staying for a long time or not."

"Don't worry though," I quickly spoke. "I'll come back and visit." I tried for a smile and must have succeeded, for Alfie's expression brightened considerably.

"Really? You will?" He looked at me, a wide grin across his face and a hopeful gleam in his eyes.

I smiled for real now. "Of course." *Could I keep that promise?*

Alfie took me at my word, grinning wider than ever. "I don't get a lot of visitors! That will be fun!" He grabbed both our plates, assuming I was finished, and disposed of them, then returned and pulled me behind him to the rec. room. With not much else to do, I challenged him to a game of chess. He was surprisingly skilled, and I had a hard time holding my own against him. In the end, he revealed a devious plot he had been weaving throughout the whole game and which I had fallen into. In a brilliant move, he cornered my king with his bishop and rook— checkmate.

"Wow, Alfie. You're a really good chess player," I complimented him genuinely. "I haven't lost a game in a long time."

My compliment was received with a shrug. "It's easy for me."

Alfie was a mystery. What was this intelligent, happy, likeable kid doing here? Sure, he could be a bit strange and apparently had no idea there was such a thing as personal space, but so far I saw nothing about him that warranted his being here, especially not for as long as he had been. What was I missing? What about him was I not seeing?

"You ok?"

"Hmmm?" I must have been staring off into space as these thoughts wandered around in my head. "Oh. Yeah, just thinking."

His busy mind didn't dwell on this topic, and soon he was talking about the possibilities of other lifeforms on other plants and invisibility and what it would mean if a creature had perfect camouflage. His thoughts on the matters were astounding.

When there was a lull in the conversation, I ventured to inquire as to why he was in the Psych Ward. In reply, he rolled up his sleeves to reveal dozens of scars on both arms. It hadn't even occurred to me that it was a bit strange that he was wearing long sleeves in the warm building. He then pulled the light scarf away from his neck to reveal fading bruises.

"I have schizoaffective disorder, particularly bipolar. I also sometimes show symptoms of schizophrenia, though that's been more under control since coming here. They keep me here because of my...suicidal tendencies and because home isn't safe. My dad...he..." His voice trailed off, but

HERE'S TO THE UNDERDOGS!

I knew what he would have said.

I stared at him. "But-but you're so happy all the time."

"It hides the pain pretty well, wouldn't you say?"

I understood where he was coming from. Over the past four years, the only one who had ever seen the pain I hid was Colette. Around anyone else, I donned a comical grin and cracked jokes so nothing would seem wrong. It had never occurred to me that there could be many others like me— or far worse off in some cases. That's when I decided I wasn't going to sit back and take it anymore. Something had to be done. Sweet kids like Alfie were suffering even more than I was, and the best that could be done for them was to hide them away in a facility. Sure, Alfie had a couple mental disorders adding to his pain, but it still wasn't right. There were treatments for both these disorders that should have allowed him to live a fairly normal life. Yet he was here for his own protection...from himself and his dad.

I was so lost in thought that I didn't notice the nurse standing over us as we sat on the couch.

"Benjamin." I was startled by her soft but firm voice as she interrupted my train of thought. "Please, follow me."

When I looked over at Alfie, he gave me a wide grin and two-thumbs up, encouraging me to follow and not worry. I gave Alfie a nod then rose from the couch and followed the nurse. She lead me to the only room in the Psych Ward that I hadn't been in yet— the psychiatrist's office. Cautiously, upon the nurse's insistence, I stepped into the office. A desk was nestled along the far wall; two plush chairs were positioned near the back of the room, turned slightly towards each other; and a couch sat a few feet from the chairs. As my eyes scanned the softly colored room, my gaze fell on the man seated in one of the plush chairs. On his lap he held a ledger, and he was busily writing something down in it when he noticed me. He looked up at me with comforting eyes and an inviting smile.

"Benjamin! I've been eagerly awaiting our time together. Please, sit." He swept his hand out toward the matching chair, two feet to his left. The chair proved to be incredibly comfortable, and I began to relax as he spoke again.

"As I'm sure you have no desire to stay here any longer than necessary, I'll make this short." I nodded in confirmation. "When you're released, where will you be staying?"

"With a friend's family."

He raised his eyebrows. "Oh?"

"Yeah." I rubbed the back of my neck as I explained. "My friend thought it would be a good idea since…my dad is never around at my house and my aunt's a little busy."

"I see. I think that's a very smart choice then."

After a few more questions, he decided I could be released. As I walked down the hall to tell Alfie, I tried not to appear too happy. I didn't want to hurt Alfie's feelings. Mulling over how I was going to tell him I was leaving, I walked back into the rec. room. He looked up from the couch, an expectant look on his face.

"I gotta tell you something, Alfie."

"You're leaving, aren't you?" The question was asked with no sadness or disappointment.

"Uh, yeah. As soon as my friend comes to pick me up."

"Good! See? I told you you'd be out of here soon." Clearly proud of himself for having predicted my early release, he gave me a wide grin.

"You were right," I chuckled.

"Don't forget to visit."

"How could I forget?" That answer seemed to satisfy him as it earned me a grin and a hug.

A nurse walked in, ending the moment, and informed me that Colette was waiting. I followed her down the hall, signed out, waved goodbye to Alfie one last time, and exited the Psych Ward. Colette smiled and smothered me in a hug as soon as she saw me.

"I wasn't gone that long."

"I know. I'm just glad to see you again. I got you something." She held out a small box.

"What is it?"

She chuckled. "You have to open it, genius."

I rolled my eyes, but opened the box. Inside was a thick leather bracelet. Gingerly, I lifted the bracelet out of the box. Colette knew me so well. She didn't have to say anything for me to understand the meaning behind the gift: for me to remember not only what I had almost lost, but also all that I had. We'd been friends for so long, she understood that something like this would help me cope.

"Ben? Are you ok?"

I stepped forward and hugged her again. "Thank you," I whispered.

"You're welcome. I knew you'd understand."

Nodding, I stepped back. I slipped my hand out of the splint and smiled as I wrapped the bracelet around my wrist.

"It suits you," Colette smiled.

I smiled at her in agreement, and we left the hospital. Turning back to glance at the building one last time, Alfie popped into my mind. Over the past few months, never once had I stopped to think that maybe I wasn't the only one suffering. It seemed foolish to me now, but it was true. The entire ride back to my house, I was silent, my mind racing.

HERE'S TO THE UNDERDOGS!

How many people did I know or pass in the halls at school every day who were going through similar things to myself?

Chapter 11: Ben

As Colette pulled up my long driveway, I realized I had been ignorant of yet another group that was hurting: my siblings. Garrett was the first to run out of the house, grinning and yelling my name. As I just sat in the car, Colette smiled encouragingly and gently urged me to get out. With much effort, I forced myself to step out of the car, and I was immediately attacked by Garrett. He bombarded me with questions as to where I had been and why I had left so suddenly. Alice joined us, remaining quiet. She looked at me knowingly, and I couldn't meet her eyes, my heart aching. Instead, I focused on Garrett and was reminded of my adopted siblings and how much I missed them. How could I have forgotten about them all this time? While I was wrapped up in how *I* was feeling and what *I* was going through, I hadn't stopped to realize that they too had lost their mother.

Colette stepped up and saved me from the tsunami of questions.

"How about we all go inside, and, while Ben unpacks, I'll explain everything, ok?"

HERE'S TO THE UNDERDOGS!

This suggestion pleased Garrett, and he dragged Colette and myself inside. I was very relieved that Colette had offered to explain things, though I hoped she would be discreet.

As Colette sat on the couch with Garrett, joined by Aunt Michelle and Joey, I escaped upstairs and started stuffing clothes into a backpack, talking to myself as I went. My mutterings were interrupted by a cough at the door, and I turned to see Alice standing awkwardly in the doorway.

"May I come in?"

I nodded, and she came and sat on the bed.

"So… You'll be staying with Colette's family? Do you know for how long?"

I shook my head. "I guess until Mr. Tance says." I paused then looked at the floor. "I'm sorry, Alice."

"What for?"

"For being a terrible big brother these past months. I didn't mean to ignore any of you. I guess I just— I got so wrapped up in my own feelings, I didn't think about the rest of you. I'm sorry for that."

I couldn't bring myself to look at her to see her reaction. She was silent for a while. Then she knelt beside me on the floor and hugged me— a very unusual thing for her.

She spoke quietly, emotion lending a tremor to each word. "I understand. You were closer to Mom than the rest of us. I'm sorry that none of us realized how much this was affecting you."

I managed a small smile. "Which one of us is the older sibling?"

That gained a chuckle from Alice. "You may be older and smarter, but that doesn't mean you're wiser, Knucklehead." She sat back and smiled at me.

I returned the smile. "I guess you're right. Don't let me forget that again, ok?"

"Deal. Need help packing?"

"Nah, I think I've got it." I tousled her hair a bit then made a more somber request of her. "Take care of Michelle and the littles, ok?"

"It's not like you're leaving the country. Colette's house isn't even ten minutes from here." She paused. "But sure. I'll watch out for them."

"How did you know?" I asked abruptly.

"Know what?"

"What I'd done."

She looked down at the floor. "Oh. That. I came home just as the ambulance arrived. As Colette went with the ambulance to the hospital, I...cleaned up the bathroom," she stammered softly.

Now it was my turn to study the floor. I wanted to say something, but I couldn't. What was I supposed to say to that? My fourteen-year-old kid sister had to deal with...yeah, I had nothing to say. I didn't even want to think about it.

"Colette will be waiting," Alice broke the silence. "You should probably get downstairs and save her from the endless questions."

I nodded, but still couldn't bring myself to say anything. Slowly, I rose to my feet and slung my backpack over one shoulder before walking out of the room, Alice following silently behind.

Downstairs, Colette was still seated on the couch. She looked up at me expectantly, and I smiled slightly, nodding once to assure her that I was alright and ready to go.

We spent probably a good five minutes hugging and saying goodbye before Colette and I were able to get in the car and drive away.

"You'd think I was leaving forever. Your house is literally a ten-minute walk from mine."

Colette smiled, amused by my lack of knowledge of kids despite having nine younger siblings. "All they know is that you left suddenly for some reason, and now you're leaving again. Also, you haven't really been yourself lately. Garrett probably misses you."

"I guess," I nodded. "Hey, do the twins know that I'm staying with you guys?"

"Not yet."

I managed a bit of a smile. "They're going to be so happy."

"Yeah. Though I don't know why they like you so much, ya weirdo." She looked over at me and smiled. I couldn't help but smile in return.

The rest of the car ride was spent in silence as I anxiously awaited our arrival. Though I loved the Tance family, it was going to be strange staying with them for however long Mr. Tance deemed necessary. I'd stayed over once or twice before, and I'd even gone camping with them, but to actually live with them was going to take some getting used to.

I wasn't too surprised to see Mr. Tance waiting at the front door of the sizable Tance residence as we pulled into the driveway. Despite having his arms crossed over his chest, he donned a welcoming smile. Seeing him made me feel a little better about the whole thing. He spanned the driveway and opened my door; before I even had a chance to step out of the car, he pulled me out and hugged me, which took me by surprise as he usually greeted me with a strong handshake.

"It's good to see you, Benjamin. I think I should warn you before you go inside that the twins are over the moon about your staying with us."

I grinned a little at his use of the phrase 'over the moon'. "I'm sure they are," I replied as I grabbed my backpack from the backseat.

HERE'S TO THE UNDERDOGS!

The twins were waiting just inside the door and attacked me in unison when I walked in. Ruby would have dragged me away to play for days if Mr. Tance hadn't saved me. Then Colette led me up the grand staircase to Marcus's room where I would be staying. I put my backpack down and looked around. An air mattress was set up on the floor next to Marcus's bed, and a small cabinet for my things sat in a corner. I noticed a new Marvel poster on the wall and made a mental note to ask Marcus about it later.

"It's been a while since I've shared a room."

"With Tony?" Colette guessed.

I nodded in answer.

"We can clean out the guest room if you want, though it may take a few days."

"No, I didn't mean that I don't *want* to share a room. This is fine."

"Alright. It's almost lunch time. Do you want to get settled then come down and eat?"

"Yeah. I'll do that."

She seemed a bit unsure, but nodded and walked out of the room, closing the door behind her. It was going to be a long...well, however long I was here for.

"Come on, Benjamin," I scolded myself. "This is the Tance's you're talking about. You know them. You like them even. So what's the big deal? Pull yourself together."

"Talking to yourself?"

I wheeled around quickly to see Morgan in the doorway.

"Jeepers, Morgan! Don't you know how to knock?"

HERE'S TO THE UNDERDOGS!

She shrugged. "I heard you talking in here so I figured it was ok to come in. I didn't know you'd gone completely crazy."

I gritted my teeth and muttered, "I'm not crazy."

"Hey, chill. Geesh, you look like you could use some 'happy-happy'." After receiving a strange look from me, she explained herself. "It's a Doctor Who reference."

"Oh…" It took me a few seconds, but I finally recalled the episode she meant. "Are you coming down for lunch or what?"

"Yeah, I'm coming."

I followed her out of the room and downstairs to the large kitchen where Mrs. Tance had lunch prepared. It was no surprise that she had outdone herself.

"Looks amazing, Mrs. T." I sat down at the table and grabbed a sandwich.

"Why thank you, Benjamin. Eat up. There's plenty here."

"Yes, Ma'am. You don't have to tell me twice." I filled my plate with potato salad, spicy chicken and cheese dip, fruit, and more little sandwiches. Both Marcus and Morgan managed to beat me in food-heaping.

"Are you feeling alright, Benjamin?" Mrs. Tance asked as she sat to eat with us.

"Just fine. Why?"

"You normally eat quite a bit more than that."

"Oh. I guess I'm just not too hungry."

She studied me, obviously not satisfied with this answer, but I turned my gaze down to my food so as to avoid hers. Thankfully, she didn't press the matter.

The day dragged on until evening. After devotions, I helped put the twins to bed as they would settle for no one else, then decided I would go to bed as well. Marcus helped me settle in, and, once he went back downstairs, I was left alone with my thoughts and the darkness. A good hour was spent staring up at the ceiling before I drifted off to sleep.

Chapter 12: Ben

Apparently, someone thought it would be a good idea to let the twins wake me up by jumping on me, something I was used to Garrett doing at home. I was reminded of my fading bruises as I sat up. In my half-awake fog, it took me a few minutes to realize what the motor was that I was hearing. I groaned and looked back at a snoring Marcus.

"Girls, why don't you wake your brother up? He sounds like a dying lawn mower."

With giggles and squeals, the twins accepted this task and began jumping on their brother. I took the opportunity to sneak away to the bathroom without their notice.

I wasn't too surprised, upon my arrival in the kitchen, to discover that Colette was responsible for my rude awakening this morning. While Mr. Tance would have been content to allow me a few days off from school, Colette insisted that I go back. She feared that if I didn't go today, I never would. And she may have been right. As much as I hated to admit it, going to school today was the best course of action.

"You'd better eat up. You're going to need all the strength you can get to power through today," Colette stated.

I rolled my eyes. "Sure, I will," I said, the sarcasm in my voice betraying my words of agreement.

She rolled her eyes in return, a grin dimpling her cheeks.

My thoughts wandered to the looks and whispers I'd be met with at school in a few hours. Aware of the uneasiness in my voice, I asked, "Can we stop by the bridge before going to school?"

The softest of smiles rested itself upon her lips. "Of course, Ben." In the next second, a glint in her eyes turned the smile playful. "But you'd better hurry up and eat, Turtle."

That memory warranted a chuckle. She hadn't called me 'Turtle' since…well, at least since my mom had died. I'm not sure why, but the nickname seemed to have been forgotten. Now it was back. The nickname had originated as a slight to my view of myself when I was nine. Turtles had become my favorite animal because I believed I was just like them: hard on the outside, soft on the inside. Ten-year-old Colette gleefully pointed out that I was outwardly soft as well, shattering my illusions of tough masculinity. For a few years, the nickname was used purely as an annoyance, but at some point it grew into more of a term of endearment rather than that of playful cruelty.

"Whatever, Lizzy," I smirked.

I thought Mr. Tance was going to die then and there as he sputtered and coughed, choking on his milk. The reason for his outburst was obvious: Lizzy was the despised nickname Mr. Tance had dubbed his daugh-

HERE'S TO THE UNDERDOGS!

ter three summers ago when all she did was lie on the driveway, roof, beach, or any other suitable surface to soak up the sun. The nickname was really her own fault. She had commented that if she were an animal, she would be some sort of reptile as she needed sunlight and warmth for energy. Thus 'Lizard' was born. I was convinced 'Rattlesnake' or 'Constrictor' or even 'Anaconda' would be better suited to her personality, but such names never stuck. 'Lizard' just couldn't be defeated.

With a bit of a chuckle, she quipped, "Just shut up and eat so we can go."

A hint of my usual, cheery attitude returning, I obliged and hastily swallowed my last bites of toast. Colette wasted no time dragging me out the door with her. The early November air was just turning chilly, but the morning sunlight slanting down on us added a welcome warmth.

Our walk was one of peaceful silence interrupted only by the chirping and twittering of songbirds as we strolled through the small neighborhood. We came to the silent agreement that we would climb down the rocky hill leading under the bridge. The sand was cool to the touch as I ran my fingers through it, seated against the stone and concrete bulwark of the bridge. The rushing water, though it looked inviting, would be ice-cold by now. Not a word was said as we gazed out over the narrow river. My thoughts wandered, as they always did, until they were shattered by a slap to my arm. I whipped my gaze over questioningly at Colette who pointed out at the water, her eyes twinkling with excitement. I looked where she was pointing to see about a dozen ducklings speeding up the river, their mother currently absent. They looked like they were running on top of the water, their stubby wings raised from their backs, necks craned out ahead of them. With amazing agility and speed, they navigated the rocks and swirling eddies, settling into the water just before the larger rapids, only to turn and race back down the river. They repeated this "game" a few times before hopping out of sight over a group of rocks.

Colette's laughter broke our awed silence. "They were so adorable! And did you see the straggler? That would have been you."

I chuckled and nodded in agreement, and we fell back into our quiet enjoyment of nature. My eyes roamed as much as my thoughts as I studied the river to our right, then turned my attention to the rapids to our left. I was surprised to see another figure seated on one of the smooth rock faces, around and over which the ice water flowed. Had I been standing, I probably would have fallen over in shock as I realized who it was. The girl with the hazel eyes and winged tattoo. I looked away as she glanced in my direction and was met with a mischievous grin from Colette.

"So? Are you going to talk to her or what?"

"W-what? Who? I don't— I don't know what you're talking about," I stammered.

She nudged my shoulder with hers. "Go on, Benjamin. You know you want to. She's cute. Besides, I'm pretty sure she caught you staring. You're not going to make things any weirder by talking to her. More embarrassing maybe, but not weirder."

"Thanks for the vote of confidence," I mumbled as I stood up and brushed the sand from my jeans.

"That's what I'm here for," she said with a wink. "Now go impress her with your charming bashfulness."

That didn't help my confidence any either. All our conversation did was get the girl's attention. I wasn't sure whether that was a good thing or not, though I'd find out soon enough. Taking a deep breath in an attempt to calm my nerves, I made my way carefully over the rocks to her. What a great first impression I would make by falling face-first into the water. She probably didn't even remember me from the beach. Even if she did, why would she want to talk to the idiot who ran into her on the beach? I was so enveloped in my thoughts, I nearly tripped over her, not realizing I had hopped the last rock to her.

"Oh. Sorry." I took a step back, aware of the short drop into the water inches away from my heel. "Hi," was all I could think to say.

"You were staring."

I shuffled one foot back, creeping closer to my possible demise. "N-no. I mean, I didn't mean to. I just— I was surprised to see you here. I haven't seen you since the beach— not that I've been looking for you! Just—" I sighed and decided silence would perhaps be a better option for the time-being.

A slight grin turned up the corners of her mouth. "That was you?"

An embarrassed blush creeping onto my cheeks, I rubbed the back of my neck and stared at the rock. "Uh, yeah… Sorry." I glanced at her to see her reaction. I was surprised and relieved to see her smiling up at me.

She patted the rock next to her. "Sit."

I sat next to her, laying my arms across my knees. "So… Do you go to school around here?"

"For the time-being. My dad's stationed here for a bit."

"Oh. Is he in the military?"

"Uh, yeah," her reply came with an uneasiness about it.

I decided to move back to the topic of school. "Westbrooke High?" She simply nodded in response, and I continued, "I haven't seen you around there."

"Today's my first day."

"Oh. My friend and I will be walking there soon." I paused, unsure of whether to offer or not. "You could walk with us. If you wanted." As I waited for her reply, I twisted the end of my scarf in my fingers.

"I'd love to."

"What?" My eyes rose to meet hers, and I tried to keep the grin threatening to spread across my face at bay. "Alright. We should probably leave now though so we aren't late." I stood and got a sense of *deja vu* as I offered a hand to help her to her feet.

Here's a tip: when you're trying to look good — or at least normal — around a cute girl, don't forget that you're standing on a slippery rock and nearly step off of said rock to plummet into the frigid water below. But what do you think I did? Exactly that.

I pulled her to her feet and took a half step back. The problem was, the rock ended a little less than a half step back. My foot slipped off the edge, and I lost my balance. Before I knew what was happening, the girl grabbed the front of my jacket and pulled me from the edge. I was practically nose to nose with her— well, nose to forehead because I was actually taller than her. A hard blush crept onto her cheeks, and she stepped away, casting her gaze to the rock we were standing on. *She's so cute when she blushes,* I thought. It took me a few seconds to stop smiling like the lovestruck fool I was and realize just what had happened.

I looked away and stammered in embarrassment, "Uh, thanks. We should, uh, we should, you know, get going, probably."

She unsuccessfully tried to stifle a giggle. "You're right. I wouldn't want to be late on my first day."

I smiled at her. "True. I'm Ben, by the way."

"Joanna."

HERE'S TO THE UNDERDOGS!

"It's nice to finally know your name." I grinned a bit and led the way back to Colette, carefully planning each step so as to not further embarrass myself.

Colette was waiting for us, a not very subtle grin on her face. She extended a hand to Joanna. "I'm Colette."

As she shook her hand, Joanna replied, "Nice to meet you. I'm Joanna."

Colette opened her mouth to speak, and I knew whatever else she had to say would not be good for me. I cut in before she could get a sound out.

"We should go. I have History first period, and Ms. Bobbin will probably kill me if I'm late."

Without giving either girl a chance to argue, I climbed up the hill to the top of the bridge and began walking down the sidewalk toward our school. I could hear the girls' footsteps behind me as they followed. Unfortunately, Joanna and I didn't get an opportunity to talk anymore before we had to go our separate ways to our classes.

Chapter 13: Ben

It wasn't until lunch time that I saw Joanna again. She was sitting at a table with a boy about my age whose tousled black hair fell about his sad eyes. He looked reserved and...prickly. A question plagued the back of my mind: *what if that's her boyfriend? If it is, then I've been such a fool and will never be able to show my face around her again.* I pushed the thought away. *No. It doesn't matter. Maybe he's just a friend. Yeah.* I took a deep breath and walked up to her table, a smile forced across my lips.

"Hi. Mind if I sit here?"

The boy narrowed his eyes at me and glanced at Joanna as if checking with her to see if I was "ok" or not. Joanna smiled at me and nodded. "Go ahead."

I set my tray down and sat on the other side of the table from them, glancing at the boy next to her. He simply glared at me as he took a bit of his rice.

"So…" I got my sandwich out of my bag and turned my attention to Joanna. "How's your first day been so far?"

"Good. I like the classes and teachers."

HERE'S TO THE UNDERDOGS!

With a nod, I replied, "That's good. Have you had Ms. Bobbin yet?"

She nodded. "She's not so bad. I actually kind of like her."

"You do? Wow. I always thought she was...well, mean, I guess."

The boy spoke, his voice just above a whisper, "Maybe she doesn't like you."

Joanna chuckled at the statement, either not noticing my annoyance with her companion or not caring. Either way, I forgot my annoyance when she directed her smile at me. Everything else seemed to fade away, and I smiled back for probably a bit too long. Colette fortuitously ended my staring as she set her tray down across from the boy. "Hi, Joanna. Who's this?"

"Luca. My older brother."

All my tension and nervousness melted away at this revelation. I could finally enjoy lunch, despite Luca's continued coldness towards Colette and myself.

Colette, friendly as ever towards new people, smiled at him. "Nice to meet you, Luca. I'm Colette, Ben's best friend."

He gave a curt nod to acknowledge that he had heard her.

"Ok... Not very talkative I see."

"Don't mind him," Joanna stated. "He has trouble socializing like a normal person."

I would have replied or tried to say something to Luca, but the bell rang, alerting us to the impending doom of our next classes. At least I wouldn't have gym class for a week or two as I had received a doctor's note to get me out of it. But gym wasn't until tomorrow anyway, and right now I had math class to deal with. As luck would have it, Luca and I had math together. (Hey, I never said it was *good* luck). Whatever type of luck, that's how our classes were laid out. We walked silently through the halls together and sat in adjacent seats without so much as looking at each other.

And without further ado, class began. I barely heard what the teacher was saying, which wasn't unusual, but the reason was that I couldn't stop glancing over at Luca in the seat next to mine. He stared ahead, his face unchanged from its imposing frown and furrowed brow. Honestly, the guy scared me. Sure, I was relieved that he was Joanna's brother and not a potential romantic contender, but brothers can hold a lot of weight when it comes to who their sisters date. I only hoped I could somehow get on Luca's good side.

Class ended, and Luca and I went to our next classes, which we did not have together. Overall, it was a pretty boring day. As soon as the bell rang at the end of the day, I grabbed my books from my locker and raced to the front doors to catch Joanna on her way out. Unfortunately, on my way there I ran into a kid. Literally. We both spilled our books and papers on the floor, and retrieving everything from amidst the race of teenagers without getting stepped on proved difficult and wasted more than five minutes of my time. As soon as my jumbled stack of books was safely in my arms again, I continued my dash to the door. Students were still flooding out of the building, and I scanned the throng for Joanna or even Luca as the two would most likely be together. I waited until the very last student had left the building, but I never spotted Joanna and her brother. Colette found me instead.

"Oh, good. You're still here," she said as she leaned an arm on my shoulder.

"Uh, yeah."

"I was looking for you. I thought you'd gone home without me. But I realized that couldn't be the case. Today is too important."

HERE'S TO THE UNDERDOGS!

"Today? Why?"

Her jaw dropped and she smacked my arm. "It's the first Monday of the month! Which means..." she waited for me to finish the thought.

As I rubbed my chest, I tried to get my thoughts off of everything that had happened the past few days and focus on what life was 'supposed to be like.' "Oh! Fro-yo!"

"Yes! How could you forget that," she scolded. "Wait... Were you looking for Joanna? Is that why you ditched me and forgot about fro-yo? I swear, if you replace me, I will come after you." She pointed an accusing finger at me.

"Of course not..." I fiddled with the leather band on my wrist without realizing it. "Ok, you could at least try to not look so guilty when you lie."

I sighed. "I'm sorry, Colette. With everything that's been happening, I just didn't even think about what day of the month it was."

"I know. Life has been kind of...messed up. Which is why we absolutely have to get fro-yo today. You need something normal. Something fun to take your mind off things."

"You're right," I agreed with a nod, the slightest smile gracing my lips. "Fro-yo sounds perfect."

She smiled and linked her arm through mine, and we walked down the road to the frozen yogurt shop together, our cars left side by side in the school parking lot to be retrieved later.

Frozen yogurt had been a tradition my mom and I had started when I was two. We used to get frozen yogurt once every other month, just the two of us. After my mom died, Colette suggested that she and I keep that tradition alive, but we loved fro-yo too much to settle for once every other month so we decided to make it a monthly tradition.

HERE'S TO THE UNDERDOGS!

With this month included, we were three for three. I knew that someday we would be too far apart to continue the tradition, but as long as we were in the same town, no matter how busy our lives got, fro-yo would be top priority.

Chapter 14: Ben

The most exciting thing that happened over the next few weeks was Thanksgiving. The Tance's invited my family over, just as they had the previous year. By now I was living at my own house again. Since my suicide attempt, Tony had been more helpful, and he and Alice got the littles bundled in their hats, coats, gloves, and scarves while I gathered the necessary food and cooking supplies that I was bringing to the Tance's house.

Aunt Michelle lead us to Colette's house. When we arrived, Garrett quickly found the twins, Colette took Joey from Aunt Michelle, and I spent the day in the kitchen with Mrs. Tance, Morgan, Alice, and my aunt. We had the most delicious Thanksgiving meal anyone could ask for. Mr. Tance had to bring the old dinner table from the basement and try to match it with their current table for all of us to fit. The tables were different heights and widths, but no one cared. We were together and having fun.

Mrs. Tance held Joey in her lap during the meal. She seemed to enjoy having a baby to take care of, which surprised me because she always seemed so serious and business oriented. But with Joey, she was completely different. She made faces and tickled him and even played patty-cake! I had seen her like this with the twins to some degree so I maybe shouldn't have been so surprised, yet I couldn't stop watching her and Joey throughout the whole meal.

After the meal, Mr. Tance gathered everyone in the living room to spend some time together. We recalled the past year and told what we were thankful for, and Mr. Tance encouraged us to thank God for His blessings. Garrett was fascinated by this idea, and even Alice was willing to listen to Mr. Tance as he talked about God and salvation. I had heard most of what he was saying before from him and Colette, and, without meaning to, I tuned him out and focused on Tony. What would *he* think of all this? When he had agreed to come with us, I had been shocked. Now I half expected him to get up and leave at the mention of religion. But he didn't. He stayed sitting on the floor, Garrett in his lap, and actually looked like he was paying attention, though he never looked directly at Mr. Tance.

I didn't realize how long I'd been staring at Tony until he happened to glance my way and lock eyes with me. He gave a sheepish smile and looked away. I forced my own attention away from him and back to Mr. T, but my thoughts still wandered from what Mr. Tance was saying. *Tony smiled at me.* I felt a smile spread across my face as a warmth rose in my chest. Despite our differences, I loved my brother and I had the hope that perhaps he was changing for the better.

Chapter 15: Colette

*I*t is my strong opinion that Thanksgiving deserves a longer recess from school. However, the school board never asked me, and, therefore, school began the Monday after Thanksgiving. It was on one of these school mornings that I met Jill and Connie, two girls who were infinitely different, yet could probably finish each other's sentences— that is if Connie spoke more. She was much quieter than Jill who seemed to never be silent for more than twenty seconds. Like a shark that dies if it stops swimming, it was quite possible that Jill would spontaneously combust if she didn't add to the conversation at least once every minute, though this could have been a myth as well.

I was out on a run when we crossed paths. Connie and Jill were stranded on the side of the road with car troubles. It turns out that having a car-crazy best friend actually came in handy as I was able to quickly identify the problem, though I wouldn't have been able to fix it had I even attempted to do so. As I pointed them in the direction of a garage, it became apparent that Jill lived up to all of the blonde stereotypes except for lacking common sense or any brains at all. She was chatty, a bit ditsy at times, and, had it not been for Connie, would never have made it to the garage without getting lost several times. But she was smart.

It was hard to learn much about Connie as she barely spoke during the ten-minute delay my run suffered, but throughout the following weeks I learned much about both of them. They had transferred to Westbrooke High, and Jill sought me out immediately at lunch on their first day. They got along well with Ben as well which was a must for any new friends I considered. And with Jill's peppy attitude, our friend group expanded quickly. Ben took advantage of this and relished the attention— once he warmed up to everyone, of course. What really endeared Jill to my heart was her ability to consistently talk Ben into coming to the Wednesday night home group meetings my church had started. She also wasn't at all shy about sharing Christ with everyone she ran into. Anytime we went out, it turned into an evangelism outreach. It was nice to have her as a friend, but I made sure Ben wasn't forgotten. We still spent the majority of our time together, just the two of us. He was still, and would always be, my dearest friend.

Chapter 16: Colette

Luckily, December 15th — Ben's birthday — fell on a Saturday. I'd set up a surprise party at my house, but I wanted to be one of the first to wish him a more personal happy birthday. I knew he'd want to sleep in and figured Michelle would want the morning with him, so after lunch I walked to his house. When Michelle let me in, I was surprised to find that Ben was still in bed. His aunt had checked on him about an hour earlier to make sure he wasn't sick, but let him be after that. I promptly journeyed upstairs to his room, knocking once before entering.

"What on earth are you doing still in bed?" I shouted as I pulled the covers from his bed. "Hey! Give 'em back!" He sat up so quickly that he hit his head on the bunk above him. I stifled a chuckle. "Oops. But you have to get up. It's your birthday!"

"Which is exactly why I'm not getting up."

He snatched a blanket and burrowed under it. Standing by his bed, I tried to decide what to do. It was obvious that he couldn't sleep the whole day, but he'd never been this difficult on his birthday before.

"What's so bad about your birthday?"

HERE'S TO THE UNDERDOGS!

"I'm a year closer to adulthood, and I don't like it. If I don't get up, no one can wish me a happy birthday, and tomorrow I can pretend it didn't happen."

"Benjamin... You're still seventeen today, and there's nothing you can do about that." I sat on the edge of his bed. "Listen. I'll be eighteen before you. I'll test out the waters and lead you through adulthood when the time comes."

He peeked out, grimacing at my smirk. "You're not that much older than me. A few months won't make you an expert."

"I know. But I'm already years ahead of you when it comes to maturity."

"Are not!"

"Who's the one hiding from their own birthday?" My question was met with a glare. "I rest my case. Now get up. Michelle made you a nice breakfast, and my family wants to see you." I left without giving him a chance to argue and joined his aunt downstairs.

"Is he getting up?"

"Of course, he is," I replied, grinning. "I told him to, and he wouldn't dare go against me."

Michelle laughed as she began reheating his breakfast. "Well, thank you."

Not ten minutes later, a tired and grumpy Ben graced the kitchen with his disheveled presence. He muttered 'good morning' to his aunt and dropped into a chair at the table.

"Food?" was the first word he spoke, looking expectantly at Michelle.

She laughed and set a plate before him. "It was fresh about three hours ago, sleepy head."

Ben didn't seem to care as he dug in hungrily, praising his aunt's cooking between bites. She and I watched in what could have been either amazement or horror. When Ben had finished, Michelle's shoulders slumped.

"An hour of cooking, and it was gone in two minutes." She shook her head and took his plate to the sink.

"Sorry," came his sheepish reply as he stood and planted a kiss on her cheek. "I do love your cooking though."

"I guess you're forgiven…" She smirked and hugged him. "Happy birthday." Ben pushed away from her and hid behind me jokingly. "The forbidden words!" Michelle simply laughed, and Ben and I joined in her joyous outburst. "You're a goof. You have to accept your birthday."

"Oh right. Like you have. You are not still twenty-one."

"Hey!" Jestingly, she whispered, "Don't give away my secret."

"Don't worry, Michelle," I jumped in. "I'll get him out of here now."

I grabbed Ben's hand and pulled him out of the house to my car, grabbing his coat along the way. Not giving him a chance to argue, I shoved him into the car and drove off.

"Ok, why was I kidnapped, and where are we going?"

"You weren't kidnapped. I'm taking you to my house."

"Oh no… This means birthday party."

"You'll be fine."

"Please let me out."

As we had successfully reached my house, I answered, "Sure. You can get out now."

"I hate you," Ben glared.

The twins ran out of the house and pulled his door open. They saved me the trouble of hauling him into the house where our friends plus Mr.

Furges were waiting to surprise him, though he'd already guessed the surprise. His siblings and aunt would join us later as well.

Ben warmed up to the celebration and had quite a good time by the end of it. A few presents had been brought, but much of the focus was on food and games. Yet the celebration had to end, and one by one people left until Ben and his family were the only ones left. Joey and Garrett were loaded into the car, already asleep. With a friendly hug, I wished Ben a final happy birthday before he drove off into the night. All in all, this had been a fairly successful birthday, and I went inside with the knowledge that I was once again the victor of Ben's birthday.

Chapter 17: Ben

Walking home in December is not fun. It's cold. Very cold. And slushy. And on this particular day it had to be icy as well. Add a gusty wind to all of that and you know what you get? Miserable. I would never again forget to have my jeep inspected. Normally, on days like this, I would have ridden with Colette, but her family had started their Christmas vacation early and were up North at their cabin in the Adirondacks. Jill and Connie were also unavailable as they had track before school and volleyball after school. So that left me to walk home from school in the cold, the wind biting at the small portion of my face that wasn't covered by my scarf and my glasses fogging up with every breath. It was also a great day to forget my contacts apparently.

I muttered to myself as I walked through town. With the wind whistling in my ear and my own bitter musings getting increasingly louder, it's a wonder how I even heard her crying. But I did. I stopped in my tracks and looked around, trying to judge the direction from which the sound was coming. *The park. That's where it is.* I opened the gate to the park I had been passing and shuffled over to the largest playset, pulling

HERE'S TO THE UNDERDOGS!

my jacket up over my nose to keep out the cold.

"Hello?" my muffled voice came. *Probably not the best idea to try speaking with your mouth covered by a scarf and jacket, Genius.* I pulled the offending clothing from my face before speaking again. "Is anyone up there?"

The crying immediately stopped. I waited a few seconds before a head appeared over the side of the structure. "Who are you? What do you want?" She brushed her sleeve over her cheeks, wiping the tears away. If I hadn't heard her crying, I would have assumed her cheeks and eyes were red from the cold.

"Are you ok?"

"Yeah. Fine. Why do you care?" She disappeared back behind the boards of her hiding place.

How can I stay without being creepy? I pondered. *I can't just leave her to cry. She probably wants someone to talk to, I just have to get her to open up.* I climbed just high enough on the ladder so that my head was poking up above the floor. "You look like you could use someone to talk to. I'm Ben."

She picked her head up from resting on her knees. "I've seen you around school."

"Oh." I climbed the rest of the ladder and sat on the edge of the playset. "You know, when someone tells you their name, it's generally accepted that you return the gesture by disclosing your own."

The smallest smile played at her lips. "Maggie."

I smiled back. "Maggie. Nice name." Pulling my legs into the treehouse-like play-structure, I continued, "With the formality of names aside, care to tell me what's wrong?"

She looked down and picked at the fur on her boots. "Nothing. I'm fine."

"Sure... Listen, my best friend is a girl, and though she doesn't get upset often, she has enough times during the course of our almost twelve-year friendship for me to know that you are far from 'fine'." The air quotes were rather pointless as she wasn't looking at me, but I felt they were needed just the same.

Her depressed exhale created a little cloud that quickly dissipated into the rest of the air. "I guess I could use someone to talk to..." She glanced up at me, but quickly returned her gaze to the wooden floorboards.

"Anything you say to me will stay with me. As the saying goes, 'what's said in the treehouse stays in the treehouse' or something like that."

Her eyes shifted up to me, her head still lowered. "You're ridiculous."

A lopsided grin tugged up one corner of my mouth. "So I've been told many times. But what's bothering you?"

She hesitated, but at last opened up and told me the problem. "My parents are getting a divorce," she sniffed. "My dad will be moving to Chicago this weekend."

"I'm sorry, Maggie. No kid should have to go through that." *And yet so many do. What a wonderful world to live in.*

She shrugged. "I'll still get to see him sometimes. But I don't want the kids at school to find out. I already get picked on cause I'm shy and an easy target."

I paused for a moment before responding. "I know somewhere you'll fit right in." She looked up at me curiously.

"At school tomorrow, during lunch, look for me at a table near the back of the lunch room. You'll be welcome there with me and my friends."

"Oh, I...I don't know... I don't really like new people..." She ducked her head again.

"I promise no one's too scary. Sure, Colette *can* be if you get on her bad side, and Joanna's brother Luca— yeah, he still scares me. But he's not around too much, so you don't have to worry about him, and even Colette won't be there. Anyway, the point is, you can hang out with us anytime you want."

Hesitantly, she replied, "I'll remember that. Thanks, Ben."

"Of course. Uh, do you want me to walk you home?"

She tugged her slouch hat over her ears, shaking her head. "Nah, I'll be ok."

"Alright. If you're sure." I flashed a quick smile before hopping to the ground. I started walking away, but stopped and called up to her, "I expect to see you tomorrow. If you don't show up, I'll go looking for you. And I'm pretty persistent so I'll eventually find you."

She poked her head out once again, her eyes lit up by her smile. "Fine... I'll see you at lunch."

Tipping my invisible hat in gratitude, I continued out of the playground and walked home, happier than I had been just twenty minutes ago. I'd never realized how nice it was to sit down and talk with someone until they felt better. It was rewarding. Sure, I couldn't make her situation better, and I really only had her word that she would show up at lunch, but she had stopped crying and even smiled by the time I left. That counted for something. But I'd still have to wait until tomorrow to see just how much of an impact I'd had.

Chapter 18: Ben

The next day in school, I made everyone aware of Maggie's possible appearance at lunch. We waited eagerly, scanning the lunch room so we could call her over if we saw her. Our plan didn't work, as we discovered when she approached our table unseen. Her quiet voice startled me and made me nearly spill my drink as she asked to sit with us. Thankfully, Joanna managed to save my precious apple juice.

"Maggie!" I leaped up from my seat and hugged her without really thinking. "Glad you made it. I would have hated to spend my lunch break looking for you."

She was taken aback by the hug and seemed even more shocked by the innocent wink I gave her as I sat back down.

Slowly, she lowered herself into a seat at the end of the table, leaving a buffer seat between herself and Connie. Everyone — except Luca — introduced themselves and expressed how glad they were that she had agreed to join our little group. As we continued with lunch, she warmed up to us slowly, smiling at different comments and even adding her opinion once or twice.

HERE'S TO THE UNDERDOGS!

***

There were only two more days before Christmas break, but we made sure to include Maggie as much as possible. Even after Christmas break had started, we all managed a few rendezvous, but it wasn't until after school started again that things really got going.

***

We integrated Maggie into our group as often as we could over the next week or so. It was encouraging to see her come out of her shell more each day, and we soon learned just what a truly sweet and amazing person she was. Though she appeared shy and reserved, and *was* for the most part, she could also be funny and added a wonderful flavor to our group. What was also amazing was the amount of attention our lunch table was getting. Other students used to ignore us, but now I was catching glances from the nearest tables, and sometimes an individual would go out of his or her way to see what was so special about the table in the back, the occupants of which were always happy and encouraging each other and didn't bother to even try fitting in anymore. Our group gained members as well.

There was Nathan, the kid with one hand. Literally. On his right arm where his hand should be, there was a stub. None of us knew whether he had been born like this or if this was due to a surgery he had had, but no one really cared enough to ask. He was incredible just the same and somehow still managed to play the guitar and piano to some degree. He was an inspiration to us all because he wasn't shy about his difference. He embraced it. It was one of the things that made him truly special, but it also made him an outcast from the majority of the students, which is why he was eager to be accepted into our group.

Becky joined next. Connie had actually found her and integrated her into our friend group. Becky was anorexic, but we were all helping her work through that and get better. Colette and I agreed to bring her along for fro-yo a few times even.

As we grew in numbers, we grew in popularity. Sort of. We certainly were nowhere near 'cool' popular, but we were being noticed more and more. Honestly, it would have been hard not to notice our group as we strode down the hall together every day. For a while, it seemed like everything was getting better. We had each other, we weren't bothered by anyone, the teachers loved us— then it happened. Deep down I always knew that there would be a breaking point, a time when Darren and the other bullies could take it no longer, but none of us were expecting it.

They started out small. Simple pranks to remind us they were still better than us: spiders or snakes in lockers, stealing homework, tipping trays in the lunchroom. But, of course, the pranks got worse. They targeted us outside of school. They even tried to break us up from the inside, but we stood strong.

Chapter 19: Colette

"Ben! Ben, look at this!" I shoved a flier into Ben's hands in the hallway. Barely was I able to contain the squeals pressing at my lips as I awaited his response, but I had a reputation of being cool and collected — and somewhat scary — to uphold at school. Thus, I waited, outwardly patient, inwardly dying with anticipation. His response was...disappointing.

"Ok… What is this and why did you attack me with it?"

"It's a flier for the school talent show!"

"I can read." Eyeing me warily, he continued, "What I mean is, and I mean this in the nicest way possible, so what?" He handed the flier back.

"So what?" I uttered an exasperated groan as my palm met my forehead. "So...you should enter, idiot."

"Ha, no thanks."

He turned away to collect his books from his locker and started down the hallway to his next class. I quickly fell in step with him.

"What do you mean 'no thanks'?"

"What would I do?"

"Um, sing maybe? You know, since you're amazing?"

I almost ran into him as he stopped. "How do you know that? When in the past half-decade have you heard me sing?"

"You lived at my house for three weeks and you sing in the shower."

Obviously, he had never considered during his brief stay with us that our bathroom was not soundproof. He waved this off.

"I'm still not singing. I don't sing in front of people. I'm not good enough."

He resumed walking, and I stepped in front of him, not weighing the risk of walking backwards in a crowded high school hallway.

"Not good enough? Ben, you're amazing! And you wouldn't be alone. Maggie sings, Nathan plays guitar and also sings a little, and I'm sure we could find others who play the drums or piano."

"Nope. Not gonna happen." He pushed past me and entered his classroom to escape, for now, anymore talk of the talent show.

I'll admit I was slightly disheartened by his cold rejection of the idea, but I wouldn't give up.

Eventually, he'd see that I was right as I usually was.

My musing was interrupted when someone crashed into me from behind. In trying to keep my balance and not fall on my face, I stepped on said person's foot. I spun around and couldn't keep a grin from tugging at the corners of my mouth.

"Jeremy! I didn't see you there. Are you ok?" From the tone of my voice, I made certain there was no way he would mistake my sarcasm for genuine concern.

The grimace on his face was the only answer I needed to that question.

He forced a smile as he stood on both feet again and answered, "Perfectly fine. May I walk you to class?"

"Even if my classroom weren't a mere three feet away, my answer would still be no." I brushed past him and ducked into my classroom before he could protest. I guess Ben and I have similar methods for avoiding unwanted conversations.

Jill accompanied me down the hall to our next class an hour later. "So, what's the deal with Jeremy?"

"What do you mean?"

"He's cute and seems pretty sweet from what I've seen of him. What happened between you two?"

I gripped my bag tighter, jaw clenched. Jeremy was the last person I wanted to talk about.

Ever. But I also knew Jill wouldn't let the subject go until I'd told her what had happened.

"Well?" She looked at me expectantly.

"We...used to...date..." I forced the words out, not meeting her eyes.

"What?" She stared at me in amazement. "Wow. I never would have guessed. I thought you didn't date?"

"I don't. But that doesn't mean I never did in the past." I quickened the pace, eager to get to our next class and avoid as much of this conversation as possible.

"Why'd you break up? I'm assuming you're the one who broke it off."

"I did. And I had a good reason."

She waited a moment for me to continue before prompting. "And that reason was…?"

"I'll tell you later." I rushed into our classroom, distancing myself from her so she couldn't pull me back out again.

A disgruntled squeal sounded behind me as she resigned to wait until another time to find out more— not that she had a choice. Of course, she sat behind me in class and, for the whole hour, nagged me to tell her more. I was sure she was going to get caught talking and passing notes and we were both going to get in trouble, but the teacher was distracted with her own problems and either never saw Jill's note-passing or didn't care enough to say anything. Either way, I was relieved when class ended without any mishaps or any detention slips being received.

We met Ben and Maggie in the hall and walked together to our lockers. This was the perfect opportunity to bring the matter of the talent show back up, though Maggie would take a good amount of coaxing to get on board. Jill, on the other hand, I was confident would eagerly agree to the idea.

I gave Ben a sly grin before speaking to the girls. "Have you two heard about the talent show?"

Jill's face lit up. "Talent show? We should perform together!"

Maggie seemed to want to hide.

"What do you say, Mags?" I looked at her hopefully.

"I...I can't get in front of people and perform..."

"But we'd all be up there together!" Jill threw an arm around Maggie's shoulders. "Just one question: what would we be doing?"

Ben hid behind his hands as a grin spread across my face. "Singing."

Jill gave a squeal of approval. "That would be so fun! We can start a band. Oh my gosh, I have to tell everyone else. And maybe we could get some other kids involved!"

Maggie stared at her, trying to catch everything she was saying, then looked at her like she had three heads.

"That's one on board. Ben? Please?" I pleaded.

He hemmed and hawed before finally, begrudgingly, giving in. "Oh, alright. I suppose I could give it a try…"

"Thank you!" I threw my arms around him. If *he* was on board, Maggie would soon follow. The others wouldn't be hard to convince.

"Yeah, ok. You can release the death grip now."

"Oh, sorry." I stepped back from Ben, still grinning like an idiot, but I didn't care. This would be good for all of us. It could be our chance to show we were more than just the outcasts.

HERE'S TO THE UNDERDOGS!

Chapter 20: Ben

Colette and her stupid talent show were going to be the death of me. Ironic considering, she was the one who had literally saved my life a few months before. But I was a nervous wreck every day for a week leading up to our first rehearsal. This would be the first time I had *knowingly* sung in front of anyone above the age of seven in, well, nearly seven years. My mom used to make me and my siblings sing at different family events, but that stopped when I was ten. Now I was about to sing in front of my closest friends— you know, the only people whose opinions really mattered? Yeah, them. My stomach was in knots, and I could see my hand shaking as I reached out to knock on Nathan's front door. We had all agreed to meet at his house since he had the best basement to practice in and his family would all be away at work.

I knocked lightly. After waiting a few moments and getting no answer, I knocked slightly harder, hoping that perhaps practice had been cancelled and I was simply unaware. My heart sank as Nathan opened the door and smiled at me.

HERE'S TO THE UNDERDOGS!

"Hey, Ben. Come on in. Pretty much everyone else is downstairs. We're just waiting on Jill and Connie now."

He led me downstairs to the basement, and I have to say it was the nicest basement I'd ever been in. To be fair, I'd only been in a few basements, and they were all the crawling-with- spiders-and-filled-with-mold kind of basements, but this basement just seemed extra cozy. It was fully carpeted, beanbags scattered along the periphery. One half of the basement had been dedicated as a game room, and the other half was divided into a gym on one side and a music area on the other with a keyboard, drum set, and a few guitars fighting for space. I picked up a guitar and played a few chords as Colette, Maggie, Becky, and Walter, our newest member, discussed songs.

Colette looked up at me and asked whether Tony was coming.

"He's not going to join the band. Trust me, I tried very hard to convince him to." I turned to Nathan. "How'd you get Walter down here? No offense."

Walter chuckled and answered, "There's another entrance with a ramp so this basement is actually wheelchair accessible."

"It was a feature of the house we never thought we'd need," Nathan put in. "Proved to be pretty handy though."

I cocked my head at Nathan. "Was that supposed to be a pun? Because it is in two respects."

He stared at me in confusion for a moment, then burst out laughing, causing the girls to look our way. His laughter was so jovial and sincere, it elicited a chuckle from me and calmed my nerves. These were my friends. Sure, what they thought mattered, but even if I were terrible, we'd all laugh about it together and then move on. Why had I been worried?

HERE'S TO THE UNDERDOGS!

Right on cue, interrupting my thoughts, Jill bounced down the stairs, Connie in tow.

"Are we ready to get this party started?" Jill questioned.

"It's more of a jam sesh," Nathan corrected as he slung a guitar over his head.

Walter wheeled himself over to the keyboard, and Connie surprised everyone by sitting behind the drum set. Maggie stood behind a mic and smiled at me.

"You've got centerstage, Ben."

Taking a deep breath, I set the guitar back in its stand and stepped behind the second mic.

"What's first on the list?"

"Do y'all know any *Shawn Mendes*?" Jill queried as she grabbed the third mic.

"Oh, come on. Really? *Shawn Mendes*?" I complained.

"What's wrong with *Shawn Mendes*?"

"Nothing, I guess. Just not my style. How about something older? Like...*Gordon Lightfoot* or *Don Williams* or *The Eagles*."

They all stared at me for a minute. Nathan was the first one to break the silence.

"Ok, I know who *The Eagles* are, but I don't think any of us have heard of the other two. Something else?"

I racked my brain for a song they would know and I could sing. "What about something by *Billy Joel*? You guys have *got* to know some *Billy Joel*."

After a general consensus of head-nodding, and deciding the particular song and key, Walter started playing. I anxiously awaited my cue to start, and after just a line or two of singing, my nervousness faded, and I donned a wide smile. The further into the song we got, the more

HERE'S TO THE UNDERDOGS!

comfortable I was singing. I loved this song, I loved these people, and I had forgotten how much I loved singing. Everyone else seemed to be enjoying themselves too. Colette even joined me in singing, wrapping her arm around my shoulders and grinning.

I laughed when the song ended, my nervousness completely dispelled and replaced with joy.

Colette and Nathan joined me in my bout of laughter.

"See? That was great! I told you you were good," Colette boasted.

The rest of the group sounded their agreement, congratulating each other.

"Ok, ok. You were right," I said as I regained my composure. "Maybe this will be more fun than I thought."

The rest of the afternoon we spent singing and laughing together. I wished Joanna could have joined us as it proved to be a great time for bonding and strengthening our little group, and we were all confident that our band would be warmly accepted at the talent show. But before we could sign up for the talent show, we needed a name.

"How about The Turtles?"

Colette turned and looked at me like I was crazy. "No. Why on earth would that be a good choice? It's a random animal!"

"So are *The Eagles* and *The Beatles*. They both became famous!"

"No. I'm not budging on this one."

"Agreed."

"Maggie!" I turned to her, feeling betrayed.

She simply shrugged. "Sorry, Ben, but The Turtles is not a good band name."

I frowned and crossed my arms. "Fine. Come up with your own stupid name."

HERE'S TO THE UNDERDOGS!

"Seriously? Are you going to pout about this?"

I didn't answer Colette, resolving to remain silent for the remainder of the afternoon, or at least until everyone acknowledged that my idea wasn't as horrible as they made it seem.

Colette sighed and shook her head. "Any other ideas?"

"What about Misfit Parade?"

Connie spoke up, "That's a song title. We can't use that, Jill."

Jill huffed but accepted the criticism with more dignity than I had.

We had a few other worthy contenders that afternoon: Shooting Star, For the People, Uprising, The Powder Puffs— the last one was suggested by Morgan when she called Colette and we asked for suggestions before hanging up. We should have known better than to ask her. Alas, we couldn't all agree on any one of them. By suppertime, everyone was tired and hungry, so we decided to call it a day and continue our name hunt at a later date. We were also tasked by Colette — who had become the honorary and unspoken president of our group with Jill seeming to act as vice president — to come up with song ideas for the talent show.

After saying a short goodbye to Nathan, the rest of us vacated his house like a bunch of stray puppies and headed to our individual homes.

My excitement to get home and eat dinner fizzled out when I realized that there would be no dinner until I had spent the time to make it. Maybe I'd settle for popcorn tonight. With my spirits thus restored, I strolled home to enjoy a relaxing evening of watching a movie and going to bed early. And for one, my plans were uninterrupted by any misfortunes, near-death experiences, or annoying older brothers. As I drifted off to sleep, I could only wonder what life was planning to throw at me next...

Chapter 21: Ben

Only two days until the talent show, and so far, there hadn't been any major mishaps. Apart from Becky's sprained wrist, everyone was in perfect health. We still didn't have a name for our

band, but we were allowed to sign up anyway. That night we were having a bonfire in the abandoned field near my house. Everyone was looking forward to it. Well, everyone ex cept Walter. He, unfortunately, had to cancel last minute and was, in his own way, moping around about it, though he still appeared chipper to anyone who didn't know him well.

"Hey, Ben, wait up!" Jill called to me in the hallway as she jogged to my side. "So, the bonfire needs music, right? Of course, it does. I volunteer to provide the music tonight."

While Jill wasn't wrong about our need for music, her taste in music was focused mostly on modern pop and slight rock and roll— not my first choices. But perhaps she'd pull through and have a few excellent choices. I devised a compromise.

"Alright. You can play DJ, but you have to include other people's music as well."

HERE'S TO THE UNDERDOGS!

"Well, duh!" she giggled.

And that settled the matter of music.

The rest of the day was spent in anticipation of the evening to follow. I practically slept through most of my classes, a fact Colette would kill me for if she knew, and lunch was even less appetizing than usual as my mouth watered for the savory steaks I'd cook at the bonfire. Gym was a war-zone, but I survived and finally made it to Chemistry— the best class of the day. This was one class I was always wide awake for. If I wanted to be a world-famous scientist someday, I'd need to get into a good college, and to get into a good college, I needed good grades in Math and Science. Hopefully no one would care about my History grades…

"Ready for tonight?" Colette asked as she looped her arm through mine at the end of the school day.

I returned her smile. "Of course."

"Joanna will be there," she grinned.

I simply nodded, hiding my glee. "Everyone will be there. Well, everyone except Walter."

She chuckled, shaking her head at my dodge. "Anyway. Do we have everything we need?"

"Yup. I'm taking care of dinner, Nathan's bringing the s'mores stuff, and Jill is in charge of music."

"That ought to be interesting."

I nodded as we exited the school together. I'd never understood how people thought we could be dating, but thinking about it now, it wasn't a ridiculous assumption. We did everything together, knew everything about each other, and here we were now walking to our cars, arm in arm.

HERE'S TO THE UNDERDOGS!

There was no other guy that Colette was this comfortable with except maybe Marcus, and even him she wouldn't be caught dead linking arms with. She and I had a special bond. I smiled at the thought.

"Penny for your thoughts?" Colette said as she looked over at me.

"Hmm? Oh. I'm just...thinking about tonight."

The way she tilted her head told me she was trying to decide whether or not she believed me.

I must have been getting better at fibbing for she shrugged and resumed walking.

We parted once we reached her car, and she drove off. The parking lot was still pretty full with student and faculty vehicles, and it took me several minutes to find my jeep. When I did, Darren and his friends were waiting for me.

"Great," I muttered under my breath.

I thought that maybe if I ignored them, they'd leave me alone. With that hope, I pushed past the pack and disregarded their second-rate slights and smack talk. Of course, my ploy didn't work.

"Hey, Connley. Where are you off to? Goin' to meet your loser friends?"

I turned to face Darren. "Losers? Yeah, maybe when it comes to being popular. But is that even going to matter after high school? In five years, no one's going to care about who was popular or who the quarterback of the football team was. What's really going to matter is who had the motivation and courage to move on with their lives. What really matters isn't high school, but rather life afterwards."

For a moment there was silence, and I had the audacity to think that maybe I'd finally gotten through to them. I was wrong.

"Nice speech," Darren sneered. "But you're wrong. High school matters." He stuck his finger in my face. "You'll see. Come on, guys." He waved for his friends to follow him as he stalked off.

A melancholy shadow fell over my face as I drove out of the parking lot. Reflecting on his words, I realized that he was right. High school did matter. Our time in high school would shape us, determine who we would become. We could give into the lies we were told by those like Darren and believe we were worthless and destined to fail or we could rise up and prove to ourselves and others that we were better than that. We were special. We were destined for greatness, not failure. And that's what I would choose to believe. I could only hope my friends would choose that way of thinking as well.

Chapter 22: Ben

Most of the crew were already encircling the bonfire when I arrived with the steaks. Marcus nearly attacked me when he smelled the food. He and Morgan would be joining us for about an hour before being sent home by Colette.

"Whoa! Relax, man. There are plenty of steaks, and they aren't going anywhere."

"I'm starving!"

"Did someone mention food?" Morgan dropped her book next to where she had been seated on the ground and hastened to the jeep, alerting everyone else that the delicacy of steak had arrived.

Rather than trying to hand out the food in an orderly fashion, I stepped back as everybody helped themselves. Colette stood next to me, arms crossed, a grin dimpling her cheeks.

"What took you so long? They were getting impatient."

"I can see that. I had a mishap with the stove."

She turned to me, her eyebrows raised in disbelief. "*You* had a problem cooking?"

"Hey, it's not my fault. Tony was messing around with the fuse box and tripped the breaker. He must have broken something because we couldn't get the power to come back on, so we are currently without electricity. I have never been so thankful that we have a gas stove."

"Oh… What are you going to do about the power?"

"I left Tony to deal with that. He said he might join us after he calls someone to fix our power."

She smiled. "I hope he can."

I narrowed my eyes and studied her. "Why…?"

"Oh, come on, Benjamin. Don't read anything into that. I just think it would be good for Tony to be around people like us as opposed to his usual friends."

"Oh, good," I nodded. "So do I."

She nudged my shoulder and grinned. "I think it's safe to eat now. The hoard has been fed."

"We can hear you, you know," Morgan piped up.

Colette chuckled. "That's the point. I was referring to you and Marcus mostly."

"And Nathan," I added as I grabbed a paper plate.

Nathan didn't even try to deny it. "It's true."

Everyone laughed except Morgan, though I did catch her smiling behind her book for a moment.

The evening continued in that manner: just a group of friends laughing and joking together. Marcus and Morgan contested Colette's decision to send them home at nine o'clock, but they eventually relented and went home. Though Colette trusted Marcus, she didn't trust Morgan to go straight home so she assured them she would call the house to make sure they made it, and we discovered fifteen minutes later that they had.

By nine-thirty Jill had started her music, and Tony arrived not long after. For about an hour we were all on our feet dancing or standing around watching everyone else as they danced. We played a few games and sat around and talked, but by eleven o'clock everyone had collapsed on blankets on the ground to stargaze. We were all quiet, Jill's music filling in the silence. Earlier that evening we had discussed band names, but we still couldn't decide on anything that we felt suited us. Then a song by *P!nk* came on. Colette immediately spoke up.

"This song? Really, Jill?"

"What? I like *P!nk*."

Colette hefted a sign. I knew she was probably irritated because of the swearing in the song, but given that she and Connie were probably the only ones who cared, she didn't protest more. I could feel the tension and barely listened to the lyrics of the song, but a certain word caught my attention, and I sat up so quickly I made Connie squeak as I startled her.

"Guys! I got it!"

Colette looked up at me. "Got what exactly?"

I turned my head to look back at her where she was lying on the blanket next to me. "Our band name!"

"Oh, no," Maggie groaned. "Please tell me it's not another animal."

Had I not been so excited, I probably would have shot her my best death glare. "No, no, nothing like that. Well, not *exactly* an animal."

"Then tell us," Nathan said as he sat up.

One word. "Underdogs."

There was silence as everyone contemplated the idea.

HERE'S TO THE UNDERDOGS!

Nathan nodded and spoke up first. "I like it."

Jill's squeal was all I needed to know I had her approval. "It's perfect!"

There was a general consensus of agreement after that, and it was finally settled that Underdogs was our new moniker. Some discussion was had concerning the name, but we eventually fell back into content silence, and it wasn't long afterward that I noticed the change in Colette's breathing indicating that she had fallen asleep. I sat up and looked around at the others, most of whom were also asleep. With a smile, I laid back down and closed my own eyes, resigning myself to the same tranquil rest.

Chapter 23: Colette

I always forget that Ben talks in his sleep; that is, until I have to sleep in close proximity to him. Then it is all too clear in my memory as I lie awake, unable to sleep because of his mumbled monologues. Hence the reason I walked home at two in the morning. We had school that day, and I needed at least a few hours of good sleep. When my alarm went off at six-thirty, rousing me from my dreams, I realized four hours of sleep was not enough, though there was nothing that could be done about it now. I debated going to wake the others, but Connie was with them, and she was sure to get everyone to school on time. Having a bonfire on a school night was a terrible idea.

By the time I arrived at school, I was surprisingly more awake and livelier than I had expected I would be. Of course, that was after I'd drunk an entire thermos of coffee. I waited anxiously in Geometry class for Jill and Ben to arrive, and, as I had thought would happen, they burst through the door with barely a minute to spare. I motioned them over, Jill taking the seat in front of me, Ben the empty seat to my left.

"Did everyone make it?"

Jill turned to face me and nodded. "Thanks to Connie. She woke everyone around six, giving us enough time to go home and prepare for today."

I hadn't realized how tense I'd been until that moment as my muscles relaxed and a smile spread across my face. "Good."

"When did you leave?" Ben queried.

"Around two I think."

"Why?"

"You talk in your sleep." I gave him a pointed look.

He raised his hands defensively. "Hey, it's not *my* fault you're the lightest sleeper in the world."

An eye-roll was all I could respond with as our teacher silenced all students and began class.

As Ben, Jill, and I were walking down the hall to our final class of the day, we happened upon Darren talking to Maggie. Ever since Ben found Maggie crying in the playset, all we knew about her family was that her parents were divorced. Now we learned the truth as Darren spewed insults and secrets of how her dad had had an affair, leading to the divorce. How he knew this was a mystery, but poor Maggie was in tears, unable to silence him.

Before I could stop him, Ben rushed to her aid— or rather to fight Darren. He took a swing at Darren's jaw. Not expecting this, Darren didn't have time to duck or block the punch and took the full force of the swing, stumbling back and staring at Ben in surprise. His surprise soon turned to rage, and, as he tackled Ben, a full-out fight broke out in the hallway. I pushed past the ring of students forming around them who were chanting "Fight! Fight!" When Maggie spotted me, she ran into my arms, sobbing onto my shoulder.

HERE'S TO THE UNDERDOGS!

The fight lasted until Coach happened by and separated the two; then Maggie, Jill, and I waited for Ben outside the principal's office. It seemed ages before Darren exited the office, pausing to glare at us before hurrying down the hall. We were all relieved to see Ben emerge a few minutes later. He kept his gaze cast downward, not even looking up at me as I took his hands in mine.

"Ben? What did he say?"

I thought he had been looking down in shame, but as his eyes met mine, I saw only anger.

"We got off with a warning. Even Darren." He spat the name out.

"You should be grateful. You could have been suspended. What were you thinking?"

Turning away from me, he shoved his hands in his pockets and started walking down the hall. I could tell Jill was about to say something to me, probably something to keep me from lecturing Ben, but I didn't give her the chance. I grabbed his shoulder, turning him to me, and began speaking, voice raised to a tone generally reserved for Marcus or Morgan.

"Answer me. Since when has getting in a fight solved anything? I thought you knew this!"

"It's not fair! I'm tired of being bullied. I'm tired of seeing others bullied. Yeah, it stopped for a little while, but it's not over."

I paused a few moments before answering, my tone soft. "I know it's hard, Ben. And I know it doesn't seem fair, but you have to trust that we'll get through this. You aren't alone."

He sighed. "Yeah, I know. And I'm grateful for you all, but sometimes everything just seems pointless. The Underdogs were supposed to... somehow *stop* the bullying. Maybe we just made it worse."

"I'm not talking about the Underdogs."

Brow furrowed, he looked at me questioningly. I waited for him to realize what — or rather Who — I was referring to.

"Oh… I get it. You mean God."

I nodded. "Yes. Of course, I mean God. I know what you and Maggie and everyone else are going through is hard and may seem hopeless, but He sees the bigger picture. If you trust Him, He'll bring you through it."

"Easier said than done," he mumbled.

"I know…" I pulled him into a hug. "But we'll make it through this."

It was no surprise to me that Jill had joined in the hug, pulling Maggie with her. The four of us lingered in each other's embrace for a few sweet moments before Ben broke it up.

"Um…that's enough group-hugging for one day." He peeled himself out of our grasp. Chuckling, I replied, "I actually agree. Let's go home, hmm?"

With a nod of approval from Ben, I linked my left arm through his right arm, and Maggie followed suit on his left as Jill linked arms with me. And, thusly, we strolled through the hall, not permitting any to separate us, though there were only a few students left in the halls, the rest either on their way home already or attending whatever after-school group they were a part of.

Upon reaching the parking lot we parted ways, giving each other final hugs to which Ben rolled his eyes, though I know he secretly appreciated the gestures.

"Don't forget about Underdogs practice tomorrow. That means you can't sleep in till noon, Benjamin."

Again, he rolled his eyes, a smirk tugging at his lips. "Yes, mother."

I returned the eye roll. "Just be there, ok? We can't practice without our lead singer."

"I know. I'll be there. See you then." With a wave, he drove out of the parking lot.

I smiled after him, lost in thought for a minute as I stood in the parking lot before finally driving home.

Chapter 24: Ben

"Ben! Wake up!"

Chubby legs straddled my stomach, two little hands pressed to my chest as I was awakened by the squeaky voice.

"Garrett... Go downstairs." As I rolled over, my four-year-old brother fell off my stomach and onto the bed next to me, delighted giggles ensuing.

"Wake up!"

"I'm awake, Garrett," I said as I buried my face in my pillow.

Garrett took this as an invitation to climb onto my back and mess with my hair. My pillow muffled my groan.

Lifting my head so I could be heard, I muttered, "Ok, ok. I'll get up. But you have to get off of me first."

"No!" he declared as he flopped forward onto my back in what I suppose was some sort of hug.

"Then you'd better hold on."

Giggling, he wrapped his chubby arms around my neck. He was used to this routine, as was I. Twisting one arm behind me so as to support him should he let go, I shimmied off the bed, careful not to hit his head on the top bunk as I stood. "Is Aunt Michelle cooking breakfast?"

"Uh-huh!"

"Then let's go eat!" I skipped down the stairs with him, the smell of bacon and cheesy breakfast potatoes hitting my senses before I even stepped foot in the kitchen.

"Morning, Michelle!"

She turned to smile at us. "Good morning, you two. Take a seat and breakfast will be ready in just a few minutes."

Wrapping my arm around my brother's middle, I swung him from my back to my front so I could put him in his chair, then I stood next to my aunt at the stove. Though she was my aunt, I rarely called her that. She was only seven years older than me, and we had grown up together, almost as though we were long-lost siblings.

"Do you want any help?"

"Sure. Would you flip the bacon?"

Nodding, I picked up a fork and commenced to watch over the bacon. Knowing Aunt Michelle preferred her bacon more on the "rare" side, I soon transferred the fatty strips to a plate and laid more sizzling bacon in the pan.

"The potatoes are ready now. Thanks, Ben, but you can go ahead and eat. You don't want to be late for your last practice," she said with a wink.

Giving her a quick hug, I made myself a plate of food and took it to the table. Garrett had already been appeased with grapes and oranges which he crammed as many of into his mouth as he could.

The three of us, plus Alice and Tony, enjoyed breakfast together before I had to rush off to Underdogs practice. I was certain on my way out the door to snag a few of the cookies Aunt Michelle had baked the day before, and I heard Joey start crying as I shut the door.

* * *

A few flurries of snow danced on the breeze as I walked from my jeep to the school. It was easy to tell which cars had been sitting in the parking lot for an extended period of time as they had a light dusting of snow on them, the pavement beneath being bare. I was a bit surprised by the number of vehicles, but I suppose it made sense. Faculty would be here preparing for the talent show, and, of course, we Underdogs wouldn't be the only group getting in a final practice.

My footsteps echoed as I clomped through the nearly vacant halls in my snow boots. After just a few steps, I had to remove my glasses as they had fogged up from the temperature difference.

The door slamming behind me caused me to whirl around, and I saw Maggie come in, cheeks rosy— well, what I could see of them. Maggie had her scarf pulled up nearly to her Rudolph-red nose, hiding half of her face. Glancing behind her, I could see through the glass doors that the snow was coming down harder now, explaining the dusting of white that topped Maggie's hat and shoulders.

"You made it!"

If it weren't for the smile showing in her eyes, I wouldn't have been able to tell if my smile had been returned as her scarf still hid half of her face. She was unable to do anything about it, her arms filled with sheet music and binders.

"Let me help you with those." I relieved her of most of the binders, allowing her to tug the checkered scarf down and tuck it under her chin.

"Thank you. Is everyone else here?"

"I'm not sure," I replied as we walked. "I only just got here myself."

"Oh, right. Of course." She flushed a bit. "That would explain why you're out in the hall."

A nod was all I had time to respond with as we turned into the band room. We'd planned to get here early enough that we would have this room to ourselves, and it appeared that our plan had worked for the only faces I saw were those belonging to my friends. Glancing around the room, scanning faces, I did notice that one person was missing: Joanna.

"Joanna's not here yet?" I asked as I set the binders on a chair.

Colette shook her head. "I haven't seen her yet, but we'd better start. She's a backup singer anyway and knows her part. Come on."

With no further talk about our missing member, assuming the snow was the reason for her tardiness, we began. Practice went smoothly for close to half an hour when it was interrupted by a scream in the hall. We all immediately raced to investigate. What we found, I was not prepared for...

Chapter 25: Ben

Joanna was glaring at her brother, arms crossed. That wasn't too unexpected, to be honest. What really astonished me and caused me to wonder if I were perhaps dreaming was Luca's response. He paid no heed to his sister's obvious irritation and instead appeared to be grinning. It was slight, almost unnoticeable, but a grin was definitely present on his face.

Jill broke our awestruck silence. "What happened? We heard a scream."

Joanna's glare intensified, warning her brother not to say a word on pain of death. This was a warning he did not attend to, however.

"Joanna saw a spider."

"Correction: a tarantula crawled across my foot."

It was all I could do to contain my laughter. "That's it? We thought someone was hurt."

Joanna's attention snapped to me, and I realized I had made a grave mistake in speaking.

"'*That's it?*'," she mocked. "That's all you have to say?!"

HERE'S TO THE UNDERDOGS!

I swallowed hard, sure to think over my words more carefully this time. "Sorry. Of course, not. How about we get to the band room, and if you see the spider again, I'll take care of it? It probably just escaped from the Biology room."

After a bit of hesitation, Joanna agreed, and we all returned to finish up with our practice. We had decided last minute to add a couple Queen songs to our talent show list, so most of our attention was focused on those. About fifteen more minutes of practice was all we could accomplish, though, before we were kicked out of the band room. It was just as well as we only had about half an hour to set up and prepare for the talent show to start. We lugged the keyboard, music stands, mics, and Nathan's guitar out of the band room. Thankfully, there was a drum set already on the stage so we didn't need to disassemble the one from the band room.

The talent show started, and everyone was excited for and enthusiastic about the first few acts; but as the afternoon dragged on, the applause died down more quickly after each act. Even the parents of the students performing seemed weary and ready to go home. Of course, we were nearly last on the list. This didn't bode well for us if we wanted to use this talent show to boost our reputation, but we resolved to make our act the best finale that the school had ever heard.

At last, it was our turn. Maggie peeked out from behind the curtain then quickly pulled her head back, cheeks flushed.

"I can't do this," she stammered. "Too many people."

Putting my hands on her shoulders, I tried to speak encouragingly. "Hey, don't worry. You're amazing. Everyone's going to love us, ok? And you've got the whole band behind you." I mustered a reassuring smile, though my own hands threatened to shake with nervousness, my insides all a whirl.

She studied me for a moment before smiling and throwing her arms around me in a hug. "Ok. Thanks, Ben."

"No problem, Mags. But you'd better get ready to sing. We're up."

She pulled back from the hug and hurried to her microphone, nodding at me to let me know she was ready. The curtain rose, and all was silent. Our audience waited in bored anticipation. For a moment, I was tempted to run, to bolt out of the auditorium and escape the possible humiliation of singing. What stopped me? My aunt. She was seated close to the front, Joey in her arms, and she was looking directly at me, smiling reassuringly. With that boost to my confidence, I signaled to Walter, and we began.

As we finished our last song, we were met with silence, my heart sank. We'd failed. *I'd* failed. We were going to go down as losers.

Then the applause broke out. It was so sudden that I took a lurching step backward. The shock quickly wore off, and a wide grin broke across my face, and, looking around, I could see that my friends all wore the same grin. When the curtain dropped, we joined in one massive group hug around Walter.

"We were incredible!" Jill proclaimed.

She had barely finished speaking before everything went pitch black.

HERE'S TO THE UNDERDOGS!

Chapter 26: Ben

"I guess the power doesn't share in your sentiment," I chuckled.

A few seconds and the emergency lights were on, casting a red glow about the backstage area and most likely the rest of the school. The flashlights from our smartphones helped to light our path far more than the emergency lights did, and we made our way out of the backstage area and into the auditorium. People were filing out of the exits on their way to the gymnasium as per the direction of the principal. The Underdogs split up to find our respective families. Aunt Michelle was waiting for me by the stage, and, after I'd taken my crying brother from her, we followed the crowd to the gym.

"Is everyone here?" the principal's commanding voice rang out. "Coach, take a few of the boys and check through the school, please. Send anyone you find, here." He paused until the coach and his favorite students had left and all was quiet again. "Now. A winter storm warning has been issued. The light dusting of snow that you may have encountered on your way here earlier this afternoon has turned into a blizzard. Roads are being blocked off, and there have already been a few car crashes due to low visibility. One vehicle ran into a utility pole, hence the power outage. Until further notice, you are advised to remain at the school. If you are a student who is not accompanied by a parent or legal guardian, then you are not permitted to leave the school building, and unless you need to use the restroom, please remain in the gym. A few of the teachers have already gone to get water and food from the cafeteria, so there should be no other reason to leave. Thank you."

As he blended into the crowd, Colette muttered, "Stupid southern drivers. If this were New York, we'd have no trouble getting out of here." Colette had found me and Aunt Michelle as soon as we stepped foot in the gym.

"I don't think that's quite fair. We never get snow like this so no one's really prepared."

"I know..." she admitted painfully. "But *I* can't even leave because I'm a student."

"Your parents aren't here?"

She shook her head. "Mom's working, and Dad stayed home with the twins and Marcus. I drove Morgan here."

"Oh. Wait, where was Morgan during our practice?"

"In here. She was probably kicking a soccer ball around."

"Ah, ok. Did Alice sit with her for the talent show?" A nod confirmed my theory. "Alright. That makes sense because I thought she had said she was coming, but then I didn't see her with Michelle."

Colette took Joey from me as he began fussing. "I'm glad they're friends."

"Me too. They seem to get along better than—" my thought was cut short as shouting broke out. "Sounds like Darren."

"That's not surprising. I wonder what his problem is?"

HERE'S TO THE UNDERDOGS!

We both peered in the direction the shouting was coming from but were unable to see through the throng. Darren was soon silenced anyway, and when Colette turned her attention to Joey, I set off to find my aunt, stopping to talk to Maggie and Walter along the way. My plans to find Aunt Michelle were thrown aside when I saw Joanna standing alone in the crowd.

"Joanna? It's not often I see you without your brother if he's around," I chuckled lightly.

She smiled at me, welcoming my company. "He went to find Colette."

"Oh. They've gotten pretty close recently, haven't they?"

"Surprisingly, yes."

I responded with a nod, leaving us in awkward silence.

"How's your aunt?" Joanna broke.

"Michelle? She's good. Trying to balance taking care of the five of us — mostly Joey — with writing. She *had* a good routine, but as Joey gets older, he gets more demanding of attention."

"I can imagine. Maybe I could help out with Joey or Garrett sometime."

"Really? That'd be great. I'm sure she'd love the help." This time it was Joanna who left us in silence, and me who broke it. "You were great today. Singing."

She snorted. "No way. *You* were amazing. I was...ok."

"Well...*I* thought you were great anyway..." I stared down at my boots, and when I chanced to glance back up at her, a touch of pink showed on her cheeks. I was about to respond when out of the corner of my eye, I saw Darren sneak out of the gym. "Uh...just a minute. I have to...go check on something."

HERE'S TO THE UNDERDOGS!

I could see the confusion on Joanna's face as I left, but I had to see what Darren was up to, partially due to my curiosity and partially due to my mistrust of Darren. Not taking my eyes off of him, I darted through the crowd of students and their relatives until I was at the exit. Looking around to make sure no one was watching, I slipped out the door and hurried into the hall just in time to see Darren round the corner. Hurrying my pace, I followed him, and when I rounded the corner, I called out to him.

"Hey!"

He stopped and turned to me but didn't say a word.

"Where are you going? We're only supposed to leave the gym for one reason and the bathrooms are back that way." I jerked my thumb behind me.

"I have to get home," he growled as he turned and continued walking. Jogging to catch up, I replied, "Darren, you can't. Principal Jones said-"

"I don't care what Principal Jones said. If I don't get home…" his voice trailed off, leaving the thought unfinished.

"What? What happens if you don't get home? Do you turn into a pumpkin?"

Darren didn't seem to receive my joke very well as his scowl only deepened.

"Sorry. I'm sure you have a reason. But, Darren, you can't leave. Just look!" By this time we were within sight of the doors leading out, and the outside world was pure white.

"I have to, Benjamin!" he turned to me, zealous eyes pleading with me to stand aside. He could have easily pushed past me, so why he didn't was a mystery to me. Perhaps he was afraid I'd tell the principal, or maybe he knew I was right— he had no chance of getting home safely until the storm let up.

"Darren, let's go to one of the classrooms. You can tell me what's going on, and maybe I can help." Turning away from him, I took a few steps toward the history classroom, trusting he would follow. A quiet relief filled me as I heard his footsteps behind me. He closed the door as he entered the room after me. Hands in his pockets, gaze focused on the ground, he leaned against the teacher's desk.

"Darren? Why are you so intent on getting home?"

He didn't speak for a minute, and when he did it was so quiet that I almost didn't hear him. "My father."

I stared at him in disbelief, not sure that I had heard him correctly. *Darren had problems at home? Maybe that's what his problem was... Maybe that's why he was so mean to everyone else.* I almost didn't want to press the matter any further. I didn't want to learn that there was anything wrong with his home life. I didn't want to feel sorry for him. Yet I had to, partially for my own curiosity, but also for Darren.

Softening my tone, I asked, "What about your dad?"

He lifted his eyes to meet mine, pain showing in them. "Let's just say, he won't like it if I'm late."

"I'm sorry." I dropped my gaze to the floor now. "I know what that's like."

"What are you talking about?"

"If I understand what you're getting at, my dad's the same way. Least he is when he's home." I brought my gaze back up to meet his.

He studied me for a moment, probably trying to gauge whether I was lying or not. "I didn't know."

"Of course you didn't," I scoffed. "You don't take the time to get to know your victims before making their lives more miserable than they already are." I gritted my teeth.

"Yeah?" He went on the defensive, standing up straight so as to tower over me as much as possible. "Well, maybe I don't care. It's just the way things are, Connley. Call it...survival of the fittest. I'm the strong, you and your friends are the weak. It's my duty to put you in your place."

I stepped back, not because I was afraid or backing down, but because with a little distance between us, I didn't feel so short. "Is that what your dad tells you?"

He winced, as though the words had physically hurt. "You'll regret those words, Connley."

He was right about that. I regretted the words as soon as they'd left my lips. *How could I say that?* I knew what he was going through and how much words like that stung. "Darren, I-I didn't mean that. I'm sorry."

"Shut it." Without another word, he exited the classroom, slamming the door behind him.

Left in stupefied silence, I could have kicked myself for my poor choice of words. No, not poor. Terrible. Awful. Any progress I had made with Darren in the past ten minutes was lost in ten seconds. I eased my anger by kicking the teacher's desk on my way out of the classroom.

"Benjamin!"

Uh-oh... That was the principal. He walked over to me, his commanding demeanor and disapproving frown making me wish I could melt into the wall.

"Yes, Principal Jones?"

"Were you not present during my speech earlier, instructing all students to remain in the gymnasium?"

"I was, Sir..."

"Then I trust you have a good excuse for disobeying that order." He crossed his arms over his chest as he awaited my reply. We both knew that nothing I said would get me out of this.

I hung my head and shoved my hands in my pockets. "No, Sir."

"I thought not. Though you aren't one to break the rules often..." I could see the wheels turning behind his eyes. He knew I was holding back. Luckily for me, he didn't press the matter. "Just get back to the gym, Benjamin. And if you see anyone else out here, be sure they find their way back."

I smiled a bit and nodded. "Yes, Sir. Will do."

When I got back to the gym, I looked around for Darren and spotted him in a corner, surrounded by his buddies. At least he was smart enough to stay in the school. Next, I looked for Joanna. I wasn't surprised to see that Luca was once again with her. Too bad. I wouldn't have minded continuing our conversation, awkward as it was, but with Luca there, I doubted the conversation would be even as good as it had been. My attention was drawn away from Joanna as a hand was placed on my shoulder.

"Where have you been?" Aunt Michelle asked.

"I uh...was talking with someone."

"Oh...I see." She smirked at me. "Looks to me like you'd like to talk with Joanna some more."

"Shh! Michelle, she might hear you."

My aunt threw her head back laughing. "How long have you known her?"

"A few months I guess," I replied with a shrug.

"Have you asked her out yet?"

My eyes nearly bugged out of my head as I stammered, "Wh-what? Why would I- why-ask her out?"

"Yes, Ben! You should ask her out."

I quickly shook my head. "No way. She'd never want to go out with me. I mean, just look at her! She's smart and gorgeous and funny. Why would she go out with *me*?"

"Because you're the smartest, most handsome, most talented boy I know."

"You're my aunt. Of course, you think that."

"It's true, Benjamin! Don't even try to deny it."

I opened my mouth to speak but was cut off once again by the principal, not that I was going to complain about our conversation being cut short.

"Listen up, everyone! The storm has let up. The roads should be open again shortly. I encourage you all to get home while you have this window to do so."

The gym was suddenly abuzz with the stampede of footsteps and cacophony of voices as everyone rushed to leave. Colette made sure Alice found her way to me and Aunt Michelle, and I nearly had to pry Joey from her arms as she was reluctant to let him go. He quickly settled into Aunt Michelle's outstretched arms and calmed down as we followed the throng out the double doors and through the halls. I considered finding Darren and offering to go home with him — I knew what it was like to be alone at home with a father like his — but I doubted he'd accept, and Aunt Michelle would probably want me to drive her home.

Before Colette and Morgan left our company, Colette informed me that Maggie, Nathan, Becky, Jill, and Connie would be meeting at her house and I was invited to join them.

HERE'S TO THE UNDERDOGS!

"I'll be there unless Michelle needs me for something."

"Alright. Have a safe drive home." She gave me a hug before leading Morgan out into the cold.

Aunt Michelle was more than happy to let me drive home. I helped her get Joey and the leftover cookies and brownies she had volunteered to make for the talent show inside, then hurried off to Colette's house.

Chapter 27: Colette

I was on my feet and racing toward the door as soon as I heard the doorbell.

"I'll get it! It's probably Ben," I called.

Upon opening the door, I found that I was correct.

"Glad you could make it, Ben. Everyone else is in the living room. Don't worry, Dad vowed to keep the twins upstairs tonight, so you won't be attacked for once."

He chuckled as he hung his coat and scarf on a hook then dusted the snow from his fedora.

"I'll have to thank your dad later."

Laughing, I answered, "I'm sure he'd appreciate that. Come on."

I linked my arm through his and lead him into the living room where he was greeted by the rest of the group. After refilling our supply of snacks, I sat on the couch next to Jill, and we all talked about the events of the day— everything from our scare that morning when Joanna had screamed, to the talent show, to the impromptu lock-in at school. Ben was surprisingly quiet throughout the discussion, and I could tell something was eating at him.

"Ben?"

"Hmm?" He looked up at me, a half-eaten cookie in his hand. "What?"

"Is something bothering you?"

"Kind of…" He sighed, rubbing his thumb over the scar on his wrist. "I talked with Darren at school today. During the storm, I caught him trying to sneak out and followed. He actually stopped and listened to me, and I learned some about his dad."

All wide eyes were on Ben.

"But I blew it. I said something stupid that ruined any progress I had made."

"We all have those moments…" I tried to reassure him. "But what did you learn about his dad exactly?"

"He didn't say anything specifically, but I'm pretty sure he deals with the same sort of thing I do."

"Whoa. That actually makes sense. Bullies are often just taking their frustrations from home out on others," Jill put in.

"Doesn't make it right," Ben mumbled.

"I know." Moving to the floor next to him, I placed a hand on his shoulder. "But, Ben… He's like us. He's dealing with something no kid should have to; he's just handling it differently."

"I guess."

Looking around the room, it was clear that this topic had brought the mood way down.

HERE'S TO THE UNDERDOGS!

"Come on, guys. Let's put all that aside for now. The last thing I'll say on this topic is that I'd like it if you all came to my church's youth group this Friday with me."

There was a bit of hushed discussion, but ultimately everyone agreed.

"Good. Now, who's up for a movie?"

That suggestion was met with more enthusiasm, and we passed the rest of the evening with a Back to the Future marathon, by the end of which many of my guests were asleep. Jill and I took the snacks to the kitchen, being as quiet as possible so as to allow the others to sleep, then we went upstairs to my room where we talked for another hour or so before falling asleep ourselves.

* * *

The week went by smoothly other than my being exhausted before church Sunday morning. But at school on Monday, and even Tuesday, we were congratulated by many of the students we passed for our performance at the talent show. Ben's mood had certainly lightened since Saturday night, a fact I was very glad of. He was the sort of person who should always be happy— or maybe I was biased because he was my friend.

By Friday, the buzz of the talent show had died down so much that you almost wouldn't know it had happened at all. What people did remember was the snowstorm and being trapped in the school for nearly an hour. In the grand scale of things, it wasn't a very long time, but apparently that's what stuck out to people most about Saturday. Then, of course, you had everyone discussing their big weekend plans. I was most excited for youth group that evening.

HERE'S TO THE UNDERDOGS!

"Hey, Ben!" I jogged up to him in the hall. "How was Geometry?"

"Not bad today. History?"

"Do you even have to ask?" I grinned, gaining a chuckle from Ben.

"I suppose not." He shook his head. "I still don't understand why you and Morgan love history so much."

"I would go into detail explaining the many reasons why, but I don't have time. You're still planning on coming tonight, right? Alice can come too if she wants. And Tony too."

"We'll be there," he smiled.

"Good." The bell rang. "I'll see you at lunch."

We both hurried to our classes and met up at lunch, then went the rest of the day barely seeing each other at all before youth group.

Chapter 28: Ben

It took me a solid five minutes to decide to wear my glasses rather than my contacts to Colette's youth group. Then I spent another ten minutes trying to choose a fedora to wear.

"Michelle! I need your advice on something!" I called out my room to my aunt who was working on her writing in the living room .

She wasted no time coming to my aid, though I wouldn't say she hurried either. "Yeah, Ben?"

"Which fedora should I wear?" I held up the three choices I had narrowed it down to: a snazzy red one with a black ribbon around it, an off-white fedora with a faded blue brim, or a green and washed-out-yellow checkered one.

"Definitely not the red. Hmm...go with the checkered one so I can wear the other one."

Chuckling, I hung the red one back in my closet, topping my head with her suggestion. "Are you going somewhere tonight?"

"Perhaps." A sly smirk tugged up one corner of her mouth.

"Where?"

"Bowling."

"Like...on a date?" I grinned.

"Maybe..."

"No fair! You can't go out on a date on a night I won't be here to wait up for you!"

We both laughed before she replied, "Sorry, Benny. Have fun at youth group tonight and don't be too late, ok?"

"I was gonna say the same to you." With a wink, I passed by her and hurried downstairs.

"You're ridiculous," she said as she descended the last stair. Now eat up and get out of here. Oh, and don't forget about Alice."

"I wouldn't forget my favorite sister."

"I knew I was your favorite," Alice walked into the kitchen at that moment.

"Well, of course! By blood relation that is," I smirked.

"Hey!"

Laughing, I dodged the sweater she threw at me. A shriek was heard from behind me, and I turned my head to see Aunt Michelle holding the sweater, laughing as well. If we had had any neighbors within earshot, I'm sure we would have sounded insane to them, the three of us standing in the kitchen laughing over a sweater.

Aunt Michelle was the first to recover. "You two had better get going so you're not late. Have fun." She hugged us both before shooing us out the door, making sure we were appropriately dressed for the chilly evening air.

HERE'S TO THE UNDERDOGS!

* * *

The church parking lot was surprisingly full. I'd accompanied Colette to church before, but I hadn't realized that so many youths attended the Friday evening youth group. Of course, the youth group was broken up into several age ranges; therefore, not all of the people who had arrived in these vehicles would be part of the young adult group, and some of the occupants would have been parents or youth leaders. Good. That meant the young adult group wouldn't be nearly as large as I had originally feared upon driving in.

Alice raced through the slush and falling snow to get to the shelter of the church. "Come on, Ben! Hurry up, Tony!"

"We're coming, Alice." I locked the jeep, momentarily debating whether that was necessary considering we were parked at a church but ultimately decided it couldn't hurt and rushed after my siblings.

We were met by the racket of young children running through the halls and various rooms. There were guys playing basketball in the adjacent gymnasium, and the worship band was practicing for the coming Sunday.

Colette spotted us almost immediately. Whether she had been waiting for us or had just happened to see us was undetermined. "You made it! Sorry about the noise," she said more quietly as she drew closer. "Once the groups split up in a few minutes, it will get a lot quieter. Alice, Morgan is in the gym if you want to meet up with her."

"Thanks!" Alice piled her coat and scarf in my arms before running off, and Tony chuckled at my predicament.

"Ah. There's a makeshift closet this way." Colette led me to the left around a corner into an open area with iron rods horizontally lining the walls so people could hang their coats with shelves for hats and such resting above the coat racks.

I hung Alice's coat and scarf before sliding my own coat onto a hanger. "As I've only come on Sundays, I never realized how large your church is."

"It can be a bit daunting, or at least confusing until you get used to it. Just...try not to get lost." She grinned, knowing I would instantly catch onto the joke. I seemed to have a knack for getting lost just about anywhere.

"I'll be sure to stick close to you, Lizzy."

My quip was met with a glare. "If anyone here repeats that after tonight, you're a dead man, Connley."

Tony snorted, but Colette silenced him once she turned her glare on him.

I simply grinned at her, to which she rolled her eyes and waved me forward. "Come on. We'll be starting soon."

The swell of excited voices died down as the youth leaders had everyone separate into their respective groups, each group immediately heading to their particular room. Upon arriving in the young adult room with Colette and Tony, I saw that the rest of the Underdogs were already there, even Joanna and Luca. Although I'm not sure Luca was technically an Underdog. I suppose he counted— he was involved in enough of our functions and get-togethers. I just didn't know much about him as the only person other than his sister that the guy had opened up to was Colette, and, apparently, he hadn't said very much to her.

Mr. Hedge, the youth leader for our group, opened in prayer then sent us to the gym where we proceeded to play a vigorous game of soccer. Though I wasn't very good, this was a friendly scrimmage, and there were a few far worse than myself. Our group was comprised of roughly twenty teens, ranging from ages fifteen to eighteen. I later learned that the youth group took place on both Wednesday and Friday, but different kids attended each. This was how the church was able to make sure each group got an equal and reasonable amount of time both for games and the message that followed. Once a month the youth groups combined for an all-night lock-in comprised mostly of games.

After half an hour of soccer, Mr. Hedge directed us to take a water/bathroom break before returning to the classroom. Nathan walked back to the classroom with me.

"Soccer is one of my favorite sports."

"Oh yeah?"

He nodded. "And I have half the chances of getting a handball compared to anyone else."

We both broke out into laughter as we entered the room.

"Maybe you should be a comedian."

"Maybe so," he replied with a chuckle as we plopped down onto one of the few remaining beanbags. I had never seen beanbags this huge. At least four kids could share one comfortably, five or six if you squeezed together.

Colette and Jill claimed the beanbag next to us and waved Becky over to join them when she entered the classroom. Tony sat on the floor between the girls beanbag and the one Nathan and I shared. I was secretly hoping Joanna would sit with me and Nathan, but she and Luca shared a beanbag across the room. How long I was lost in thought about Joanna I didn't know, but I was brought back to reality as Maggie sat next to me. Not long after she did, the remaining youths filed into the room and Mr. Hedge began his message. I must say he was an engaging speaker.

Though my mind wanted to wander, it didn't take much concentration for me to remain focused on his words.

He spoke on Romans eight, emphasizing verse seventeen: "And since we are His children, we are His heirs. In fact, together with Christ we are heirs of God's glory. But if we are to share His glory, we must also share His suffering."

I scribbled that reference down on my hand, borrowing a pen from Maggie. That night, I wrote the verse out on a piece of paper and taped the paper to the bottom of my top bunk. I stared at it for an indefinite amount of time, running over Mr. Hedge's message in my head. *Suffering.* A word I knew all too well. A word most of us in the Underdogs knew much about. A word apparently Darren knew something about other than how to cause it. A word that Jesus Christ, God Himself, understood better than I had ever realized before.

These thoughts floated around my head until I drifted off sometime in the night to a dreamless sleep. But before sleep claimed me…I prayed. I didn't say anything eloquent— most of what I said was just my jumbled thoughts put into words. But I felt different after. A refreshing peace filled me, and even though my prayer would have received a failing grade had it been for an English assignment, I felt certain that it had been heard.

HERE'S TO THE UNDERDOGS!

Chapter 29: Ben

Most Saturdays I didn't see the light of day until at least noon. Aunt Michelle was kind enough to keep Garrett out of my room with the condition that I watched him the rest of the day so she could write or go out. But this morning I was awake before eight o'clock and in the kitchen cooking breakfast by eight thirty. Aunt Michelle stepped into the kitchen not long after.

"Ben? What are you doing up? Not that I'm complaining— whatever you're cooking smells amazing."

"I just couldn't sleep. And…I wanted to talk to you about something."

"Oh?" She took a seat at the island. "What would that be?"

"Breakfast first," I stated, handing her a plate of eggs benedict. "I'll agree to that," she said as she took a bite.

Getting myself some breakfast, I sat next to her, and we ate in silence. The ticking of the grandfather wall clock in the living room seemed louder than usual. Outside, the sun sparkled off the half inch of snow we had. Nearly all of the snow we received during the snowstorm had melted

HERE'S TO THE UNDERDOGS!

over the course of the past week. Chickadees flitted past the kitchen window, and squirrels raced up and down the trees.

"Ok. Talk now."

Aunt Michelle drew my thoughts from the outside world as she again sat next to me, having just taken our dishes to the sink.

"Right." I turned my attention to her. "I haven't really talked to you about how youth group went."

"I'm sorry we didn't get the chance to talk last night, but Joey wasn't the best at the bowling alley, and I was too tired to stay up much later."

"Oh, I understand. I was tired too. And I can't believe you took Joey on a date with you."

"Ok, it wasn't exactly a date. There were several of us hanging out, and Ashley was bringing her daughter so I figured I'd bring Joey rather than trying to find a babysitter."

"It was still a date." She rolled her eyes, but I cut her off before she could offer a retort. "So, youth group. It was actually a lot more fun than I had expected."

"What did you do? I'm assuming there was a message."

I nodded. "There was. We played soccer first, but there was a message after."

As I paused, Michelle prompted me to continue. "And...what was it about?"

"Romans eight. It was really good, actually."

"Oo, yes. I love that Chapter."

"Really? Why haven't you ever mentioned it? Verse seventeen is amazing."

"I know it is. But, Ben, I stopped trying to talk to you about these things too often a few months ago. Remember? You stopped listening, so I stopped talking."

"Oh... I guess that's true. Sorry."

"It's fine, Ben." She smiled at me and put a hand on my knee. "I'm glad you're talking to me about this now."

I gave a small nod, looking down at the counter.

"What is it?"

"I uh, I prayed last night. I don't really know why, but I felt like I should." I glanced up at her to see tears in her eyes, a proud smile on her face. "So, um, I wanted to talk to you about that."

"Of course, Ben. What did you pray about?" She quickly added, "You don't have to tell me if you'd rather keep it private."

"No, I don't mind. I don't even really know... I just talked. Mostly about my friends." I paused briefly. "And Mom."

"Do you think it helped?"

I shrugged. "I guess I'll find out." Aunt Michelle gave me time to collect my thoughts and figure out how to continue. "Michelle? I...I want to be a Christian." I was taken by surprise as she leaned forward and hugged me tightly.

"You don't even know how long I've waited to hear you say that." She hugged me even tighter, and I returned the hug, burying my face against her shoulder.

All was silent for several minutes, the silence ending only when Garrett toddled into the kitchen, babbling to himself. At that point, my aunt pulled back from the hug, wiping her eyes.

HERE'S TO THE UNDERDOGS!

"Ben, I couldn't be happier. This is the best news I've heard in a long time."

A bit of a smile tugged at my lips. "Would you— would you pray with me?"

"Of course."

And she did. We prayed together and afterward had a long talk about what it really meant to be a Christian and where to go from here. Alice was kind enough to take care of Joey during the two and a half hour discussion, by the end of which Aunt Michelle had decided to come to Colette's church with me the following day. Since moving in with us, she had been without a church. As her faith went beyond attending a weekly service, she hadn't been bothered by this, but she was eager to attend Colette's church and see what she thought of it.

"Do you think Alice will come along?" she asked.

"I think so. She'll like the opportunity to see Morgan, and she seemed to really enjoy youth group too."

"That's good. What about Tony?"

"Um...he might take a bit of convincing. Where is he anyway?"

"He left early this morning, but I'm not sure where he went."

"Typical."

My comment was met with a frown.

"What?"

"Speak kindly of your brother, please."

I caught myself before rolling my eyes at her. "Fine..."

"Thank you. Now, you should probably tell Colette the good news."

Just thinking about Colette's reaction made me laugh. "You're probably right. She'll kill me for waiting *this* long. Thanks for everything, Aunt Michelle."

HERE'S TO THE UNDERDOGS!

With one last hug, I rushed to get my coat and ran out the door. By now the snow was turning to slush that splashed onto my jeans as I ran through it. I ran the whole way to the Tance household, surprising myself by how quickly I arrived.

Though I knew the Tances well and was always welcome, I generally at least knocked before entering their home. Not this time. I burst through the door, scaring Mrs. Tance so bad that she screamed. I had never heard Mrs. Tance scream before, and I almost laughed, but quickly decided against that.

"Sorry, Mrs. T. Is Colette here?"

Taking a moment to compose herself, she answered, "She is. She's in her room."

"Thanks." I hugged her before rushing upstairs. That was probably more surprising than my bursting through the door. At least I had more sense than to barge into Colette's room.

"Entrez s'il vous plaît," was her response to my impatient knocking.

"Guess what!"

I commenced to tell her all about my talk with my aunt that morning and my decision of salvation, at the end of which she nearly knocked me over with a hug.

"Ben, this is amazing!"

"I know! I'm excited too." That fact I'm sure was evident from the grin on my face.

As soon as Colette was done squealing in delight and excitement over my decision, she pulled me downstairs by the hand to announce the news to her family. I had never received so many hugs in such close succession in my whole life. I even received a hug from Morgan, something I never would have expected. It was nearly half an hour before I was able to convince the family to let me leave.

Colette walked me to the door. "Thanks for coming over to tell me, Ben."

"I value my life now."

Grinning a bit, she punched my arm playfully. "Be quiet." Her face grew more serious. "But really, I am *so* happy for you."

"I know. Thanks." I gave her a final hug before walking back to my house.

Chapter 30: Ben

A few weeks passed, and we were approaching Valentine's Day. In past years I had done nothing more with the holiday than giving flowers and chocolates to my sisters. This year though, my thoughts were of someone else, and at this very moment, I was seated across from her at lunch, listening to her talk about something. Honestly, I hadn't *really* been listening for the past five minutes, so I had absolutely no idea *what* she was talking about. That was probably not a good thing, but my thoughts were so distracting. As was she. Her long, always-braided, brown hair; her hazel eyes; her perfect smile— *oh shoot. Did she just ask me a question?* I could have tried to play this off like I was listening, but by the time I'd stared at her with a dumbfounded look on my face for fifteen seconds, it was too late.

"Ben? Have you been listening?" Joanna asked, already guessing the answer. "Huh? Oh, yeah. Of course."

She sighed. "Forget it. It wasn't important anyway." She started to get up, holding her tray so as to dispose of it.

"No!" Without thinking about it, I grabbed her wrist. "Don't go. I was listening; my mind just wandered for a minute..." *Or five or ten or...how long had we been sitting here?* It felt like hours, yet also like only seconds.

My hold on her wrist loosened as she sat back down, but I didn't pull my hand away. "Alright... I was just wondering what your plans were after high school."

"Oh. Well, I've been accepted to the Rutherford Institute of Science Technologies, so I'll start there in the fall." (Remember that email I got along the lines of "You're an idiot, why would we accept you"? Yeah, as it turns out, that was a mistake. Some punk hacked into the college email and thought it would be fun to send that email to everyone on the waitlist. RIST soon contacted me to apologize and inform me that I'd been accepted!)

Slowly, she nodded. "Good. What are you going for?"

"An art degree." My joke was not appreciated, and I quickly amended my statement. "My masters. I'm not sure yet what classes I'll be taking exactly, but I'm figuring that out. There's still a bit of time."

She smiled. "You'll do great in college."

I returned her smile, absentmindedly running my thumb over her hand. "Thanks. I'm excited to go."

A nod was all she could respond with as the bell rang. Realizing my hand was still placed over hers, I quickly withdrew it and grabbed my tray, standing and stuttering.

"We, uh, we'd better get to, um, class."

She grinned slightly at my lack of eloquence, but I noticed the blush that crept onto her cheeks as she nodded in agreement. We walked together to dispose of our trays, then I further accompanied her out of the lunchroom. The hall is where we parted ways, not catching more than glimpses of each other throughout the rest of the day.

Upon arriving home, I kicked off my boots, tossed my light coat and scarf over a chair, and collapsed face-first on the couch.

"Long day?" Aunt Michelle asked as she sat on the arm of the couch at my feet, a mug of apple cider in hand.

"Not really," came my muffled reply.

This apparently baffled her. "Why the couch comfort time then?"

"I have a dilemma."

"Oh? If you're going to tell me about it, you're going to have to get your face out of the couch." She sipped her cider as she waited.

With a muffled groan, I turned my head, hugging the throw pillow it rested on. "I guess it may not really be a dilemma. But...Valentine's Day is coming up."

"I like chocolate. That's all you need to know." She winked at me, lightening my mood.

"I'll let your boyfriend buy you the gifts," I smiled.

"That may be best... So, what's your problem?"

I hesitated. Nearly whispering, I replied, "Joanna."

"I see..." I knew she must be grinning from her tone. "You don't know what to get her?"

I shook my head. "That's not it. My problem is, I don't know *if* I should even get her anything. It's not like we're dating or anything. We're friends."

"Benjamin Arminius Connley, when are you going to ask her out on a date?"

"Maybe never," I mumbled.

"Why on earth not?"

A shrug was all I replied with, an unacceptable answer to my aunt.

"Speak, child."

Heaving myself to an upright position, I replied, "I'm not sure a high school relationship is worth it. They never last, and if that were the case then we'd only have a few months before I graduate."

"Never, Benjamin? Are you sure? What about your Uncle Zeb and Aunt Ashley? Or your grandparents? Or Joel and Cassie? They all met and dated in high school, and now they're happily married. It obviously worked out for your grandparents."

"I guess... But more often than not, it doesn't."

"You're looking at this from a scientific viewpoint. Data shows that these relationships fail, barring a few exceptions. But you can't use science on matters of the heart, Ben. Stop listening to your head, and listen to your heart instead. Otherwise, you may never find the right person for you." She paused. "Though there is something else to consider now..."

I turned to face her. "What?"

"You're a Christian now. That should affect your standards for who you'll date..."

"Oh..." My mood dropped once again. "Then I guess it's good I didn't ask her yet."

Troubled as to how to rectify this, my aunt bit her lip in thought. "She goes to the youth groups, right? And I've seen her in church. Does she express any other interest in God and Christianity?"

"She's a rather active part of the devotional group Colette started with just those of us in Underdogs."

Michelle nodded thoughtfully, then sighed. "Honestly, I can't really counsel you to pursue a relationship right now, despite what I said five minutes ago. I was caught up in how adorable you two would be. But…I'll make an exception for Valentine's Day. Even if you just go out as friends, I'm sure she'd appreciate that."

I mulled this over, a smile creeping onto my face. "Yeah. Maybe I'll do that. Thanks, Michelle."

"That's what I'm here for. Now, you'd better get started on your homework. I'm taking care of supper."

I stood with a groan. "Can we switch? I'd rather cook."

Standing as well, she laughed. "Sorry, nephew. You have to do your own homework. And you'd better pull your grades up in history. If you need help studying, don't hesitate to ask."

"But you hate history too."

"That doesn't mean I can't help you study it. Now get started on your homework." Not giving me time to argue further, she returned to the kitchen.

* * *

Three days were spent planning the perfect dinner with Joanna, leaving me with one day to actually ask her to go out with me. More specifically, it left me with three hours to do so as it was now lunchtime on the eve of Valentine's Day. *Why did you wait so long? What if she has other plans?* I berated myself for my procrastination, but since not much could be done about it now, I scanned the lunchroom for Joanna. The whole period, I barely ate anything as I waited for her to come in. Just my luck. She didn't show.

HERE'S TO THE UNDERDOGS!

All day I looked for her in between classes. Finally, just before my final class, I saw her at the end of the hall. As I was hurrying toward her, I was stopped by the principal's receptionist. She'd always reminded me of a secretary bird: tall, thin, sometimes-crazy hair, neutral expression, but seriously beautiful eyes.

"Benjamin, there's a call for you in the office. It's your aunt."

My mind still partially focused on Joanna, I followed Ms. Brown to the principal's office. I hadn't the slightest idea why Michelle would be calling me at school, but it had me worried.

Chapter 31: Ben

Bursting into the waiting room at the hospital, I looked around for Aunt Michelle. She ran to me, throwing her arms around me, and I returned the hug tightly.

"Where's Alice? How is she?"

Holding back tears, Michelle answered, "She's-she's in surgery now. I don't know when we'll hear anything."

"What happened?"

Aunt Michelle took a moment to compose herself. "Her appendix burst in school. She didn't complain about the pain, but when she became feverish and was puking, the school nurse asked if she had any pain and called an ambulance when Alice told her where." She hugged me, burying her face in my shoulder.

After over an hour of waiting, I was running low on energy. The adrenaline of the crisis had worn off, and comforting Aunt Michelle had taken quite a bit out of me, though perhaps now she was comforting me more than I was comforting her. Nevertheless, I was relieved when Colette walked into the waiting room. I hugged her tightly, needing the reassurance of my friend. I could have called any or all of the other members of the Underdogs, but I called Colette. Neither my aunt nor I would have wanted a crowd of people, and no one would have been able to strengthen my hope as Colette could. She sat with me, held my hand, and prayed. It's amazing how calming that was. Praying. I'd been at the hospital for over an hour, and not once had I thought to pray, though I'm sure my aunt had been praying continuously.

Gideon, Michelle's boyfriend, came as soon as he'd finished work, unable to leave beforehand. He comforted her, and Colette stayed with me. My eyes were glued to the clock. Ten minutes passed. Twenty. Forty. Another hour. Fifteen more minutes before a doctor finally came out and we all stood to meet him. He informed us that Alice would be just fine, and I didn't hear anything he said after that. I was so relieved that my sister was going to be ok, nothing else mattered. Having stayed relatively strong throughout the two and a quarter hour surgery, I now allowed myself to cry. The truth of the matter is, I wouldn't have been able to stop the tears no matter how hard I tried. I wasn't balling or sobbing, but several tears did find their way down my cheeks.

We had to wait a bit longer before being allowed to see Alice. She looked tired, but well. For an hour, we all sat around her bed and talked, keeping the mood cheery. Colette had to go home around four-thirty, but the rest of us stayed late into the evening, then Aunt Michelle sent me home to take care of Joey and Garrett. She'd left them with Mrs. Tance when she heard about Alice, but she didn't want the Tances to have to watch them all night, so I left the hospital and took care of my little brothers.

The next morning, taking the day off from school, I brought Joey and Garrett to the hospital with me. I learned that Gideon had stayed with my aunt and Alice all night, and he was only just leaving for work as I arrived. The poor guy looked exhausted. He placed a hand on my shoulder and gave a meaningful nod before leaving.

It wasn't long before I realized that bringing Garrett may have been a bad idea, but I hadn't really had many other options. He was hardly still for more than thirty seconds at a time and complained about being hungry every ten minutes despite the enormous breakfast I had fed him not even an hour earlier. Thankfully, Aunt Michelle took over taking care of him, allowing me to talk with Alice in a brother/sister heart-to-heart.

It's funny how time works. When you're waiting for something, minutes feel like hours, but when you're engaged in something enjoyable, the opposite is true. Waiting for Alice to come out of surgery the previous day had felt like ages, but talking with her now, the hours flew by, and before I knew it, it was two o'clock in the afternoon. I only knew because Aunt Michelle had to take Garrett and Joey home for a nap, leaving me at the hospital with Alice. We talked for a while longer before running out of things to say. When that happened, I got out the chess board I had brought, and we played several games of chess. Alice had gotten a lot better since I last played her, and, at times, I had difficulty staying ahead of her. She eventually tired of chess, and I sat on the bed with her as we watched a movie. With her head resting on my shoulder, we flipped through the channels on the hospital TV before finding something acceptable. Near the end of the movie, I could tell from her change in breathing and the new heaviness with which her head rested on my shoulder that she had fallen asleep. When the movie ended, I let it roll into the next movie for fear that any movement would wake her.

HERE'S TO THE UNDERDOGS!

I hadn't realized I'd fallen asleep until Aunt Michelle woke me later, speaking in a hushed tone. "Ben. You should go home and rest. I'll stay with Alice."

I yawned. "I'm resting pretty well here."

"But you need better rest. And food. Don't worry, she'll be home tomorrow."

I perked up. "She will?" The slight rise in my voice caused Alice to stir, though she stayed asleep.

Aunt Michelle smiled and nodded. "She'll basically be on bed rest, but she can come home."

"That's good. But I still can't go home yet. I don't want to wake her by moving..."

"Ah. Alright. What have you two been up to other than sleeping?"

I told Aunt Michelle about our time throughout the afternoon, and she listened, nodding and making comments at certain intervals. Just about the time I finished, Alice woke up. She was even more excited than I was to hear that she would be returning home the next day. With the news delivered and Aunt Michelle present to keep Alice company, I bid my sister farewell and returned home where I ate a quick dinner before going to bed, falling asleep almost instantly. For once, I was grateful to Tony as he was taking care of Joey and Garrett.

Chapter 32: Ben

After seeing how Alice was catered to during her recovery, not to mention the fact that she got to stay home from school, I considered having an appendectomy just so I could get a break. The third quarter of the school year had gone by, and we were into the final quarter— every seniors' most loved *and* most hated quarter. Finals, college, adulthood, taxes— all were within sight when the fourth quarter started, and the only one I was excited for was college. Even that was slightly terrifying when I considered the fact that I'd be living in a dorm with someone I had never met, but that I would get used to. Hopefully. Being an actual adult though? No way. I was already dreading my eighteenth birthday, and it was ten months away. Maybe I could put it off. Or everyone would forget. Probably not. So, the only option was an appendectomy.

"Ben?" Maggie drew me from my thoughts as she poked her head over the side of the wooden play structure.

"Hmm? Oh, hi."

She ascended the rest of the way up the ladder and sat across from me. "What are you doing up here?"

"Thinking."

"I thought you did that at the bridge," she questioned.

"Normally, yes. But I decided to change things up." I gave a lopsided grin.

"Ah. I can leave if you want..." She started slinking away.

"Wait!" I grabbed her wrist to stop her. "You don't have to leave. I actually wouldn't mind the company."

She smiled as she sat back down, and I pulled my hand back into my lap. I didn't really have anything to say, but I'd been alone long enough already. Having someone to chat with would be nice. Apparently, having someone to remind me to go to school was necessary as, after several minutes of talking, she said,

"We're going to be late if we don't hurry."

"Oh... School... You know, I think we should all take a day off as a senior skip day."

"Well, you and Colette and Jill could, but most of us will have to wait till next year or even the next."

"Oh, right." I heaved a sigh before crawling toward the ladder. "Come on then. I'll have to plan it for another day."

With a soft chuckle, she followed me down the ladder and we rushed to get to school on time, parting ways once we'd arrived.

Walking through the halls alone, I was again left to my thoughts. On my mind most were the students I passed in the halls. Their sideways glances and whispering didn't go unnoticed— not that this was anything new. I was used to the whispered conversations, but what had changed was the topic. Before, the things people had to say were always demeaning, and I felt like they were solely about me, though I now knew that I was wrong. But lately, the conversations were focused on the change in certain members of the Underdogs— a change for the better. Though this change was only evident in a few members of my group, it was nice to know that it was noticed. And we made sure that the reason for the change was clear: Christ.

* * *

For myself, I noticed a change mostly in my speech. Before, had I dropped my tray in the cafeteria, dumping my food on my boots, able to feel it trickling down my shins, I probably would have cursed. I'm not talking about something minor like a 'heck'. I mean full on swearing, maybe even dropping an f-bomb. I didn't even curse out of anger most of the time; it was just a habit, though I was always good about not swearing around Colette as she made her aversion to swearing very clear. Otherwise, I really didn't care. But now, as I stood in between two tables, tray at my feet, I stayed quiet, a sigh being all that escaped my lips. I stooped to clean up my tray and as much of the dropped slop as I could.

As I crouched there, my gaze focused on the floor, a pair of boots came into view. As my eyes traveled up to the wearer's face, I was dismayed, though not surprised, to see who it was.

"How's it going, butterfingers?"

"Just great, Darren." I straightened, knuckles white as I gripped my tray in anticipation for him to try to knock it to the floor again. Thankfully, his hands stayed in his pockets as he smirked down at me. I spoke again, "What's on your mind?"

"Nothing you won't find out soon enough." With that most helpful bit of information, he pushed past me.

HERE'S TO THE UNDERDOGS!

* * *

Darren's final words to me proved to be a complete lie. All day I waited anxiously to discover their meaning, and all day nothing out of the ordinary happened. The anticipation was killing me on my drive home. So distracted were my thoughts that when I pulled into my driveway, I didn't even remember the drive there. It's instances like these that solidify my theory of wormholes even more in my brain.

The house was quiet, unusual for a Tuesday afternoon— or most afternoons for that matter unless Aunt Michelle had decided to take the littles somewhere. When she did, she usually planned the outing far enough ahead of time to tell me at least by the morning of. I'd heard of no such plans today.

Slinging my backpack over my shoulder, I entered the house. "Aunt Michelle? Garrett? Tony?" It was doubtful that Alice would be home yet as her bus route was fairly long.

When no one answered my call, I started searching. The downstairs was quiet so I dropped my backpack and skipped up the stairs. I was met with silence. My mind raced with the possibilities of where they could be or what could have happened, none of my ideas being the most likely, of course. Had it not been for Darren's foreboding words, I wouldn't have worried. I still shouldn't have been worrying. Did I really believe that Darren was capable of anything so devious as to involve my family? Not really. Did that matter now? Absolutely not.

I scoured the upstairs before returning downstairs. *Where could they be? If they were going out, why hadn't Michelle told me ahead of time?* I ran both hands through my hair as my gaze roamed aimlessly around the living room. The rational side of my brain was telling me not to panic, that there was a good reason for their absence, that Aunt Michelle had probably just gone out and forgotten to tell me; but my worry outweighed my rationale.

A famished growl sounded from my stomach, but I ignored my hunger. My family was more important than food. Well, at least at the moment they were. That wasn't the point. My focus was figuring out where they'd gone, and with that focus a brilliant idea came to me. I could simply call my aunt. Mentally facepalming for the amount of time I had wasted worrying, I dialed my aunt's number— or rather tapped her contact name. Thank you, technology.

I waited for her to pick up. Two rings. Five. Six. Voicemail. Ok, if I wasn't freaking out before, I was now. Aunt Michelle *always* had her phone with her and the ringer on when she was out. At a loss as to what to do, I plopped down on the floor, resolved to sit crossed legged until another brilliant thought invaded my brain.

Chapter 33: Ben

With my being a genius, coming up with an idea shouldn't have taken long, but I sat in the middle of the living room floor, shoulders slumped, for so long that I fell asleep. I was pulled from my slumber by a voice calling me.

"Ben. Yo, little bro."

"Huh...?" Blearily, I looked up, able to make out the form of a human standing over me. "Are you ok? What are you doing on the floor? Were you sleeping?"

It sounded like Tony. I rubbed the sleep from my eyes and looked again. Yup. My big brother was looking down at me with a puzzled look on his face. It took a few seconds for me to wake up enough to register what he had said.

Good question. What was I doing here?

I jumped to my feet as the memory of my missing aunt and brothers flooded into my mind.

In my haste, my head connected painfully with Tony's chin.

"Ow!" Tony exclaimed as he rubbed his jaw. "Watch it!"

HERE'S TO THE UNDERDOGS!

Rubbing the bump on my head, I mumbled, "Sorry."

"What were you doing?"

I fumbled over my words, trying to explain myself without sounding like an idiot. "Uh...trying to figure out what happened to Aunt Michelle and everyone..."

"What do you mean 'what happened'?"

"If you hadn't noticed, they aren't home." I swept my arms in a general gesture to the empty house. "And Michelle didn't answer her phone when I called. She always answers, and she always tells me when she's going out."

"But she *did* tell you..."

"I would have remembered if she had."

"Ben, she left you a note. Go check the fridge." He nodded toward the kitchen.

Confused and curious, I went to the fridge. Upon opening the door, I spotted it— the note Aunt Michelle had left on a plate of leftover pizza. Clever. Usually, I would have enjoyed the peace and quiet of having the house to myself, and my first stop would have been the fridge. Perhaps I should have listened to my stomach after all.

Tony stood in the doorway, arms crossed, an amused smirk plastered on his face.

"Shut up," I muttered, closing the fridge, pizza in hand.

"I didn't say anything." His words were dripping with amusement.

"But you're going to. Don't."

He pushed off from the door jamb he'd been leaning against and strolled up to the island. "Why were you freaking out?"

I turned to Tony and spoke in a tense, high-pitched tone. "I was just worried, ok. Darren said something today, and I guess it messed with my head."

"Oh? What was it?"

"He made an ominous threat of something to come. I guess it was more of an empty threat."

Tony arched an eyebrow. "You thought he'd done something to Aunt Michelle and Joey and Garrett? Darren's a jerk, but I don't think he'd ever risk that."

"I know, I know." The microwave beeped. "I couldn't help worrying anyway."

Tony clapped a hand on my shoulder. "Then I'm glad I could come home to ease your mind."

I smiled at him, surprised to see him smile back.

"Hey, we should get out of the house. Michelle won't be back till after dinner, and you're right— it is really quiet here. We could go bowling."

"I thought you hated bowling."

He shrugged. "I do. But you like it. And the last time I got you out of the house and we did what *I* wanted, things didn't go so well."

"True." I shivered at the memory of that night. "Ok. Bowling it is." A grin spread across my face. "You're going down."

"No way. I'm not losing to you in anything." He grabbed a slice of my pizza before bolting out the door.

"Hey! Thief!" Wolfing down the last of my pizza, I dashed after him, struck by the cold as soon as I stepped outside. "Nope. Too cold." Not ten seconds later I was back in the warmth of the kitchen.

Through the door, Tony called, "Come on, little brother! Aren't you coming?"

"I have to get my coat. And scarf. And gloves. It's freezing."

"It's really not that bad, but whatever. Don't forget a fedora," he smirked.

"Oh, never." I raced upstairs to grab a hat and scarf then ventured outside, sufficiently bundled up to defend against the cold.

"I'll drive."

I leaped in front of him to take the driver's side first. "Over my dead body."

"Ok, go stand in front of the jeep and that won't be a problem."

Shoving him back with an eye-roll, I stepped into the jeep. "Just get in before I leave you behind."

"I'm not a bad driver." He shut his door a little too harshly for my liking.

"Maybe not, but I'm better and this is my car."

"You're really stingy about your car, aren't you?"

"Yes, because if anything happens to it, I'll be the one paying for a new car."

Tony didn't disagree.

* * *

The bowling alley was under fifteen minutes away, and we arrived in what seemed like half that time. I was tempted to make a comment about wormholes when Tony remarked on the seemingly short trip, but decided against it. No theories this evening. Just two brothers enjoying a few rounds of bowling in which I would utterly destroy my older brother.

It had been a long time since Tony and I had done anything together that didn't involve arguing, but we survived the night without so much as an unkind word except those meant in fun. After all, what's bowling without some friendly banter? By the end of two rounds, Tony was all bowled out and tired of losing to his little brother, so we turned in our bowling shoes and went to the diner across the road to get some dinner. Before leaving the house, we probably should have left a note for Aunt Michelle…

* * *

It was nearly eleven o'clock by the time we stepped through the door to the kitchen. I jumped as the screen door slammed.

"Tony!" I scolded in a harsh whisper. He grinned and shrugged off my rebuke, searching the fridge for a late-night snack.

Avoiding the squeakiest floorboards, I stepped into the living room only to find Aunt Michelle still awake and waiting for me and Tony. She sat with her arms crossed, looking up at me expectantly for an answer.

"Uh…hi. You're still up."

"Very observant. Where were you?"

"Out with Tony. We went bowling, got dinner, then caught a movie."

Her expression softened. "Did you have a good time?"

"We did," I answered, smiling.

She stood and walked over to me. "I'm glad, Ben. You and Tony should spend more time together."

I could sense the 'but' that would follow.

"But you have school tomorrow and should have been in bed over an hour ago. Both of you."

I nodded. "Ok, Michelle. You want me to tell Tony?"

"Nah, I'll talk to him. Goodnight."

"Night."

Chapter 34: Colette

"Colette, wake up."

My eyes stung with exhaustion as I opened them just enough to see who had awakened me. My surprised scream was cut off by Ben's hand on my mouth.

"Shh! It's just me."

Slowly, he removed his hand.

Rubbing my tired eyes, I sat up next to him. "What are you doing here? In my room?" As my eyes adjusted to the darkness and I was able to see him better, I could see the anger on Ben's face. "What happened?"

He looked down at something clutched in his hands. It was so shredded that it took me a moment to realize that it was a child's fedora.

"Oh, Ben… What happened to it?"

"It was Darren. I know it was." His grip tightened on the fedora, fingers digging into the tattered fabric.

"Is that…?"

He nodded. "The one Mom got me when I was seven. The-the only thing I have left of her besides her memory."

His anger changed to sorrow, and I could feel his shoulders shaking as I pulled him into a hug. As he spoke, his voice shook as well. "He warned me that something was gonna happen. I thought he was bluffing. I never— I didn't imagine he'd do *this*."

"How did he know about it?"

"I don't think he did before tonight. My room was torn apart, other things destroyed as well. But I keep this in a special place. It wouldn't have been hard for him to see the meaning it holds."

Knowing that anything I said to comfort him would be disregarded or go unheard at the moment, I stayed quiet, leaving him to pull back from the hug or speak more when he was ready. I was sure that wouldn't be for a while as I knew how important that hat was to him. I remembered when he had first gotten it, and how proud of it he was. He had pranced up my driveway, deliberately standing where he could best block the sun that I needed for my chalk drawing. As I scowled up at him, he grinned back, his missing front tooth adding to the adorableness of his chubby face. With the shadow from his hat added to his shaggy hair, his eyes were hidden, but I didn't need to see them to know the twinkle that they held, and seeing him so happy made my scowl fade to a smile and finally to a gleeful laugh.

He picked up a few fedoras in the years following, but it wasn't until his mother passed that he really started his collection. Each fedora held a memory, but none as special as the first. And it could never be replaced.

Eventually, he sat back, pulling his sleeve across his cheeks to dry the tears that had rolled over them. He stared down at the tattered felt in his hands. Amazingly, the hat still held some of its shape, but it was far from the condition that Ben had been able to keep it in for nearly a decade. A smile touched my lips as I looked at the hat. I touched a tear on the brim.

"Look." I kept my tone soft. "This wasn't from Darren. Do you remember that?"

His brow furrowed thoughtfully, as he turned the fedora so the spot faced him. A hint of a smile was all of an answer that I needed, but he reminisced about the memory.

"Yeah. You never should have let me watch Robin Hood right after getting me a bow and arrow set."

"That poor snowman. You hit him in the face at least three times before nicking the hat."

"Wasn't it William Tell who shot an apple off someone's head anyway?" I nodded. "His son's head actually. I think I told you that at the time."

"You were such a know-it-all. Still are." He smirked, hoping to get a reaction out of me. I obliged, of course, by smacking his arm.

"Watch it, Robin Hood. I'm usually right."

His eyebrows arched in mock surprise. "Not always?"

"Oh, shut up." I gave his shoulder a playful shove before we fell silent. "Ben? Do you remember how you felt after you shot the hat?"

"I was devastated." He paused. "Oh. I think I see your point. You think I'll get over this, and we'll look back on it and laugh someday?"

"Maybe not laugh, but it just gives the hat a new memory. It will be a reminder of this time of your life: your friends, your struggles, all you went through and overcame."

He sighed, but I saw that he wanted to believe me. "I guess. Not much I can really do about it now anyway…"

"Mhmm. So let's hope for the best." I rubbed his shoulder.

"Thanks, Colette."

"You don't have to thank me, Ben. I've been here for you for most of your seventeen years, and I'll continue to be here when you need me for the rest of our lives."

"I know. But I didn't just come here to talk and feel better. I came so I didn't go after Darren."

"Oh… You made a good choice. I'm better company than Darren." I nudged his shoulder, grinning a bit.

"Yeah, whatever." His light-hearted chuckled betrayed his grumpy reply. "Can I stay here tonight? I left in such a rush I forgot my coat, and it's cold outside. And…my room's still a mess."

I gave his hand a squeeze. "Sure, Ben. You know where the extra blankets are, just be quiet." I tossed the extra pillow from my bed on the floor before laying down as he journeyed into the hall to get a blanket. By the time he returned and made up a bed for himself on the floor, I was nearly asleep again. I stayed awake just long enough to hear the clock in the hall strike one, then drifted off to sleep.

* * *

It wasn't unusual to wake to the sound of giggling, but the reason for the giggles this morning was different than that of most mornings. Rolling over to face the expanse of my room, I could see Sapphire and Ruby sitting on the floor by Ben's head, taking turns decorating his hair with frilly ribbons and bows. They were so engrossed in their activity that I was able to sneak my phone from my dresser and get a few pictures and videos before having to put an end to their joyful enterprise.

HERE'S TO THE UNDERDOGS!

Waking Ben was such an endeavor that I began to question whether I should have just let the twins wake him. But I eventually caught a glimpse of his deep green eyes as he looked up at me, sleepy and confused.

"I'll call your aunt to let her know you're here. You might be better off just borrowing some clothes from Marcus as we're likely to be late already." I waited for him to get up, and when he didn't, I stooped to my last resort— tickling. That did the trick, and it was mere seconds before he was on his feet and running out the door, shouting as he ran, "Ok! I'm up! Meanie!"

I laughed at his childish name-calling and frantic flee from my "torture" as I called his aunt. Poor Michelle had been worried since she'd woken up to find his room trashed, Ben himself missing. She had called his phone only to discover that he'd left it at home in his rush to get to my house. The relief was evident in her voice as she responded to my recount of what had happened and my assurance that Ben was safe at my house. Thankfully, Michelle wasn't one to talk on the phone for too long, and I quickly got dressed and hopped downstairs for breakfast. Ben was seated at the table, a twin hanging on each arm making it difficult to eat. By now Ben had removed all but one of the bows from his hair. The remaining bow looked as though he must have put it in himself as neither of the twins were adept enough at hair to have positioned a bow so perfectly as to give Ben a toddler-like pigtail in the very center front of his hair.

"Please tell me that's not your new ponytail."

"Hey, you won't let me grow out my hair any longer than this, but apparently I don't need to. I think this is perfect, right, girls?"

The twins giggled in unison, nodding their heads fervently and making their curls bounce.

HERE'S TO THE UNDERDOGS!

"You know, it's growing on me. You should definitely keep that hairstyle." Grinning, I turned to grab some fruit from the counter.

"Then it's settled. This is my new look. And who knows, maybe it'll catch on."

"In your dreams, Benj." I took my seat across from him. "How do you expect to eat without the use of your arms?"

He looked down at each girl then back up at me and shrugged. A grin spread across his face, and he didn't even have to open his mouth for me to know what he was thinking.

"I am *not* feeding you like a baby bird."

His grin turned down into a pout. "Please…? You don't want me to starve, do you? Breakfast is the most important meal of the day."

I glared at him. "Fine. Open up."

Of course, Morgan had to walk in on this crazy scene. "What the heck? When did he get here?"

"My favorite thing about your question is that it was about my being here and not about your big sister feeding me," Ben said, obviously not seeing the need to swallow first.

"Both seem pretty normal except I didn't hear you arrive."

He shrugged. "I guess you're right. I came last night."

"Why?"

"Cause."

"Cause why?"

"You're nosey this morning. Though I guess you're always nosey."

Morgan rolled her eyes, but dropped the subject. "Ruby, Sapphire, Mom wants you."

"Aww…." The girls were really in sync today.

"Go on now. You don't want to get in trouble," Ben urged the girls.

"Ok!" They jumped up from the table and raced upstairs.

"What is their fascination with you?" Morgan asked as I set Ben's fork back on his plate as he now had the use of his arms back.

"I have no idea," he chuckled.

"I do. You're fun and amazing." I took our plates to the sink. "Now come on, we're going to be late. I'm driving."

Besides grumbling about having to ride shotgun, Ben made no further complaint about going to school. I took the opportunity as we drove to talk to him about the events of last night and how he would handle the culprit this morning.

"What are you going to do about Darren when you see him?"

"If he stays away from me, then we won't have any problems."

"And if he doesn't? I wouldn't be surprised if he approached you and tried to start trouble."

He took a moment to think before answering. "I don't know. I guess I'll do my best to be civil. I'm not as angry as I was last night at least."

"Just don't let him bother you."

Ben nodded as we pulled into the parking lot.

"You also need a haircut."

"No. I like it like this."

"Ben, it's getting too long. I can barely see your eyes anymore!" I reached over and pushed his hair back from his forehead to solidify my point.

Swatting my hand away, he retreated out of the car. "Fine. You can cut it tonight."

"Of course, I can. I always win," I boasted, linking my arm through his as we walked into the school.

"Sure you do…"

HERE'S TO THE UNDERDOGS!

"I do!"

He laughed and gave in. "Alright. I guess you're right."

"You're dang straight I am." I smirked at him, and he very maturely stuck out his tongue.

"Good morning, you two." Jill strolled down the hallway and linked her arm through mine, completing our usual trio. "I see that you two are up to your usual shenanigans."

"Shenanigans? Us? You must have us confused with another good-looking couple," Ben quipped.

"Oh, right. I don't know what I was thinking."

Chuckling, I cut in, "Well, I know what I'm thinking and it's that I don't want to be late to class. I'll catch up with you two later." Unhooking my arms from theirs, I headed back down the hall to my locker and eventually to class, excited for history as always.

Chapter 35: Ben

Every time I passed Darren in the halls or saw him in class, my blood boiled. He looked so smug yet said nothing. I kept expecting him to say something in passing to rub in the destruction of my most cherished possession, but all day he said nothing. Finally, I could take it no longer.

"Darren, I wanna talk to you," I commanded as I passed him and entered a vacant classroom.

He followed, closing the door behind him. "Yeah, Connley?" His ever-present smirk was getting tiring.

"I know what you did."

"Well, I can't personally take credit for most of it. Just the hat."

"Figured as much. But why? Why this continued feud? Don't you think it's about time it ended?"

"Not a chance." Without another word, he returned to the hallway.

"Great conversation," I mumbled.

"Ben?" Colette poked her head in the classroom. "I thought I heard you. Was that Darren I saw come out?"

I nodded. "I was hoping to be able to talk to him and make peace. It didn't work. I don't think I've ever had a shorter conversation in my life."

"Are you surprised?"

"Not really. I'm not even disappointed."

"It's admirable that you tried, but I think it's going to take more than talking to change Darren." She took my hand, pulling me with her into the hall. "Come on now. Last class of the day."

* * *

I loved the days that Aunt Michelle was in a baking mood. As soon as I stepped into the house I was blasted by an array of delicious smells: fresh pumpkin bread, chocolate chip cookies, potato soup, apple pie, and more.

"You're baking without me?" I called, hanging up my coat. "That's not allowed!"

Michelle's laugh sounded from the kitchen. "I have another helper today!"

The kitchen was one big, floury mess, Garrett situated in the middle of it on the island.

"Hi! Yook!" He held up his sticky hands to show that he'd been helping.

"Wow, Michelle. What happened in here?" I chuckled.

"Your brother, that's what. But hey! You're just in time to help clean up," Michelle grinned.

"You know, I just remembered a huge project that I have due next week that I should probably work on..."

"Come on... At least get your brother in the tub for me."

"I guess I can do that..." Upon picking Garrett up, I found that it was going to be impossible to stay clean whilst carrying him. Maybe that's why Aunt Michelle wanted me to take care of him...

I looked around the kitchen. Nope. The kitchen was a much bigger job, and she was already covered in flour.

After getting Garrett situated, I retired to my room with the intention of doing homework...until I stepped into my room and was reminded of the disaster area that it was. Cleaning would have to come first…

Not five minutes into cleaning, I was startled by a knock at my window.

"Colette! You nearly gave me a heart attack!" I opened the window to let her in. "Since when do you not use the front door?"

"You always enter my room through the window; I figured I'd try it for once. Wow." She surveyed my room. "Need some help?"

"That'd be nice. Thanks."

Cleaning went much faster with Colette, mostly because she kept me from getting distracted by throwing pillows at me when I did. That backfired, though, when I retaliated and started a pillow fight.

"Ben! We're supposed to be cleaning!" she laughed, berating me with a pillow.

"I must have vengeance!" I jumped on my desk chair for an advantage.

"What is going on here?" Michelle stepped in the room just in time to get a face full of down pillow. "Oh, I want in on this." Not skipping a beat, she snatched the final pillow from my bed and joined in the battle. At some point during the fight, Michelle and Colette ganged up on me. Being attacked from two different directions, I was unable to keep hold of my pillow, and once it had been snatched from me and I was left undefended, I curled into a ball on the floor, laughing as they continued their assault.

"Ok! I give up!"

Thankfully, both girls were laughing too hard to continue the barrage anyway, and I sat up unhindered.

"Hey, I think I hear Garrett calling."

"Oh!" Aunt Michelle exclaimed as she dashed out of the room, no doubt because she'd forgotten the child in the tub.

Colette had been sitting on the floor and now fell onto her back laughing. "I love your aunt."

I chuckled. "She's great. And we really failed at cleaning up my room…" Looking around, I was amused to find it even more of a disaster than it had been.

"Yeah… Sorry. I've still got a few minutes before I have to go home for dinner though. Help me up?"

I grabbed her outstretched hand and pulled her to her feet. "You know, I think I could live like this. Maybe we should just quit."

"No way. I'm not letting you leave it like this."

"Why not?" I whined.

"Just help me."

We attempted to straighten my room, this time with more success, finishing just in time for some freshly baked pumpkin bread.

"Mmm… Smells delicious, Michelle."

"Of course, it does, Ben," Michelle winked.

"It's not fair that your family got so much cooking talent," Colette pouted, stuffing a slice of bread in her mouth.

"We should have a baking day, Colette," my aunt offered.

"I'd like that."

"So would your mom, I'm sure."

"I heard that, Benjamin." Colette shot a playful glare in my direction. "Anyway... I should get home. Thanks for the pumpkin bread."

"You're welcome. Would you like to take any home? I made plenty."

"Enough to feed a small horde. Please take some, Colette," I added.

Colette laughed. "If you insist. With Marcus and Morgan in the house, it won't take us long to eat it."

Aunt Michelle packaged up some baked goods and sent them off with Colette. "What shall we do for the rest of the evening?"

"Uh...homework?" I wasn't sure whether I was answering her or asking my own question.

"Oh... Yeah, that's important."

"Or so we've been told."

Aunt Michelle chuckled. "Just go on. The potato soup is for supper, and I'll keep Joey and Garrett downstairs."

I showed my reluctance by groaning and whining, "Do I have to...?"

"Yes!" Michelle laughed. "Now go!"

I didn't have much of a choice as she shoved me toward the stairs. "Fine... But I'll be down for supper."

"Of that, I have no doubt."

With an eye roll, I ventured upstairs to tackle my dreaded homework. I ended up getting so engrossed in my Chemistry homework that I lost track of time, and Aunt Michelle had to remind me about supper. And from that moment onward, no more homework was done for the rest of the night. Alice, Aunt Michelle, Tony, and I played a few rounds of the card game Pepper as Garrett sat on my lap, convinced he was my helpful partner. He and Joey fell asleep, saving me and Aunt Michelle the trouble of putting them to bed. We probably would have played late into the night, but when Alice nearly fell asleep at the table, Aunt Michelle ended the game and strongly advised that we all get some sleep. I didn't even argue, eager to get some shut-eye myself. After tucking Garrett in and making sure Alice made it to her room without falling asleep in the hall, I snuggled up in bed, having no trouble falling asleep.

Chapter 36: Ben

A few weeks passed without incident. Graduation grew nearer, spring began to warm our corner of the earth...and Jill would not shut up about prom. I usually dreaded the event, but since the Underdogs would be providing some of the music, I figured prom might not be so bad this year. But that didn't mean I wanted to hear about it all day long. Most of the time I ended up zoning out, leaving Colette to respond to our crazy friend.

A week before prom, we Underdogs were all gathered at Colette's house for a Friday evening movie marathon: The Hobbit edition. It had become regular for Marcus and Morgan to join us for many of our get-togethers, and tonight we were also joined by Tony and Alice.

Throughout the evening I noticed Connie glancing at Tony, an occurrence that thoroughly confused me. I'd have to talk with Colette about it later.

Per usual, Marcus and Becky had fallen asleep before even the second movie was over, but we continued the marathon without them. Halfway through the second movie, Luca was purely focused on the movie, and

HERE'S TO THE UNDERDOGS!

I took the opportunity to scooch closer to Joanna (over a reasonable amount of time so as to not be too noticeable, of course). At least I hoped it wasn't noticeable. Whether or not Joanna caught onto my plan was irrelevant when she slid next to me and leaned her head on my shoulder. I swear, at that moment, my heart stopped beating. The noise of the movie faded into the background, as did the friends surrounding us. All that was on my mind was Joanna. I felt her even breathing on my arm; the stray hairs that had fallen from her braid brushed against my neck. I ventured to put my arm around her shoulders, and she snuggled closer. I noticed Colette grinning at me, but chose to ignore her, hoping Joanna wasn't paying attention. As her breathing slowed and became more even, it was evident that she indeed wasn't paying attention— she'd joined the others in slumber. I dared not move for fear of waking her up, though my arm began to ache as the movie neared its end.

"Daww... You two are adorable," Colette whispered from where she was situated on the couch above me.

"Oh, hush." I paused. "Sitting on the floor was a bad idea. I at least should have sat on a pillow."

In her attempt to not laugh aloud, Colette snorted. "That would've been smart. But you two really are adorable." She slunk from the couch and knelt in front of us to get a picture, an act that I could not contest for fear of waking Joanna.

"Be warned, I will get you back for this. Actually, Joanna will probably beat me to it."

She grinned. "You're probably right, but I'll take my chances." She returned to the couch, laying her head on the arm of the couch. Raising her voice for the others to hear, she said, "I vote that we all just sleep here."

"I second that..." Jill responded.

A few mumbled agreements, and the matter was settled. The floor and couches were soon covered with sleeping teens, but I found myself unable to even doze. I was too focused on the beauty leaning against me, fast asleep.

It wasn't until near one-thirty that Joanna woke up, blinking up at me sleepily. In return, I smiled at her. Rather than moving, she snuggled closer, speaking softly.

"Are you comfortable?"

Unable to speak, I simply nodded, sure I must be blushing.

She frowned in disbelief. "Really?"

I shrugged half-heartedly, and her frown deepened, her brow furrowed adorably. Lifting her head from my shoulder, she reached up to get the last pillow from the couch before lying on the floor, pulling me down next to her so my head rested on the pillow. She snuggled into my arms, her head on my chest.

A few moments passed and she looked up at me, eyes barely open. "I can't feel you breathing..."

Heat rose up in my cheeks. "Oh..." I released the breath I hadn't realized I was holding. I couldn't help but smile at how cute her sleepy, slurred speech was. It was probable that she hadn't been quite awake even just a few minutes ago when she moved us to this position, and now she was once again fast asleep. Wrapping my arms loosely around her, I closed my eyes, completely aware of each breath she took, each tiny shift in her position, each mumbled secret she uttered. I was so attuned to her, I felt sure I would never fall asleep. Not five minutes later, I was lost in my dreams.

Chapter 37: Ben

For once it would have been nice to wake up early because, by the time I woke up, Joanna was already in the kitchen helping Colette with breakfast. At least I wasn't the last one up—that honor went to Marcus.

I walked into the kitchen and was immediately met by a glare from Luca. If I had to guess, I'd say he woke up before Joanna…if he'd even slept.

"Hey, Luca… How's it going? Sleep well?"

Colette interrupted before he could answer, which was probably for the best.

"Ben, would you make the pancakes?"

"Sure. What kind do you want?"

The vote was almost unanimously chocolate chip, and I set to work cooking. Colette had put just about everyone else to work: Tony and Connie were making smoothies, Jill was in charge of the scrambled eggs with Alice and Morgan as her sidekicks, Becky and Nathan were flipping the bacon, and Luca was helping Colette and Maggie butter toast. That

HERE'S TO THE UNDERDOGS!

left Joanna as the only one without a job, and she was more than happy to help me with the pancakes.

To no one's surprise, Marcus woke up just as breakfast was finally prepared. With so much food, we decided it would be better to serve ourselves in the kitchen before moving to the dining room rather than bringing all the food to the table. We had such a feast that it was almost a shame Mr. and Mrs. Tance had taken the twins camping for the weekend— we could have used their help eating it all.

Jill all but monopolized the conversation during breakfast, talking about the upcoming prom. As head of the decorating committee, I suppose she had a right to be obsessed with the event, but we all agreed that we needed a new topic.

"Well, we still have to decide what we're doing today," Nathan pointed out.

"True. Ideas?" Colette asked before taking a bite of bacon.

"I say we hang out around town doing lots of things. We could go to the mall, stop by the beach, maybe check out the new skate park— the possibilities are endless."

"I'm not sure *endless* is the word I'd use, Nathan... But sure. That sounds fun. Anyone opposed to that?"

Other than Morgan, no one contested the idea and it was decided that, after cleaning up from breakfast, we'd take over the mall.

* * *

The mall was as busy as would be expected on a Saturday, but our group was like a mob going through. That is until the girls wanted to go clothes shopping and the guys wanted to browse the sporting goods store. At that point, we decided it might be best to split into groups.

Surprisingly, Luca joined the guys rather than sticking with his sister as I would have expected him to. I avoided him as much as I could, though perhaps there was no reason to. I just couldn't shake the feeling that he was scrutinizing my every move as if making sure I was good enough for his sister. There was really no reason to— it's not like we were dating or anything...unfortunately.

Before any of us realized it, we had spent two hours looking around the store and the girls were waiting for us outside. We only knew this when Colette was sent into the depths of the store to drag us out. Most of us went willingly, but Colette almost had to physically remove her brother from the gun counter.

We boys had no say in the decision to move on to our next venue— the beach. As it was still early spring, the beach was nearly vacant when we arrived, and we ran up and down the shore before collapsing in the sand.

Our rest didn't last long. After just a few minutes, Jill was on her feet, urging the rest of us to get up for a game of beach volleyball. Nathan was the only one who had slight qualms about the game, but he joined, and we all had a great time for well near an hour. Upon finishing, we realized that we had forgotten to pack any lunch, and Tony and Marcus volunteered to get some subs for everyone.

While they were gone, we had an unwelcome visitor.

Chapter 38: Ben

Jeremy strolled down the beach, hands in his pockets. Passing the rest of us without a word or second glance, he approached Colette. Knowing she could handle herself, I watched in amusement, ready for the show to begin.

"Jeremy, what are you doing here?" Colette questioned, crossing her arms.

"I was just going for a walk when I saw you all here and thought I'd say hello."

"Well, now you've said it. Bye."

"Hang on just a minute. We've really got to put whatever this is behind us."

"Believe me, I'm trying, but you just keep on popping back up."

Jeremy gently took Colette's arm and lead her a few yards from the group, spoiling my fun. A tap on my shoulder made me jump.

"Oh. Jill. Hi."

"What happened between them?" She gestured to Jeremy and Colette.

HERE'S TO THE UNDERDOGS!

"They used to date. Colette really loved him. Then one summer Jeremy and his family went on vacation, and a few months after he got back, Colette found out about some girl he'd been seeing. He had met her that summer and stayed in contact, and when she and her family moved to a town not far from here, he started dating her."

"Oh... No wonder Colette doesn't like him..."

"Yeah. He soon learned how stupid he'd been and has been trying to get Colette back ever since."

"Wow. Has she dated anyone since?"

I shook my head. "I don't think she ever will; not for a long time at least. She has...big plans for her life and feels that dating would just get in the way."

"Yeah, what *is* she doing after high school? She seems like the type to have the next five years at least figured out, but whenever I ask, she sidesteps answering."

I grinned, feeling special being the only person Colette had told about her plans— outside her immediate family, of course. "Oh, she knows what she's doing."

Jill would have asked more questions, but Jeremy and Colette finished their conversation just then. As Jeremy walked away, Colette joined me and Jill, hooking an arm around each of our shoulders.

"What'cha talking about?"

"Nothing." Jill answered so quickly that it was doubtful Colette had any question as to what our topic of discussion had been.

"Ok... I take it Tony and Marcus aren't back with the food yet."

"Not that I've seen," I replied this time.

We joined the others to wait for the food to arrive. After Tony and Marcus had been absent for well over half an hour, we began to worry,

HERE'S TO THE UNDERDOGS!

and I called my brother. No response. I wasn't too worried though—Tony would definitely be irresponsible enough to not answer the phone, and it was likely that he and Colette's brother had simply gotten distracted or sidetracked. Still, after they'd been gone an hour, it was more difficult to stay calm.

"I bet Marcus is to blame."

"Wow. Way to throw your brother under the bus," I chuckled.

"Well, it's probably true!"

"Wait a minute... Did they take *my* jeep?? If anything happened to that, I will kill Tony!"

"Now who's full of brotherly love?"

Before our dispute could continue, our brothers arrived, the jeep unharmed.

"What took so long?" Morgan demanded.

"Never trust Marcus for directions. We took his so-called shortcut, and, well, you can see the outcome."

"Yeah, never trust Marcus for anything," Colette laughed.

Her brother protested the sentiment, but it didn't much matter as everyone was too busy getting food to pay attention. Seeing his argument was in vain, he relented and pushed through the group to grab a sandwich.

Storm clouds rolled in as we ate, putting an end to the rest of our plans for the day. Most of the group decided to go to their respective homes, leaving me and my siblings, Colette and hers, and Maggie to figure out what to do with the afternoon. I thought surely Connie would have stayed, but Jill convinced her to help with last-minute prom details. Poor Connie.

HERE'S TO THE UNDERDOGS!

The seven of us agreed to see a movie then head to Colette's house for some games as her parents would still be gone until late that evening.

* * *

As strange as it was for my house to be quiet, it was even stranger for the Tance house to have been quiet for so long. Still, it was rather nice. We spent the evening playing board games and eating popcorn, forgoing dinner. Maggie had to leave around eight, but when Alice fell asleep on the couch with Morgan during Monopoly, Tony and I decided to stay at least until Mr. and Mrs. Tance came home. That proved to be much later than we had anticipated— after midnight in fact. Mrs. Tance offered to have us stay the night, but we had to decline as Aunt Michelle had wanted us all together for church the next morning. I discovered that my sister was just as heavy of a sleeper at times as I was, and Colette enjoyed my struggle in trying to wake her. I soon gave up and carried her to the car instead.

Aunt Michelle was a bit irritated at how late we arrived home, but I appeased her with the promise that I would make breakfast and take care of Joey the next morning. With that assurance, she bid me goodnight and went to bed. I followed suit after a quick snack…

Chapter 39: Ben

Thursday. Only one more day until prom, and Jill officially had a one-track mind. She had gotten to the point of obsession where I started avoiding her as much as possible. Unfortunately, I was forced to be in her presence for at least half an hour during band practices which had become more frequent and lengthier the closer we got to prom. Though, as the realization hit me that prom meant only three weeks until graduation, her droning on about the subject became a welcome distraction in the final hours of the evening. But after practice, when everyone else had gone home, and Michelle and I were the only two in the kitchen as I baked a cheesecake, I was reminded of the coming end of my life as I knew it.

"Are you excited for the college visit next week?"

"Mhmm," I replied, distracted.

"That's it?"

"What? Sorry, I wasn't really listening…"

She gave me a "really" look and repeated herself. "I was asking about your college visit. Are you excited?"

HERE'S TO THE UNDERDOGS!

"Oh... I guess."

Rising from her place at the island, she stood by my side. "Are you nervous?"

Not looking directly at her, I nodded as I put the cake in the oven.

"Why on earth are you nervous? You're the smartest kid I know, going to visit a school where, though it's full of genius kids, you're going to stand out."

"That's what I'm afraid of," I mumbled.

"Ben... I didn't mean you'd stand out in a bad way. Go blow them away with your brilliance."

I grinned as I continued the colloquialism. "And if I can't do that, I'll baffle them with my—"

"Ok, yes, I know the rest of the saying," Aunt Michelle cut me off, glancing at Garrett on the floor. The child would repeat anything and we didn't need him going around the house saying *that*.

Chuckling, I responded, "Anyway... You really think I'll like it at college?"

"I do, Ben. I really do."

"Ok... I guess so."

"I know so," she grinned at me.

I couldn't help smiling back. "Alright. I'll trust your judgment."

"Good. Now how's that cheesecake coming?"

It wasn't long before the cake was done and we were sitting at the island, discussing life after graduation. Aunt Michelle had a way of making things seem like they were going to be ok.

HERE'S TO THE UNDERDOGS!

***

The next morning at school, it seemed as though only one thing was talked about: prom. The posters for king and queen that had been hanging all week were straightened, the candidates were vying for votes, and I was trying to stay calm about performing that night. I tried to rehearse every moment I could, even if I was just recalling lyrics and tunes in my head. Colette wasn't making rehearsing easy as she hummed Christmas songs next to me.

"Worried about tomorrow?" she asked, looping her arm through mine.

"What do you think?"

"Ben, the talent show was a success. Don't worry about this."

"I know... I'm not really too worried. I'd just rather not waste my Friday night doing this."

"What else would you be doing?"

A shrug was all I could manage to respond with.

"That's what I thought," Colette grinned. "You'll have fun, Ben."

"I guess... I'll just be glad when it's over."

"I'm with you there."

Our conversation was cut short when we arrived at our classroom, and we had to wait nearly an hour to continue it— not that it was a very important conversation.

"Do you think there will be any trouble tonight at prom?"

"Not really," Colette doubted. "Other than maybe someone trying to spike the punch or something."

I nodded thoughtfully, and then my mind moved on to something else. "You got nominated for prom queen you know."

"I *what?* Who did that?"

"I dunno," I answered.

Colette half snarled through gritted teeth, "I'm gonna strangle whoever it was. Who are the prom king nominees?"

"The only one I remember is Jeremy..."

This new information made Colette stop in the middle of the hallway. "You have *got* to be kidding me."

"Afraid not." I paused, thinking up a plan. "You know... We could always just ditch prom, and then you wouldn't have to worry about dancing with him if you both win."

She was too smart to fall for that. "Nice try, Benjamin, but no. You're going and singing."

"Yes, mother," I grumbled to which Colette responded with an eye roll. "Hey, what about a senior ditch day today?"

"You know...no." She shook the idea from her head. "Not today. History test, remember?"

"Gee, I completely forgot. That was totally not the reason I wanted to ditch," I responded.

She ignored the sarcasm and quipped, "I hope you didn't also forget all the answers. And this time, if a question says to explain, do so. Don't just change your answer."

"That was one time! And I had a headache."

She gave me a look to convey her annoyance with my excuses. "Stop pouting. Just get to class and ace that test."

"Ha! Hell would freeze over before I ever aced a history test."

"You're impossible."

HERE'S TO THE UNDERDOGS!

"So I've been told."

"Just go..." She drew out the last word, shoving me into my classroom and waving before continuing down the hall.

Time to flunk out of history for the year, I thought as I took my seat by the window. *Maybe staring out at the parking lot will help me think.*

It didn't. I knew as soon as I placed the test on the teacher's desk that I had definitely not aced it and had probably come closer to failing than anything else. At this point, I'd be happy with a seventy. Good thing RIST had already accepted me and didn't care about my failing grades in history. But Colette cared. And my aunt cared. They'd both have something to say about this test...whenever we all found out my grade. Maybe that'd be Monday when I'd be gone.

"How was the test?" Colette asked as she fell in step with me.

"Guess we'll find out when I get it back with a grade. Hey, where's Jill?" It wasn't that I missed the constant babbling on about prom, but at least her incessant talking would keep Colette off my back about history.

"She's probably working on some last-minute planning and setting up."

"Oh... Probably."

The lunchroom was as noisy as ever when we entered, scanning the crowded room for our friends. Colette pointed out Walter and Nathan at our table, and we hurried to claim our seats after getting some food.

"How's it going?" Nathan asked as we set our trays down.

"Alright, I guess," I replied before filling my mouth with food, thereby excusing myself from answering any more questions.

Nathan grinned. "Less than seven more hours now."

I groaned to show my displeasure with his countdown. "You're worse than Jill," I responded after swallowing.

He simply laughed, and Walter saved me any further stress by jumping into the conversation and updating us on the latest news in the political sphere.

* * *

"I almost want to walk home," Colette stated as we exited the school building at the end of the day.

I looked at her like she was insane, which I was pretty sure she was after that sentence. "What? It's not that cold out, and I missed my morning run."

"You're still doing that?" I almost thought I'd heard her wrong, but in a way, it didn't surprise me. I just thought she'd lost it.

"Of course. I can't stop just because we had a cold snap in the weather."

My sigh created a cloud in the frigid air. "You're crazy. Though I do admire your dedication."

Her lighthearted chuckle almost seemed to warm the air around us. "Why thank you. You could join me some mornings you know."

"No thanks. I appreciate my sleep."

She nodded. "I guess there wasn't much point in offering."

"Not really," I replied, grinning despite the pain it caused my frozen cheeks.

"I see you enough anyway," she nudged my shoulder, her grin creating dimples in her rosy cheeks. "And I'll see you back here in a few hours."

We stopped by her car, and I opened her door for her, nodding, yet refusing to verbally acknowledge the event that was a mere four hours away. After giving me a hug, she got in the car and waved as she drove away.

HERE'S TO THE UNDERDOGS!

Hands in my pockets, I strolled to my car, debating whether or not to go straight home. As soon as I got in the car, it was decided— I was going home. My drive home was powered by the hope that Aunt Michelle would have hot cocoa waiting and perhaps a surprise trip to Hawaii for that night. The latter was certainly less likely, but far more desired.

Aunt Michelle picked Joey up and waved as I pulled in the driveway. Joey was so bundled up that not much other than his green eyes and cherry red nose could be seen poking out. Garrett's eyes lit up when he saw me, and he ran from Michelle's side as I approached.

"Hey, buddy!" I picked him up and carried him inside. "You're up from your nap early."

"Uh-huh!" was the only intelligible part of his reply, but he continued babbling, presumably about the events of the day.

Aunt Michelle must have only planned on keeping Joey and Garrett outside for a short time as there was a pot of water nearly boiling on the stove. I aided her by setting out three mugs and Joey's sippy cup then removed Joey's coat, hat, scarf, and gloves. Despite his excessive clothing and his short duration outside, his cheeks and hands were freezing. The weather this week had been uncharacteristically cold, but that didn't stop my little brother — or Colette for that matter — from enjoying some fresh air every day.

Upon smelling the hot cocoa Aunt Michelle was fixing, Alice skipped down the stairs and hopped up on a stool at the island. I set out an extra mug, and Aunt Michelle topped each mug with whipped cream and cinnamon then pushed two of them to me and Alice. Joey complained about the lack of whipped cream in his sippy cup until Aunt Michelle quieted him by squirting some in his mouth, an act she repeated for Garrett.

After chugging my hot chocolate, I raced upstairs for some downtime. With *Billy Joel* playing through my headphones, and my favorite hobo sweater (as Colette called it because of the many holes perforating it) keeping me warm, I sat on my floor, surrounded by my Legos as I built new creations. I would have much rather spent the evening thusly, but Aunt Michelle commanded I leave my room and eat dinner before heading back to school. She didn't fall for my false complaint about a sore-throat, and I was on the road by quarter after six, giving me plenty of time to set up and prepare once I reached the school.

Jill snagged me as soon as I stepped foot in the door, dragging me to the gym. I stood in amazement at how the gym had been transformed over the past two days. Paper lanterns hung from the ceiling, keeping the lighting soft. Twisted streamers lined the walls, balloons separating them every few feet. Beneath one of the basketball hoops were the refreshment tables— one was topped with finger sandwiches, fruit trays, chips, and several other snack foods. The adjoining table held the drinks: sodas, punch, water, and iced tea. Jill would certainly have someone on standby to make sure the tables were kept stocked.

"The stage is all set up, we just need to do a sound check," Jill drew me from my awed stupor, her silver heels clicking on the cement floor as she hurried gracefully toward the other side of the gym.

As I followed behind her, the shimmery jewels in her curls caught my eye. I had no idea what they were or how she got them to stay in her hair, but their purple hue matched her knee-length dress perfectly. Her silver dangle earrings sparkled as she turned to me.

"Jeff's in charge of sound tonight so he'll get you set up." Her attention was drawn to the refreshment table as a bowl clattered to the floor. "Sarah, what are you doing?" she called to the redhead left standing over the scattered cheese puffs. "Just talk to Jeff." She barely looked at me as she responded before hastening to rectify the snack disaster.

It didn't take long for me and Jeff to figure out the sound arrangement, and by the time we had, the gym was filling up with students. Right at seven o'clock, Jill took the stage and the festivities began.

Chapter 40: Ben

Prom actually wasn't as terrible as I had been anticipating. The evening passed rather quickly, the Underdogs providing music during most of it with short breaks in between every few songs. So far, no one had caused any trouble. Jill had allowed two freshmen to attend prom on the arrangement that they guard the punch bowl with their lives. The two took turns standing at the table, the one off duty enjoying a few dances before returning to the table to relieve the other.

I was glad to steal a few dances with Joanna, but alas, a slow dance was not one of those treasured few.

Finally, it was time to reveal who our class-men had chosen as king and queen. The nominees were called up on stage, Colette being among them. Though the fake smile she wore on her face didn't add much to her beauty, she was the most dazzling girl on stage. Her ginger hair was piled on her head tastefully save for the few curled pieces framing her face. I recognized the pearl earrings and necklace adorning her as being her mother's, and they complimented her iridescent blue dress nicely.

HERE'S TO THE UNDERDOGS!

She was wearing heels, but they were hidden beneath the flowy fabric of her dress.

Jill took the stage, this time with an envelope in her hand. In past years the principal had revealed the "lucky" two, but he allowed Jill to oversee absolutely everything this year. So, microphone in one hand, envelope in the other, she read off the names.

"Colette Tance and Jeremy Hudson."

An excited grin on her face, Jill turned to Colette and waved her forward, placing the crown on her head once she'd stepped up. Jeremy didn't need any coaxing as he took his place at Colette's side, ducking so Jill could adorn his gelled hair with the other crown. After their picture was taken, Jeremy offered Colette his arm, a gesture she reluctantly accepted as she followed him off the stage. One dance was all that was required, and there was no doubt in my mind that Colette would make sure that one was all Jeremy got.

He respectfully placed a hand on her back, the other extended to hold her hand. With an apologetic look in Colette's direction, I lead the group in the romantic song that had been selected for the king and queen dance. I couldn't help thinking that Colette and Jeremy made a good-looking couple, and maybe they would have been a good match, had Jeremy not messed up.

Now he'd be hard-pressed to find anyone better, and from how persistent he'd been in trying to win her back, I could see he knew that. The old saying was proven true in this moment— "you don't know what you have until it's gone."

I'd hardly heard the words I'd been singing as the song ended. No sooner had Walter stopped playing the piano than Colette separated herself from Jeremy and hastened toward the exit into the hallway. I glanced at Maggie, and upon receiving a knowing nod from her, hopped from the stage and pushed through the throng, following my friend.

I found her sitting against the lockers in the hallway, face buried against her knees. Quietly, **approached.**

"Colette?"

She looked up as I spoke softly.

"Are you ok?" I slid down next to her, one leg stretched out in front of me, an arm resting on my other bent knee.

Colette nodded and leaned her head against my shoulder, shifting her position to be more comfortable. I draped my free arm across her shoulders, drawing her closer and planting a kiss on her head, my cheek brushing against the bun atop her head as I did so. Her hair smelled like mint and strawberries.

"How come your hair always smell like strawberries?"

She looked up at me, her brow furrowed in confusion at my random question. "I dunno. I thought it'd smell like mint, like my shampoo."

"Oh, it does, but it also still smells like strawberries. I theorize that the reason is that your hair is magical and therefore the scent matches the color." I grinned down at her, certain that she knew I was joking.

A slight smile tugged at her pink lips. "You're such a weirdo. Why do you even know that my hair always smells like strawberries? Do you smell it regularly?"

My grin widened as I responded. "Why, of course. I sneak into your room nightly and smell it to make sure it still smells of strawberries."

She laughed at that before replying with a simple, "Creep."

Chuckling, I crossed my other arm over her, resting it on her arm. "Are you sure you're ok?"

She nodded again. "I am now. Thanks, Ben." After a pause, she scowled up at me. "Why'd you wear that suit?"

"Why not? I like green. And it matches my eyes." I waggled my eyebrows at her, turning her scowl into a playful chuckle.

"Maybe so, but it doesn't match me. We should have matched."

"You could've worn green."

"And be Christmassy? No way."

I cocked my head in confusion until it dawned on me— her hair. Then I threw my head back laughing. "Fair enough."

"Exactly." Tilting her head back down, she snuggled into me. It wasn't often she got like this, but I didn't mind when she did. She was cute when she was pouty and all snuggly. I made the mistake of telling her that once, and she proceeded to hold me in a headlock for the next ten minutes until I relented and took back what I'd said.

"Ready to go back in yet?" I rubbed her back as she took a moment before answering.

"I suppose..."

"We don't have to. Maggie's covering for me, and I won't be missed by anyone else."

"No... I should go back." Lifting her head from my shoulder, she pushed herself to her feet, smoothing her dress before offering me a hand.

I chuckled and accepted. "Shouldn't I be helping *you* up?"

"Not when I'm stronger."

"You are not stronger! Just cause you fight better, doesn't mean you're stronger." I crossed my arms, frowning at her.

The curls around her face danced as she tossed her head back and laughed. "I'm kidding! I know you're stronger. Now. Shall we?" She linked her arm through mine and ushered me back into the gym. Maggie smiled at me from up on stage where she was still singing solo.

A few yards into the gym, Colette stopped and turned to me. "Will you dance with me?"

I gave a lopsided grin as I answered, "I'd be honored to dance with the prom queen."

I led her onto the dance floor and got two dances more than she had allowed Jeremy, after which I relieved Maggie for a few songs. And that's when the trouble started…

HERE'S TO THE UNDERDOGS!

Chapter 41: Colette

Ben was in the middle of the second verse of a song by *Fun* when someone turned on the oversized fan, spewing glitter everywhere. It wouldn't have been so bad had the food and drinks been saved from the explosion, but the little particles found their way onto nearly every surface, leaving the gym a shimmery mess.

After everyone's moment of surprised silence, the gym erupted in an uproar of cheering and shouting. Jill assured everyone that the glitter was planned, but I'd seen the look on her face when it first filtered out from the fan, and it told me that glitter had not been on the agenda. Still, it was a nearly harmless prank except for the loss of some good food and punch, both of which were soon replaced. The night continued as though nothing had happened, until the next unexpected calamity.

I already had an idea of who was behind the glitter fiasco, and my suspicion was proven correct when several of Darren's closest friends ran into the gym throwing water balloons at everyone. The prank wouldn't have been too detrimental had the water balloons just been filled with water. But they weren't. They were filled with several different liquids, all of which were guaranteed to stain any fabric they touched. The wielders of said water balloons were unfortunately accurate, and not a single balloon was squandered on the floor. Hundreds, even thousands of dollars were essentially wasted as dozens of dresses and suits were ruined. There was still a chance for prom to be salvaged though.

Or so I thought. Not fifteen minutes had passed before students began leaving, complaining of upset stomachs. I accompanied Jill as she hurried to investigate. As many students as we could stop all admitted to drinking the punch within the past half hour. Jill then proceeded to interrogate the two freshmen overseeing the punch. Both insisted that one or the other had been stationed at the refreshment table for the extent of the evening, but had one of them been distracted for even a few seconds, it would have been easy enough for something to have been slipped into the punch unseen. Jill was quick to dispose of the punch and didn't even dare to refill the bowl for fear that the rest had been contaminated as well.

And thus ended the 2016 prom of Westbrooke High. After an hour of cleaning glitter off of everything, I went in search of Jill and found her sitting, defeated, on the school steps. The raw night air bit at my skin, and the cold from the concrete steps crept through the thin fabric of my dress, thoroughly chilling my legs as I sat next to Jill.

"Well, at least this prom will be remembered," she mumbled, not able to stay quiet no matter how devastated she was.

"None of this is your fault, you know. You couldn't have foreseen any of it."

"But I was still the one in charge. This will go down as the worst prom of Westbrooke High, and *I* was the one in charge. The details won't matter in five, ten years."

"Jill, *prom* won't matter in a few years. Do you really think we're gonna look back on this as an important night in our lives years from now?"

She gave me a sideways glance before replying, the words seeming almost painful. "I guess not..."

"In fact, we'll probably laugh about the glitter and the water balloons. Food poisoning...maybe not so much. But with things like this, people tend to romanticize the good and forget the bad. Sure, the students who actually got sick might remember that most about the evening, but everyone else will probably recall the excitement of the other pranks."

At last, she smiled. "I guess that's true. Thanks."

"No thanks needed for being wiser than you," I smirked.

"Oh, that is so not true," she grinned back, rising to her feet.

As I rose, I rediscovered just how cold it was. "Can we please go back inside?"

"Who's the city girl now, huh?"

I defended my honor with a most dignified eye roll as I grabbed her arm and pulled her inside. "Just hush. This dress was not meant for cold weather."

"That I will agree with."

The gym was beginning to look normal again. I estimated that two more hours were needed before it would be acceptable to the principal, but with the dozen of us left to clean up, and the music that poured from the speakers keeping us energized, that time would pass quickly.

With no interruptions or disasters, we finished just on schedule and didn't spend much time on goodbyes as we were all eager to get home to our beds. On my way out of the building, I noticed a lone trash bag in the hall just outside the gym. Not in too much of a rush to get home and not wanting to leave any bit of a mess, I resolved to dispose of it before

HERE'S TO THE UNDERDOGS!

heading home. It was as I was rounding the back corner of the school on my way to the dumpster, holding the trash bag of mostly glitter as far from myself as I could, that I encountered Darren. He was leaning against the building looking as though he hadn't a care in the world.

"I'm surprised you're still here. I figured you'd leave after seeing your plans carried out, ruining tonight for everyone." He opened his mouth to speak, no doubt having planned some smart retort, but I didn't give him the chance as I continued. "That was really low, making everyone sick. The glitter and water balloons weren't enough? What if someone gets seriously ill? You could probably get suspended if this gets traced back to you."

"I wasn't behind that. The glitter and water balloons, yeah, but not the thing with the punch. One of the guys got carried away."

"You expect me to believe that?"

He gave a half-hearted shrug. "Innocent until proven guilty, right? As the daughter of a lawyer, I'd expect you to know that inherently."

His response surprised me. "Why do you even care? I thought you'd want the credit for that stunt whether you orchestrated it or not."

"I don't wanna be known as the guy that got everyone sick on what was supposed to be the best night of their high school lives. Ruining prom with harmless stunts is one thing, but causing an epidemic is a bit too extravagant for my taste." He seemed to notice the trash bag I carried for the first time. "Here, let me take care of that." He practically snatched the bag from my hand before I had time to respond or even comprehend the gesture.

"Thanks..." I was skeptical but grateful for the assistance.

"Tell anyone about this and you'll regret it."

There's the Darren I know. "I'd expect nothing less."

HERE'S TO THE UNDERDOGS!

Casting a suspicious glance over my shoulder, I walked back into the school to do one last check of everything before locking up. Jill had been bequeathed the keys by the principal and then passed them on to me when I offered to stay behind for a few extra minutes. I made sure all the interior lights were off and all the doors were closed before exiting the building, the door clicking shut behind me. Making doubly sure I'd completed my task, I jiggled the locked handle and was satisfied with its security.

The moon was full, and it illuminated the parking lot so brightly that my shadow stretched out clearly in front of me as I walked to my car. The moon and my shadow were my only companions in the early morning— not even the spring peepers made their calls down in the pond less than a mile away.

Darren's reason for helping was revealed to me as I reached my car. The first thing I noticed was that it was covered in cotton balls, but beyond that, upon opening the door I discovered that Darren had apparently disposed of the massive bag of glitter in my car. How he managed to get into my car in the first place was a mystery, but I didn't much care at the moment. All I cared about was the glitter spread around my feet and over the seats of my car. There was no way I was riding home in my car with it like that. I only hoped that Ben was still awake as I called him.

He finally responded after the fifth ring and agreed to pick me up. The sleep in his voice made me worry he would fall asleep at the wheel, but he arrived safely and reluctantly allowed me to drive on the way home— not that he had much of a choice. I had to keep poking him on the drive to his house to keep him awake and thought I'd have to drag him inside once we arrived. Fortunately, he woke up enough to stumble through the front door which was good enough for me. After he'd disappeared into the house, I walked home alone, the streets lit by yellow lamps every few yards. I avoided the moths fluttering around each lamp as I passed by. As I neared my house, my neighbor's cat crept from the shadows and rubbed up against my leg, curling around in front of me and causing me to stop. I stooped to gather the gray tabby in my arms, stroking his cheeks as I continued up the hill.

I released the cat into his yard before crossing into my own and entering my house silently, careful to avoid the one squeaky step that Dad had yet to fix as I ascended the stairs. Passing by each bedroom on my way down the hall, I could hear the rhythmic breathing and snoring that assured me all in the house were asleep.

I decided, as I changed into my cozy PJs, that I wished Mom had still been awake. I spent several aggravating minutes trying to get the zipper of my dress un-snagged from the delicate cloth. At last, it gave way, and I was soon in bed, snuggled deep in the blankets.

Chapter 42: Colette

Ben had only been away visiting his college for two days, and I already missed him. How were we ever going to survive being apart for months on end after high school? I didn't even want to think about years down the road when both our lives were too busy and invested in other things that we only saw each other once or twice a year.

"Sweet Potato? Are you alright?" Dad queried as I picked at my chicken.

My nod may have satisfied him had it not been accompanied by a sigh.

His light chuckle made me smile a bit. "I assume your despondent spirit is caused by Ben's absence?"

I nodded, a bit shyer this time.

"Isn't he coming back the day after tomorrow?"

"Yeah..."

Dad's left eyebrow quirked up, increasing the few wrinkles on his forehead. "So...why the long face?"

HERE'S TO THE UNDERDOGS!

Mom rose, taking up her plate. "Twins, help me in the kitchen. Marcus, Morgan, go do you your homework." Having given her commands, she walked to the kitchen, fully expecting her wishes to be respected with no qualms. Morgan shot a pleading glance at Dad, but he stood by his wife. "Go on now. You have half an hour before devotions."

Suddenly remembering his extensive amount of homework, Marcus shot up from his chair and dashed up the stairs, lazily followed by Morgan. The twins had already bounced after Mom, leaving me and Dad to talk in peace.

"What's this about?"

"I was just thinking about the inescapable future when Ben and I aren't so close and hardly see each other."

"Do you really think either of you would let that happen?"

"Dad, how are we going to avoid it? He'll be in college, and I'll — hopefully — be on missions in the CIA. It's not like we'll have an endless supply of time."

"But you'll make time. I know you both very well, and I'm certain this is a friendship that will last."

He stood and placed a kiss on my head before taking our plates to the kitchen. We'd had enough discussions that I was used to the sudden endings when he believed the issue had been solved, for it generally was. But not this evening. Ben wasn't the only thing on my mind...

* * *

Mom called up the stairs to Morgan, Marcus, and I when it was time for devotions. I hadn't been able to focus on homework, and my mind wandered just as much during family devotions. This must have been evident to Dad as he stopped more than once to get my attention. When we finally closed with prayer, the others dispersed, but Dad called me into his office to talk some more.

"I see I concluded our previous discussion prematurely. What's on your mind? You can't be this distracted simply because of Ben."

"I'm not... I'm also thinking about Jeremy and Darren."

"That's an interesting combination."

I did a half eye-roll before catching myself. "Not at the same time, Dad. Just in general."

"And what exactly have you been thinking?" He leaned back in his chair, arms crossed thoughtfully.

My dad was in his late forties, but he seemed much younger to me at times. He still looked youthful and was just as energetic now as he had been nearly twenty years ago when I was little. His dark hair was just beginning to gray, but in the right lighting, it still held its reddish tint; and his eyes were still youthful and jolly.

"Umm..." I decided to talk about Darren first. Maybe Dad would forget about Jeremy... "Why won't Darren just leave us alone?"

"People do things for reasons that I will never understand."

I nodded thoughtfully before answering. "I imagine as a lawyer you see people who do all sorts of things." I couldn't help thinking about my own uncle.

"I do. But you know my favorite part about being a lawyer?"

"The justice you see dealt."

"Exactly." Dad paused, brow furrowed slightly. "I believe we have gotten off track."

My laugh was so infectious as to cause him to laugh along with me.

"You have a habit of doing that when we talk."

Dad's laugh fizzled out to a chuckle. "Maybe it's your fault for saying things that distract me."

"The blame game? Really?" I crossed my arms, raising an eyebrow.

He responded in kind, a boyish smirk tugging at his lips. "Really."

"Which of us is the adult here?"

He laughed. "Ok. Back on topic. What was this about Jeremy?"

Of course, he remembered. I tucked my hair behind my ears as I replied, "I've just been seeing a lot of him lately…" I untucked my hair, sweeping it over one shoulder.

"Oh? Has he been bothering you?"

"Not so much that I can't handle him."

"That I know. You could handle just about anyone." He smiled thoughtfully, his brows furrowing ever so slightly.

"What?"

"Hmm? What what?"

Repressing an unamused frown at his attempt to avoid the question, I clarified, "You've got that look you get when you're not sure whether you should regret something or not."

"I don't have a look like that."

"Do too! It's also your 'kinda-guilty' look. Like when you've done something you maybe should feel guilty about, but you don't really feel guilty. That's how Mom knows when you've eaten all of her brownies or cookies." I couldn't help smirking a bit.

"Well, thanks for that revelation. I'll have to be more careful," he chuckled.

"Just don't tell Mom that I'm the one who let you in on the secret."

"Deal."

"Anyway… The look. What's it for?"

"I wonder sometimes whether it was right of your mother and me to indulge your fascination with defense and fighting."

"Why wouldn't it be?"

"It wasn't the most normal childhood."

"Normal is boring." When my quip wasn't met with a smile, I added, "It was the perfect childhood for me, Dad. I was always happiest when training. And after everything that happened with Uncle Tommy...well, I was a lot more at ease having additional training." To further convince him, I leaned forward and wrapped my arms around his neck in a hug. "I love you."

Now he smiled, returning the hug. "I love you too, Jellybean."

"Hey... You haven't used that nickname in a while."

Dad pulled back from the hug purely so he could grin at me as he replied, "It's making a comeback."

I chuckled. "That's ok. I like that one."

The sound of someone knocking caused us both to turn our attention to the study door.

With a "come in" from Dad, the door opened a crack, and Mom poked her head in.

"The twins are in bed and wish to see you, Dear."

With nothing more to say, she left as quietly as she'd come, closing the door with a soft click. Dad and I rose and exited, him going upstairs while I plopped down on the couch in the living room.

"Will you be going with Michelle to pick Ben up from the airport?" Mom asked, her fingers deftly working the pink yarn for Ruby's hat over the knitting needles resting against her crossed legs.

"I believe so. Alice is coming here after school, right?"

"Yes, and I'll have Joey all day."

HERE'S TO THE UNDERDOGS!

"We need a closer airport. Three hours is too long of a drive," Dad added his opinion from the foot of the stairs. "If I didn't have a case to attend to, I'd fly and pick him up myself. It would probably be quicker."

"I know, Dad. But it's not *that* bad of a drive... It'll give Michelle and me a chance to talk."

"And you and Ben..." Morgan grinned.

The other three of us present gave Morgan the same look: Dad looking over his reading glasses, Mom glancing up from her knitting.

"Morgan, leave your sister alone," Mom instructed, her eyes turned to the unfinished hat again.

"Fine..." my sister grumbled in reply.

"Anyway..." I cut through the silence that followed. "You gave Principal Jones the note for my absence, right, Daddy?"

Dad looked up from the newspaper he'd been reading. "Hmm?"

"You know... The one that'll keep me from getting in trouble for skipping...?" I prompted.

"Um..." For once, he was speechless as he removed his glasses, folding them in his hand. "You know, all week I've had the feeling that I was forgetting something."

"Dad..." I sighed. "Ok, next time I offer to deliver something like this myself, please let me."

Rubbing his chin, Dad chuckled. "Will do. Remind me tomorrow morning to take it in before court."

"Thank you." I stood and kissed Mom on the cheek then crossed to Dad's chair, stooping to place my arms around his shoulders. "Thanks for talking with me today. I love you." I pressed a quick kiss to his temple before heading for the stairs. "Night, love you both!"

"Goodnight, Sweet Potato."

Mom smiled up from the half-finished hat and gave a slight wave. "Goodnight, Colette."

Chapter 43: Colette

When I got home from school, Dad was waiting for me. He took my hand and sat me down on the couch, looking quite upset.

"Dad? What is it?" I doubted whatever was on his mind could be worse than the suspense of not knowing, but I was wrong.

"Your Uncle Tommy… He gets out of jail soon and wants to see you. Says he wants to make things right. Sweetheart, you are under no obligation to go, of course, but I thought you should know."

All I could do was stare at my dad as I processed the meaning of his words. Memories of all that had happened a few short years ago flooded my mind, and unsolicited tears dripped down my cheeks.

"Oh, Colette… I'm sorry, Sweetheart." Dad hugged me tightly as my tears wet his shirt.

Not a sound passed between us for several minutes until I broke both the hug and the silence.

"Can I think about it?"

"Of course. The choice is yours; I can't advise you either way."

I nodded, numb as I stood. "I think I'll go for a walk." Without so much as a glance in my dad's direction, I left the house.

I'd been walking no more than ten minutes when I ran into Luca. What he was doing in my neighborhood I couldn't guess, but I was relieved to see him. He noticed right away that something was wrong and lead me to a bench to talk.

It was a few minutes before I could explain to him what was troubling me, and I feared how he would take it. Still, I felt I needed to talk to someone, and with Ben away at college, Luca was the best option.

"My uncle gets out of prison soon. He wants to talk to me, but I don't know if I want to see him…" Luca remained silent, leaving me to continue at my leisure. "I don't know if I should because of the reason he's in prison…" I had to pause and take a few breaths before continuing. "He's in prison for…child molestation." Another pause for breathing. "Me."

I couldn't meet Luca's eyes for fear of the pitying look I was certain I'd receive. He hugged me tightly, whispering, "I'm so sorry, Colette."

Sniffling, I replied, "It's alright now. That was years ago. And, if he really wants to apologize and make things right, maybe I should talk to him. What do you think?" I looked up at his well-cut features.

"I can't tell you what to do."

"You sound like my dad now," I grumbled. "I guess…I guess I'll go. Maybe it'll give me closure."

He nodded slowly, rubbing my shoulder. I remained in his arms for a few minutes longer before returning home. Dad was, of course, waiting to hear my decision. He didn't seem quite pleased with my conclusion, but he allowed it and agreed to come with me the following day.

HERE'S TO THE UNDERDOGS!

***

"How did things go?" Luca asked as we walked down the street together. I had called him as soon as I got home from meeting with my uncle, and he insisted on talking face to face to make sure I was okay.

"Surprisingly well. He seemed sincere."

"Good."

By the time Luca walked me home, it was nearing dinner time. Mom enveloped me in a hug, from which she refused to release me for several suffocating minutes. She and Dad watched me worriedly until I scarfed down my dinner, thus satisfying them that I was doing okay.

I should have gone straight to bed after devotions, but I ignored the rational part of my brain and stayed up till nearly two thirty binge-watching TV. When my alarm went off at seven forty-five, I nearly threw my phone across my room. Groaning, I dragged myself out of bed and downstairs.

"Well, good morning."

I dropped into a chair at the table, head barely propped up in my hand.

Dad chuckled. "Do you require coffee?"

Opening my eyes a crack to look at him, I nodded, stretching out my free hand.

"Patience, Jellybean. I haven't made any yet."

My hair spilled out on the table as my head fell onto my crossed arms. Dad was usually good about having coffee ready for me and my mom, but as I had woken up late today and liked my coffee fresh, it appeared that he had waited to make it. I would have appreciated the thought had I not been so tired.

"How late were you up last night?"

A mumbled reply was all I managed.

"I guess that means it was pretty late."

Finally, I heard the clink of my coffee mug meeting the table on which my head rested. As soon as Dad had released the mug, my head popped up, and I thrust out my hand to receive the treasured caffeine. Dad couldn't help but laugh, and I glared at him sleepily over the rim of my fox mug. This gesture only caused him to laugh more.

"Despite your tactical training and threatening looks, you can be quite cute sometimes."

I nearly spit my coffee out in surprise. "Cute? Since when do *you* say cute?"

He shrugged, stirring the oatmeal on the stove. "Since it applies. Right now."

As his back was turned, I took the opportunity to give a proper eye roll, purposefully slurping my coffee. This caused him to face me, a frown creating wrinkles by his mouth.

I grinned back, hunched over the table with my coffee cup at my lips. "Yes? Something wrong, Daddy?"

My dad was unfortunate enough to have had four girls: not unfortunate because we were badly behaved, but because he could never stay mad at or refuse one of us anything we wanted when we called him "Daddy". His frown slowly flipped around to a smile as he shook his head.

"Morgan may appear to be the most devious of you five, but I still hold that you are far more crafty than she at times."

"Like a fox," I reminded him of my favorite animal.

"Exactly like a fox. Whereas Morgan is more of a...weasel."

HERE'S TO THE UNDERDOGS!

I had to sit up as I laughed. "That's true! And Marcus is a chipmunk."

"What about the twins?"

"Baby bunnies."

Dad chuckled. "Perfect."

"If we're going to assign animals to everyone, you and Mom both need an animal."

"True... Your mother would be a cat."

I nodded thoughtfully, head tilted slightly as I studied Dad, coming up with an animal for him. "Hmmm... You're like Aslan. Or Bagheera."

"Those are specific animals."

"But they fit. Especially Bagheera," I grinned, assuming he'd prefer Aslan.

He frowned thoughtfully before nodding. "Alright. I'll allow it."

"Hey, you're a lawyer, not a judge."

"Very true. It is also true at this very moment that your oatmeal is ready, young lady."

Making a grabbing motion with my outstretched hands and looking as adorable as possible, I pleaded, "Bring it to me?"

Dad gave a helpless groan. "Ok..."

My expression turned into a victorious grin. "Thanks, Dad. With brown sugar and milk too?"

"Now, I'm not so sure about all that..." One pleading look from me, and he had no choice but to fix up my breakfast as I had requested. "Oh, alright... But not a word of my coddling to your mother, you hear?"

"Of course not. My lips are sealed." I cupped my hands around the steaming bowl he brought me. "Thanks."

HERE'S TO THE UNDERDOGS!

* * *

As I sat waiting for Michelle fifteen minutes later, I realized that I had once again allotted myself more time than was needed. She wasn't due to arrive for another ten minutes— not enough time to get much of anything done, but too much time to be content sitting around waiting. Mom returned from dropping the twins off at gymnastics a few minutes later, and I busied myself talking to her as she prepared a soup in the crockpot. I made sure to keep watch out the kitchen window as I conversed with her, not wanting to cause Michelle any delay when she arrived.

She pulled in the driveway a few minutes early and came to the door with Joey and Garrett. The toddler threw himself into my arms and was grieved to learn that I wouldn't be babysitting him that day. Many tears were shed as I passed him off to my mother and ducked out the door, grabbing my coat as I waved to my parents, Garrett, and Joey.

* * *

The first few minutes of the trip were spent in silence, but Michelle and I soon held a conversation that was interrupted only by our bouts of laughter at what the other had said. The entirety of the drive was spent in this manner, and the three hours passed quickly. Sooner than it seemed possible, we had arrived at the airport, and I jumped from the car, practically sprinting to the building in anticipation of seeing my friend.

Chapter 44: Ben

I didn't even have time to take in the bustle of the airport as I exited the terminal before I was tackled, barely keeping my balance as I dropped my backpack.

"Whoa! I was only gone a little over two days." I pried Colette's arms from around my neck. "I just missed you, ok? And I want to hear all about the college."

Colette retrieved my fallen backpack as we approached my smiling aunt. She stretched her arms out to me for a hug, and I gladly obliged, squeezing her just a bit too tight.

"Ben!" she squealed. "I'd like to breathe if you don't mind."

Grinning, I released her. With my best show of puppy dog eyes, I pouted, "I missed you…"

She planted a hand on her hip. "I think you just like being a pill."

I couldn't help chuckling. "You may be right."

She laughed softly through her nose, waving Colette and me forward. "Let's go eat. I'm sure you're hungry."

"You know me too well," I grinned. Realizing Colette still carried my backpack, I turned to her, holding out a hand. "I can take that now."

"I don't mind carrying it."

I frowned at her. "That's not the point. You *shouldn't* be carrying it."

She stopped short, causing me to turn back. "Why? Because I'm a girl? Honestly, Benjamin, haven't you known me long enough to know that I hate that kind of reasoning?"

With an exasperated groan, I stepped closer to her. "Please just let me carry it. This has more to do with my being a guy than it does with your being a girl. Just hand over my backpack." I held out my hand expectantly.

When she simply walked on past me, brushing against my shoulder, I reached out and snatched the pack from her shoulder. Luckily for me, she had it slung over only one shoulder, and it was easy enough to slip it from her arm. Having secured my backpack, I sprinted past Colette and my aunt, dodging the other individuals in the building.

"Ben!" Colette called as she raced after me.

"Wait! Look out!" Aunt Michelle tried to stop us, but we were too caught up in our chase to notice or care.

I should have paid more heed to my aunt's warning for, as I glanced back at Colette, laughing goadingly, I tripped over someone's luggage, tumbling to the floor and angering the owner of the luggage responsible for my spill.

"Ow..." I groaned, spread out on the grungy floor.

Colette jogged to my side then stood over me, laughing at my mishap while my aunt apologized to the poor patron whose luggage I had disrupted. "I hope you didn't have anything breakable in your backpack." The chuckle in her voice betrayed her concern.

HERE'S TO THE UNDERDOGS!

"Just my laptop…" I suddenly remembered another treasured object and sat up quickly, scanning the ground around me for my pack. My eyes alighted on it, and I snatched it up, pawing through the front pocket.

"Um… Did your laptop shrink while you were away? I wouldn't have thought it would fit in there," Colette queried.

Distractedly, I replied, "I'm looking for something I made on this trip." At last, my fingers brushed the cool metal, and I grasped the circular object, relieved that it hadn't fallen out or gotten smashed.

"What is it?" Colette crouched beside me curiously.

"Nothing." I opened my hand, dropping the treasure back into my backpack, and buckled the flap over the pocket before shouldering my backpack and standing.

Colette eyed me suspiciously as she stood. There weren't many secrets between the two of us— none really aside from the times one planned a surprise for the other. Guilt nagged at me as we exited the airport. I didn't like keeping secrets from her, but this was my special project. I eased my conscience with the knowledge that she'd find out eventually.

"I'm driving home!" I stated, racing to the car. Slinging my backpack in the back seat, I started the car and honked at Colette and Aunt Michelle. "Slowpokes!"

"You're such a child," Colette grumbled, sliding into the back seat.

"Always. Ready to go?"

Aunt Michelle closed her door. "Yup."

"Ok. Where are we going to eat?"

"Anywhere you want."

"Hmmm…" I browsed the eateries we passed. "Oo, Subway! Let's go there."

We enjoyed a meal together at Subway as I recalled the events of the past few days. There wasn't much to tell: I went to classes, met some of the faculty and students, and spent the nights that I was there in one of the dorms. Despite this, Colette wouldn't rest until I had told her every detail. It took me fifteen minutes to eat a sub that I could have devoured in less than three.

I was finally released from my interrogation, and we were on the road again with a three-hour trip ahead of us. It would have been smart to have saved the college talk for the ride home, and I made this clear to Colette. She, in turn, proceeded to call me a brat, but that was nothing new, and I simply grinned at her through the rearview mirror.

It was nearing dinner by the time I pulled in Colette's driveway. I offered to retrieve Joey and Garrett as my aunt continued home on foot, getting a head-start to cook dinner. The twins were home, and I was held up at the Tance's for nearly fifteen minutes as they crowded around me, pulling me in every direction. Finally, Colette scooped up one, and Mr. Tance held the other, and, with Joey holding tightly to my neck and Garrett at my side, I said my farewells and walked home, greeted by a lovely dinner and my semi-adoring sister, having to once more recount my uneventful stay at college.

HERE'S TO THE UNDERDOGS!

Chapter 45: Colette

Maggie and I were on our way to our next class — a study hall period — and decided to take a less crowded route, though it would add a few minutes to our trek from one end of the school to the other. A few students were scattered throughout these barely used halls, most likely having had the same idea we did, but we came to a stretch of hallway that was completely vacant— or so we thought. As we rounded a corner, we ran into Darren and another student. The shaggy-haired boy, not surprisingly, looked terrified as Darren towered over him, fists in his face. It took me a few seconds to realize what was going on, and by that time it was too late to stop Maggie from getting involved. She pulled at Darren's arm in an attempt to get him to leave the boy alone. In response to her action, Darren swung his hand back, inadvertently catching her on the cheek. Maggie let out a pained yelp and stumbled back, her hand flying to her cheek, eyes wide with fear and surprise. Darren looked just as surprised as he realized what he'd done. A look of horror washed over his face as he stood stunned, mouth moving to speak with no words coming out. Finally, he turned and ran down the hall, disappearing around a corner. Over the initial shock, I rushed to Maggie's side.

"Are you ok?" A large red mark was revealed as I removed her hand from where it had been fixed on her cheek.

Shaking her head to pull herself from her stupor, she replied distractedly, "I'm ok. It doesn't hurt much." She was still staring after the direction Darren had gone.

"There you are!" Jill came down the hall. "When you didn't show up for study hall, I was sent to find you." Noticing Maggie's cheek, Jill gasped. "What happened?"

I now realized that Maggie's lip was bleeding too.

"Darren hit her."

"He what?!"

"Not on purpose!"

Jill and I stared in surprise as Maggie jumped to Darren's defense.

Fiddling with the hem of her shirt, Maggie continued, "It's the truth..."

Still unsure as to why she was defending him, but knowing she was right, I decided to move on. "Do you need to go to the nurse's office?" She shook her head but said nothing. "Ok...

We should tell the principal. At least about Darren harassing that boy."

Giving a slight nod, Maggie started down the hallway in the direction of the principal's office, Jill and I trailing behind. As she walked, Maggie kept touching the tips of her fingers to her cheek and lip.

Maggie hardly said a word in the principal's office other than to restate that she was certain Darren hadn't meant to strike her. Nearly our entire study hall was used up by the time the ordeal was over, and the principal allowed us to simply move on to lunch where we met up with Ben and the rest of the crew.

HERE'S TO THE UNDERDOGS!

Ben was outraged when he learned what had happened to Maggie, but he was also the most understanding and knew the right things to say— not that Maggie was angry or freaking out. But she seemed to relax as Ben talked. Connie was the first to move the conversation onto a new topic which proved to be a good idea as Maggie calmed even more after that.

After eating, we all walked Maggie to her next class, a gesture that she tried to convince us was unnecessary. I'm sure she was right, but the rest of us insisted on walking her. It was actually rather fun being her bodyguards.

* * *

No one saw Darren for the rest of the day, and it was assumed that he had gone home. I also managed to lose Ben by the end of the day and noticed that his jeep was absent from the parking lot as I pulled out of the schoolyard. This worried me...

Chapter 46: Ben

Per usual, I didn't have a plan as I drove to Darren's house. Well, other than confronting him as calmly as possible. I knew that I was setting myself up for a potentially colossal amount of pain, but what he'd done to Maggie, accidentally or not, was unacceptable. I was also a bit more protective after learning that I hadn't been there for Colette when she needed me over the weekend.

I'd known where Darren lived for years, but I'd never actually been to his house, and I was surprised by what I found. It was a beautiful Victorian style house with a weeping willow in the yard and flower boxes in the windows. I assumed his mother was responsible for the flower boxes.

I wasted no time going up to the door and knocking, hoping Darren would answer and not his parents or siblings— if he had any. That thought made me realize how little I knew about Darren, not that I had any reason to know more.

I jumped when the door finally opened, having been lost in thought. Darren looked surprised to see me and stumbled over his words.

"Connley? What are you doing here?"

"I saw what happened to Maggie."

The color drained from his face as he stuttered, "I— that was an accident. I didn't know she was there."

"Yeah, so she said. Don't you think you should apologize anyway?"

He quickly shook his head. I'd never seen Darren scared of anything, but the prospect of talking to Maggie again evidently terrified him. "I can't. She probably wants to stay as far away from me as possible, and that's best."

"You can't avoid her for the next month of school."

"I can if I don't go."

I blinked at him. "You have to go to graduate."

"Then I won't graduate."

"You're seriously going to drop out over this?"

"Why not? No one thinks I'll make it anyway."

"Prove them wrong!" The amount of heart to hearts that we'd been having lately was a bit concerning.

"Just leave me alone, Connley." He shut the door in my face, and I doubted he would be opening it again any time soon.

Hands in my pockets, I walked down the steps to my jeep, having failed. Not only that, but I was more confused now than when I had arrived. As I drove home, I kept replaying in my mind how scared he had looked and acted. What was so terrifying? Why did he even care about what he'd done to Maggie? It didn't make sense to me, and I doubted I'd ever find out. That bothered me. I didn't like not knowing things.

Aunt Michelle was baffled as well but didn't spend much time dwelling on the matter as there wasn't much she could do about it. She tried convincing me to leave the matter be, so long as Maggie was safe, but I couldn't help thinking about it that evening. I guess Colette was right— I did overthink things.

Despite my overthinking, my sleep was as peaceful and deep as ever. Had I remembered to close my door before going to bed, I could have slept much longer, but instead, my slumber was interrupted by Garrett wandering into my room and climbing on top of me. Apparently, he had woken up before Aunt Michelle this morning. I checked the time and was discouraged to find that it was not even seven o'clock. So much for sleeping in this Saturday.

"Garrett, you gotta get off of me so I can get up." He had me pinned by laying on my back.

"Nope!" he giggled.

"In that case..." I slid out from under the top bunk, holding Garrett on my back. "Let's go make breakfast."

When Aunt Michelle came down, she took in a deep breath to fully appreciate the smell of sausage and cheesy potatoes cooking on the stove. She was also incredibly grateful for the cinnamon latte I'd made her, remarking on how delicious it was between sips.

My plot to energize her with coffee worked as she suggested afterward that we get out of the house that day, perhaps doing some shopping. Though shopping wasn't quite what I had had in mind, I did want to spend the day doing something with my family. When my other two siblings came downstairs and Aunt Michelle had gotten Joey, our day of shopping was agreed upon.

Chapter 47: Maggie

If I had known it was going to rain, I would have brought an umbrella with me. So long as it did not pour, I suppose I would be ok. My beret kept my hair fairly protected from the sprinkling of water, but my shirt and skirt were already splotched with wetness. Keeping my head down, I avoided the puddles that were already forming; but as I walked through the park, I just had to look around at the flowers decorating the trees and bushes. Not many insects or birds braved the weather to gather sweet nectar from the blooms, but I occasionally spotted a little wren or sparrow, flitting from bush to bush, their brown coloration contrasting nicely with the vivid green leaves.

I had been watching my steps carefully, but I got distracted by a bird in the tree above me and knew I must have stepped in a mud puddle as my left foot slipped, nearly throwing me off balance. I was able to stay upright, but my sneaker was now perfectly brown as opposed to the cheery pink it used to be. It was not something that was going to distract me from my purpose, however, and I continued until I reached my destination.

The purple flowers beneath each window caught my eye, and I admired them from the sidewalk before approaching the elegant house. A gold knocker hung in the middle of the door, and I lifted the metal ring, tapping it gently against its adjacent plate. A few minutes passed before the door opened, and I nervously bit my lip, forgetting about the cut until pain shot through my lip. I looked up as the door opened, expecting Darren to answer. Instead, my gaze met with who I assumed was his father.

"What do you want?"

"Oh, I— is Darren here?"

I adjusted my beret as he yelled over his shoulder for Darren. Scowling, he studied me as we waited. I lowered my gaze to my shoes, purposefully letting my hair fall over my bruised cheek. I never would have thought that seeing Darren would be a relief, but I found myself letting out a held breath as I heard him tromp down the stairs.

"What—" his question was cut off when he saw me. "Maggie? Why are you here?" His brow furrowed, but whether it was from anger or panic I could not tell.

Without so much as a nod or word of farewell, his father turned back into the house. Darren quickly stepped through the door and pulled it closed behind him, shoving his hands in his pockets. He stared at my cheek for a few seconds before catching himself and dropping his gaze to the porch on which we stood.

"I...I just wanted to let you know that...there are no hard feelings. What happened was an accident." As an afterthought, I mumbled, "Though intimidating that boy was not right…"

He straightened, hardening his features. "Yeah, well, he had it coming. He owed me for something. And if you hadn't gotten in the way, I'd have gotten what was owed me."

My previous timid demeanor was now replaced with anger, and I squared my shoulders, frowning up at him. "That doesn't excuse threatening kids and making them miserable and scared. You could try being nice for a change."

My tone and sudden outburst must have surprised him as he simply blinked at me, shoulders slumping a bit. I crossed my arms, waiting for a reply. "Well? What do you have to say for yourself?"

Shaking his surprise away, his scowl deepened. "I don't answer to you."

"I think you owe me some sort of explanation."

"Oh yeah? And why's that?"

I gestured to my bruised cheek, and the color drained from his face as he stuttered, "O-oh."

I kept my stance of having my arms crossed, head tipped back to look up at him. His eyes dropped to the porch. It was evident that he was not going to say more without a bit of prompting.

Heaving a sigh, I dropped my arms to my side. "Like I said, no hard feelings about this, but I can only forgive you if you actually want forgiveness."

"I don't need your forgiveness," he grumbled, not looking up at me.

"Are you saying you're not sorry about hitting me? Because your demeanor suggests otherwise."

He shot a glare in my direction before saddening. "I didn't mean to…"

"Is that an apology?"

He sighed then nodded so slightly that I scarcely could even call it a nod. But I accepted it.

"Good. Then I forgive you. But you can't go on bullying people, Darren."

His eyes shot up to me as I said his name. It was as though he had not realized I knew what it was. He made no reply though, and I decided to change the subject, hoping to ease the atmosphere some.

"I noticed the flowers as I came up the driveway. Is your mom responsible for that?" He shook his head in reply, and I prompted further, "Who then?"

His reply came in a whisper. "Me."

My eyes widened as I stared at him in disbelief. "You?"

He raised his voice defensively. "That's what I said. You got a problem with that?"

I tried not to slink back into my shell, but despite my moment of courage before, Darren still intimidated me, and my reply was timid. "I was just surprised..." Again I forgot about my cut lip until it was too late to avoid the pain of biting it. Darren's guilt was triggered as I flinched and touched my fingers to the cut.

His tone was soft as he clarified, "My sister likes them. They remind her of our mother."

"What happened to your mom?"

There was a long pause before he replied, "She left a few years ago. We used to see her a lot, but recently not so much."

"Oh... I'm sorry, I-I didn't know."

"Of course, you didn't. It's not something I talk about ever. And we don't really talk anyway."

"That's because all you ever do is bully my friends." I inadvertently furrowed my brow angrily.

One corner of Darren's mouth turned up in a smirk.

"What?"

"You're kinda cute when you're angry."

My frown deepened. "You're not even sorry, are you? How can you do those things and not feel bad?" I sighed. "Since this is obviously a waste of both our time, I'm leaving."

I spun on my heel, stepping out from under the roof that covered the porch and into the rain. Before I could get very far, a tight grip on my arm stopped me.

"Wait. Did you walk here?" A nod was all that I responded with, and Darren continued, "Are you really going to walk home in the rain? It's raining pretty hard now..."

"Why do you care?" I yanked my arm from his grasp.

"I just... You know what, I don't care. Go ahead. I won't stop you." Though his words rang true with what I would have expected from him, his demeanor suggested that he was not being completely truthful in his harsh reply.

Tilting my chin up defiantly, I took a few decisive steps down the driveway before realizing that Darren was right and this was a bad idea. Within seconds, the rain had soaked through my clothing, even reaching my hair through my hat. I glanced back at Darren to find him leaning against one of the columns that held up the porch roof. Smirking, he waved at me.

"Nice day for a walk. Have fun."

I stuck my tongue out at him which only served to heighten his amusement at my predicament. I stood in the rain for a few seconds before huffing and stomping back up to the porch. Crossing my arms, I stood with my back to him.

"Change your mind?" he chuckled.

"Obviously."

"You know, in school, you always seem so timid, but right now you're different."

I could feel heat rise in my cheeks as I looked down at my feet— heat different than the consequence of the slap, but no more welcome.

"And...you're back to 'school you'. Why's that?"

All I could manage was a shrug.

Darren grinned a tad. "Are you embarrassed?"

"No..."

"Could've fooled me. So, uh, are we just gonna stand here all day or should I drive you home?"

I snapped my gaze up to him, but was unable to speak.

"Cat got your tongue? I need an answer."

I summoned my remaining courage to answer him. "Why should I accept a ride from you? You've been a terrible person all year— for the past four years even!"

It was almost as though I had dealt Darren a physical blow.

He took a stumbling step back, staring at me in shock before stuttering, "I-I know I have." Suddenly, his face hardened. "Don't you think I know that? Do you think telling me that will help anything?"

"Then why do you do it?" I raised my voice to match his as best I could.

"I don't know!" He raised his arms in defeat before pressing his hands over his face. His voice was almost a whisper when he next spoke, "I don't know."

I stood in shocked silence, blinking at him as I tried to process his sudden change in tone and attitude. Finally, I stepped forward and placed a hand on his arm. I had no idea what I should say, but it seemed as though I should fill the silence somehow.

"I think I know…"

He flinched at my touch before slowly pulling his hands from his face. "What?"

Despite having been reminded of my cut twice that day, I bit my lip again, shutting my eyes tightly for a moment before looking at Darren to reply shyly, "When my parents got divorced, I lashed out at my closest friends until I realized that I was only doing that to cope with what my dad had done to my mom and to our family. I don't know why your mom left, but I'm guessing you act the way you do as a way to cope."

Darren pondered the words before furrowing his brow. "Let's just go." Brushing past me, he stepped from the porch and to his truck, slamming the door once inside.

Worrying that I had only made things worse by speaking up, I stood on the porch for a long moment before reluctantly climbing into his truck, having to shut the door twice as I was too gentle on my first attempt.

The drive home was uncomfortably quiet. I nearly started singing several times just to fill the void. The only times there was any communication between the two of us was when Darren needed directions. Then it was back to silence. When my apartment complex came into view, I almost jumped out of the truck; but when Darren finally did park, I found myself unable to leave the vehicle. I had something I needed to ask him first.

HERE'S TO THE UNDERDOGS!

"Hey, Darren? Would you, um...would you wanna come to this special youth group thing on Friday? It's gonna be mostly just a bunch of teens hanging out and playing games..."

For a minute he looked at me like I had slipped into speaking French, but after considering, he slowly nodded. "I guess I could do that."

My eyes must have brightened noticeably. "Really? That would be wonderful! I could meet you at your house maybe..."

"Sure, whatever."

"Alright." By this point, I was grinning. "It starts at six so I'll probably be at your house around five-thirty. Bye!"

I hopped from his truck and began ascending the stairs to my apartment. Looking back to wave, I couldn't keep back a few giggles. He sat motionless in his truck, staring at me and looking completely lost as to what had just happened. My giggles were stifled when I realized that I was perhaps the first person from school to ever show him any kindness...

Chapter 48: Colette

I'd happily agreed to go visit Alfie — the kid Ben met while staying at the psych ward — with Ben after church, but as we exited the elevator, stepping onto the psych floor, I felt like I had tiny, nervous butterflies in my stomach. Ben had hardly told me anything about this kid or why he was here for so long. I shook these thoughts aside as I followed Ben down the hall.

My nervousness was contrasted with Ben's excitement. He'd been feeling guilty about not visiting for so long and was eager to make up for his absence. His fingers tapped on the front desk as we waited for the receptionist to return with a sign in sheet. When she returned, Ben scribbled down his name and urged me to hurry with my own name. As soon as I had, he grabbed my hand and pulled me down the hall to Alfie's room.

After knocking, Ben slowly pushed the door open, poking his head inside. "Alfie?"

The small kid on the bed looked up, and his sad demeanor flipped instantly, a concerningly wide grin spreading across his face. He shot up from the bed and raced to tackle Ben in a hug. "You came!"

Wrapping his arms tightly around Alfie, Ben responded, "Of course, I came! I said I would, didn't I? Sorry it took so long."

"That's ok," Alfie looked up at Ben. "I'm just glad you're here now."

"I'll come back more regularly from now on for as long as I can."

Alfie nodded then seemed to notice me for the first time. Having not let go of Ben yet, he nodded in my direction. "Who's she?"

I stepped into the room. "I'm Colette. Ben's friend."

Alfie finally released Ben only to latch onto me. "Hi! Ben's my friend too!"

I couldn't help chuckling. "I see that. It's nice to have finally met you."

"Let me show you around!" Alfie released me only to grab my hand and pull me into the hall, dragging me around to every room. Ben simply watched and laughed, having already gone through this months ago.

The hours passed quickly as we talked, Ben and Alfie dominating the conversation with complicated science talk that I eventually gave up on understanding. Most of it made sense to some degree, but when they began talking of black holes and time travel, I stopped caring.

When we were nearing dinnertime, I almost had to drag Ben away. Poor Alfie looked as though he could cry as he waved back at us before the closing door hid him from view. As Ben and I exited the building, searching for our car, we decided that from now on, we would visit Alfie every other Saturday as we were able. We had two reasons for doing so, both relating to Alfie's own benefit. We would visit him simply to lift his spirits and make his stay more bearable, but we also had hopes of drawing him to Christ. During the ride home, Ben and I talked about future visits.

HERE'S TO THE UNDERDOGS!

"Do you think Alfie will be open to religious discussions?" he asked.

"I don't know, Ben. I hope so," I paused then said more confidently, "I think so."

"He's kind of like me in the way he thinks. If I can just show him how much my own...relationship with God has changed my life, maybe he'll consider...accepting Christ."

It was still difficult for Ben to say everything I wanted to when it came to this topic. Certain terms and phrases sounded awkward to him, I'm sure, but I understood what he meant and tried to help him find the right phrasing when I could.

I nodded and replied, "He trusts you, so I think he'll listen."

"Yeah, but *I* don't even believe it sometimes. How different everything is." He clarified, "Well, not every day circumstances. But how I react to them, and how I *feel* now. I think about people differently now too."

"You mean with more grace? You don't immediately hate them for the choices they make, but rather wish they had what you did so maybe they'd make *different* choices."

"Huh. I wouldn't have thought of it that way, but, yeah." I smiled at him briefly. "I'm really proud of you, Ben."

He shrugged off the praise with a sarcastic comment, but I could tell he was very pleased.

One day, hopefully, he'd be able to give Alfie the same praise.

* * *

On weeks when much happened, I wished for more uneventful days; then on weeks like the one that had just passed when nothing had happened, I wished for something more in each day. At least each dreary day that passed brought us one closer to the lock-in at youth group that Friday.

And alas, that day had come. Marcus was certainly more excited than I was as he bounced around the house. Morgan was the complete opposite as she sat on my bed, book in hand. Why she had chosen to read in my room, I had no idea.

"Please tell me you aren't bringing that book tonight," I implored as I applied a light coat of mascara to my lashes.

"I might need it. What if I'm bored?"

"It's a lock-in. There are activities planned for twelve straight hours. I promise you won't be bored."

I glanced over to see her staring at me, her eyes wider than usual.

"What?"

"What if you poke yourself in the eye?"

I eyed her with confusion before looking down at the mascara wand in my hand. I then responded with an eye roll before completing my task at hand. "It's called being careful."

"I think it's weird. What's the point anyway?"

My attention snapped back to her. "What's the point of you being in my room? All you do is ask stupid questions."

"Bothering you is fun— it's always a mystery what your reaction will be, unlike Marcus who always ends up chasing me and yelling."

Not attempting to hide my annoyance, I answered, "I could always kick you out, you know."

"But you won't. Because you're a good si—" Her voice cut off suddenly, and I slowly turned to face her, grinning.

"I'm what? Were you going to call me a good sister?"

"No way! I would never say such a thing." She crossed her arms, sticking her nose in the air.

"You totally were going to." Facing the mirror again, I made the finishing touches to my light makeup.

Morgan grumbled something about annoying sisters, her nose in her book again. Chuckling, I exited my room, leaving her to her grumbling. Marcus was racing down the hall at that very moment and crashed into me, knocking us both to the floor.

"Marcus! Get off me!" I shoved him, and he toppled onto the carpeting beside me with a groan. "This is why you're supposed to *walk*. Or at least look where you're going," I grumbled, rubbing the already-forming bruise on my lower back.

"You are not a soft cushion to land on," he mumbled, unmoving.

I glared down at him. Weighing the consequences, I decided against smacking him as that would only serve to get me in trouble in the long run. A hand planted on the floor, I pushed myself to my feet and stepped over my incapacitated brother.

"Help me..." he groaned weakly.

"Stop being dramatic. You're fine."

His groaning continued until I had disappeared down the stairs, at which point I heard him get up and continue his tromp to his room.

"What happened up there?" Dad asked, looking up from the dinner he was cooking on the stove.

"Marcus ran into me." I dropped myself onto a stool at the island.

A light chuckle was my dad's response as he resumed stirring the hamburger meat.

"Is that for tacos?" I asked hopefully.

"It is."

"Do you need any help?"

"Well, the cheese still needs to be grated."

I was on my feet as soon as he said 'cheese'.

"Not too much now..." he cautioned as I retrieved a rather large bowl from the cupboard.

"There's no such thing as too much cheese."

Dad shook his head, knowing there would be no convincing me of an alternative view on cheese. If he had tried, he would have had the rest of the family to convince as well. Dad didn't understand our love of cheese as he couldn't stand the delicious food himself. I sometimes wondered if Dad were adopted... Jokingly, of course.

The smell of well-seasoned hamburger brought Marcus nearly tumbling down the stairs. "Foooood!!"

Dad caught Marcus before he could devour everything by throwing an arm across his chest and holding him back.

"Not so fast, son. Go wait at the table."

Marcus groaned, but one look from Dad was all it took to send him scurrying to the dining room. Once he'd left the room, Dad and I both laughed before finishing up with dinner prep.

"Please call your sisters to dinner."

I nodded and skipped up the stairs to round up my siblings. Once I announced that we were having tacos, no further prodding was needed, and they stampeded down the stairs and to their seats.

Discussion at the table was mainly focused on the events that would take place that night. Marcus had endless questions about the lock-in and what it would entail. Eventually, my answer became an irritated 'you'll see soon enough'. Dad, picking up on my annoyance, changed the subject to my mother's approaching birthday. As she was working late, this was the perfect opportunity to discuss our plans— though nothing too secretive could be discussed in the presence of the twins...or even Marcus for that matter.

Once all had finished eating, the twins helped clear the table while Marcus and Morgan got ready for the lock-in. By quarter after six, I was ushering the two out the door. If we arrived too late, we'd miss out on the secretive preplanning. Those who arrived at least half an hour early had the option to be included in special "missions" that were to be carried out throughout the night. These missions could be anything from covertly spreading messages around the school, putting together a special gift at an appointed time, or going on secret food runs. Only a handful of teens arrived by six-thirty and were appointed as the "secret service" of the lock-in. It was just as well though, as having too many made things less secretive.

About ten minutes to seven is when most started arriving. Though the lock-in was supposed to start at seven o'clock sharp, it was generally delayed until quarter after or so as young people trickled in late. I hadn't expected any surprises until well into the lock-in, but as Maggie ventured shyly through the doors, I found I was wrong.

Chapter 49: Ben

My jaw dropped when I saw who stepped through the door after Maggie. "Is...is that...Darren? What's he doing here?"

Colette looked just as surprised as I did. Turning back toward the door, I saw Maggie approaching us, Darren following behind and looking as scared as I had ever seen him. Maggie, on the other hand, wore the widest smile I'd ever seen, which only accentuated the fading bruise on her cheek.

"Hi, guys," she waved.

Colette and I remained in our confused stupor.

"Wow, Ben. You're hardly ever speechless."

"I just... I didn't expect to see *him* here." I nodded to Darren to clarify a statement that was perfectly clear.

"I knew this was a bad idea," his gruff voice sounded.

As he turned to leave, Maggie grabbed his hand to stop him. "Please stay. I think you'll like it."

I expected Darren to shove Maggie away and storm out the door. Instead, he nodded slightly and stood beside her, pulling his hand from hers. I had never seen Darren this chummy with anyone outside his gang; I'd never seen Maggie this comfortable around someone so much bigger than her for that matter.

I almost laughed when I looked over at Colette to see her still standing in shock. Not much could shake her, but this apparently baffled her beyond reason. Jill bounded up and broke the silence.

"You! What are you doing here after ruining my prom?" she yelled at Darren.

Darren's fists clenched at his side. It was evident that he was trying his best to be civil, but why? Could it possibly for Maggie?

"Jill, just give him a chance. Isn't that what we do?" Maggie came to Darren's defense.

Jill backed down, looking almost ashamed for her outburst. Tony had stood by and quietly surveyed the whole scene. The mood having sufficiently dropped, everyone was relieved when the chaperones announced the first game and the lock-in officially started.

* * *

We played games for over an hour before taking a break for the message. Teens filed into the fellowship hall — the only room big enough for us all to sit comfortably throughout the message — snagging snacks and drinks before sprawling out on a beanbag chair or blanket on the floor. Once everyone was seated and had quieted down, one of the youth leaders pulled a chair out for himself near the front of the group, facing us, and began speaking. He was good about including us in the message so it seemed less like a sermon and more like a discussion.

There were two types of lock-ins that Colette's church held: one focused on discipling current members of the church and youth group who had accepted Christ, the other geared toward reaching young people and helping them learn more about beginning a relationship with God. This being the latter type, the message was about forgiveness and God's love. Though these were important topics for anyone to hear many times throughout their life, I found my mind wandering more than usual as the message went on. I scanned the room, studying each occupant, and my eyes finally rested on Darren. At first, I thought he wasn't paying attention at all, his gaze fixed on his phone which was cleverly hidden from the youth leader's sight. Yet as I continued watching him, I realized he was paying better attention than even I was. He glanced up at the young speaker from time to time, typing something on his phone immediately after. Upon watching him repeat this action several times, I realized he must be taking notes on the message. This surprised me beyond belief.

What unimaginably surprised me more was the emotion on his face. Rather than looking mean and, well, almost emotionless as he normally did, he looked…remorseful. But when he hurried out of the room not ten minutes later, I figured he must have had enough of this "Jesus stuff". The youth leader looked up, but otherwise, no one paid him any attention.

It was, of course, possible that he had left for such reason as he had to use the restroom, but as time wore on and he still hadn't returned, I began to wonder whether he had just gone home. Apparently, I wasn't the only one who was concerned.

Maggie had been checking the time every few minutes since he left, glancing at the door in hopes that he'd return. She had evidently had enough of waiting when fifteen minutes passed, and rose to her feet, silently stepping through the group and exiting the room, most likely in search of Darren.

Chapter 50: Maggie

I only had to walk down the hall a little way to find Darren. He was sitting against the wall by the water fountain, knees tucked up, his arms resting on them and his face hidden against his arms. He was silent and still.

"Darren?" my voice came quietly as I approached. Though I could not see his face, he looked so vulnerable slumped there on the floor at my feet. I slid to the floor next to him, repeating his name before continuing, "Are you ok?"

His reply came as a muffled, "Do I *look* ok?" Nothing more and no movement of his person.

Keeping my tone gentle, I asked further, "What happened? You left so suddenly... Did...did something upset you?" I paused, waiting for his reply, but it did not come. A third time I spoke his name. "Darren?"

This time, he lifted his head slightly, making his words less muffled. "Why are you being nice to me?"

Though his face was still hidden, I could have sworn from the shutter in his voice that he had been crying before I arrived. Silent, I pondered his question before answering, collecting my thoughts.

"It's like the youth leader was saying. We've all been forgiven of a far greater sin. And...if God can forgive us, we should forgive others. You may have made many mistakes, but I still have hope that you can change."

Hesitantly, I slipped my hand into his and gave it a reassuring squeeze. This act caused him to first look at our hands before raising his eyes to meet mine. When he did, it was evident that he had indeed been crying as the tears on his cheeks glistened in the light.

"No one...no one's ever treated me like that. You and your friends are the first... I've been nothing but awful to you — all of you — and yet you're the ones who are kind. You're...different."

"Thank you."

He cocked his head questioningly.

"We try to be different, Darren. Different from most of the world at least. So it's...nice that someone noticed."

"Why? Being different generally doesn't turn out well for people..."

"Well, because of Christ. We strive to be different to show His life."

Darren simply looked confused.

"I forgive you, Darren. For everything you've done. And...so does God..."

He scoffed. "I'm not sure about all that God stuff."

"You don't believe it?"

"I didn't say that exactly... I'm just not sure what I believe yet. And I certainly don't believe or feel like He loves me at all."

"Darren... I can assure you He does."

He replied with a shrug and nothing more.

"Do you think... Would you come to church with me on Sunday?"

His mouth dropped open slightly as he stared at me. "You want *me* to go to church?"

I gave a slow nod, a bit unsure now whether or not my question had been such a good idea.

"I...I could..."

"Really?" I brightened.

"I mean, just to kinda make up for, you know, hurting you," he tried, unsuccessfully, to shrug it off.

I could not help the smile that spread across my face nor did it seem possible to keep from throwing myself at him in a hug— a hug which greatly surprised him. He tensed up, but awkwardly returned the hug rather than sitting limply. Regaining myself, I pulled back from the hug, staring at the ground in silent embarrassment.

"Um, we should probably go back in before people worry..."

Clearing his throat, Darren nodded and stood, hesitating before offering me a hand up. I could feel the blush that crept into my cheeks as I accepted, and we rejoined everyone else.

I had the opportunity to talk with him more during the ride home that morning. He also kept his word and showed up at church the next day. Once again, all were surprised to see him, but he received a warmer welcome this time.

The next day at school was rather unusual. Rather than avoiding Darren, a few of us purposefully sought him out throughout the day. This shocked the other students and even the teachers, a few of whom approached us privately, concerned Darren had coerced us into this act.

When we assured them this was not the case, the look on their faces was always the same: pure shock.

Despite this, the day went smoothly, and Darren accompanied me home afterward. I was certain my mother would have something to say about that, but Darren was so sweet in asking that I could not refuse him.

He was different when it was just the two of us: thoughtful, not as rough, and almost shy. I caught him stumbling over his words, cracking his knuckles nervously, and glancing away from me often. Even now as he was speaking to me, I was focused more on *him* than his words. The way he brushed a hand over his close-cropped hair, the shifting of his weight from one foot to the other, his frequent glances at the ground—all were noticed by me as his words got lost in my subconscious.

"Maggie?" Darren softly drew me from my thoughts, his brown eyes searching mine. "What? Sorry, I guess I got lost in my own thoughts... What were you saying?"

Darren paled, looking as though the prospect of having to restate what he had said only moments ago might possibly cause him to pass out right there on my porch. "I uh, I just wondered if maybe you wanted to..." His voice trailed off as he dropped his gaze to his feet.

"Darren?"

Taking a deep breath to gather his courage, Darren looked up at me and asked, "Do you like coffee? I mean...would you wanna get coffee sometime?"

I stared in shock, jaw dropped just slightly. It was several minutes before I was able to recover my voice enough to croak out a reply. "I-I guess..."

"We don't have to," Darren said quickly.

I cleared my throat, finding my words at last. "No, I'd like to. I think it would be nice." I smiled to further convince him of my sincerity.

A grin spread across his face. "Really? Great!" He cleared his throat in an attempt to hide his eagerness. "I mean, cool. When?"

"Thursday after school?"

"Perfect. It's a date then."

Color rose to my cheeks, and I nodded, taking a step toward the door. "See you in school tomorrow."

"See ya then." Smiling at me once more, he stepped from the porch and walked down the street, disappearing behind a house as he turned onto the next street.

As I had expected, I was met at the door by my mother, arms crossed over her chest disapprovingly.

"Who was that?"

"Just Darren," I answered timidly.

"Darren..." Mother pondered the name, attempting to place it. "The bully you told me about?"

I nodded slowly, awaiting her next question.

"What was he doing here?"

"He walked me home."

Mother raised her eyebrows as she looked over at me. "And he lingered why?"

My voice grew quiet. "We were just talking..."

"About?"

"Stuff..."

"How intriguing." Despite the light tone of her voice, Mother did not seem amused.

"He asked me to get coffee with him..." I chanced a glance up at my mother, trying to read her face, a task which proved rather easy. Written in her features was, in a word, vexation.

"You declined, of course." The phrasing of her words and the tone in which they were said made it difficult to distinguish whether they were meant as a question or a statement.

"No... I offered to go with him Thursday."

"Maggie..." Mother shook her head, her hands falling to her sides. "Why would you go out with someone like him?"

I found myself glaring at my mother. "What's that supposed to mean?"

With a sigh, she replied, "You know what I mean. I'd rather you were interested in someone...better. Someone good."

"He is good! At least, he's trying to be..."

After studying me for a moment, she said, "I'll trust you on this, Maggie. But be careful." She opened her arms for a hug, and I happily obliged.

"I will be, Mom." I knew she was trying to protect me and keep me from the same fate she'd suffered from with my father.

HERE'S TO THE UNDERDOGS!

Chapter 51: Colette

The school was abuzz with talk of graduation, but there was a more pressing matter on my mind: Jeremy. As the school year came to a close, and he realized that I would most likely be leaving soon, he became even more persistent in his pursuit of me. I found notes in my locker and gifts by my car, and he called me nearly every day. It was time to put an end to this; convince him that I was not, nor ever would be, interested in dating him again.

This was my plan as I entered the school building the Thursday before graduation. As I had expected, Jeremy was waiting for me by my locker, his left shoulder against the cold metal. When he spotted me, his lips curled up in a smirk and he shoved off from the locker, turning to face me as I went around him to put in my combination.

"Excited for graduation?" he asked, just a bit closer than I would have liked for him to be. "As excited as anyone else I suppose."

He nodded, probably not even having heard my answer as that wasn't what he really wanted to talk about.

"Why can't you just give me another chance?"

HERE'S TO THE UNDERDOGS!

I shut my locker a bit harder than I had intended. "We've been over this. We're not right for each other, Jeremy. Looking back on when we dated, we fought a majority of the time. Plus having a boyfriend would just get in the way of my plans at the moment."

"I thought we worked pretty well... Listen, I'm sorry I cheated on you. But can't we get past that?"

"Did you not listen to what I *just* said? I'm not looking for a relationship right now."

"Why not?"

"Jeremy. You have to stop. Move on and find someone else. I'm not interested."

"Come on..."

I resorted to raising my voice, hoping a harsher tone would get the point across. "Drop it, Jeremy! We just didn't work out. That's the end of it."

His face hardened and he clenched his fists at his sides. "You know, if you hadn't been such a prude while we were dating, I wouldn't have cheated on you."

At this, my body tensed, a fierce heat building. "I'm the same now as I was then, so why would you even want to date again? Go find someone down at your level."

He stared at me for a long time and I dreaded what else he could possibly say, but he remained silent, turning away a moment later to go to class. I let out a forced groan to dispel my frustration and anger before going to my own first class of the day, hoping that would settle my issue with Jeremy.

HERE'S TO THE UNDERDOGS!

* * *

A few members from the original Underdogs met at my house after school, that title now including not only those in the band, but also anyone who had found their way into our group. Maggie and Darren assured us they would come after their date. I still wondered why Maggie went on a date with him.

Those of us who were going to be graduating had wanted to get together and make plans for a graduation party. It had already been decided that the party would take place at my house directly after graduation. Dad had agreed to put some money toward the party, but none of us wanted to go overboard with decorations and such. Food would be the biggest expense. We decided that all senior attendees could bring either a snack or drink, and my family would provide the necessary ingredients for sandwiches, therefore not heaping the burden onto a single person or family.

Maggie and Darren arrived shortly after all the planning was finished, which was perfectly fine as Maggie still had a year of school left and it's doubtful Darren would have been of much help. Both were equally smiley as they walked in the door, though Darren's smile was quickly masked.

"Glad you could make it. Just in time to miss party planning," Jill joked.

Maggie blushed slightly. "Sorry... Did you get everything figured out?"

"Thanks to Jill we did," I commented to which Jill protested that *I* was the one who had done most of the planning.

Ben saved us from an argument by stating that *he* was to thank for everything getting planned. That drew a laugh from everyone, Ben grinning like the child he was. When the laughter died out, Maggie cleared her throat to say something.

"Darren had an idea for something he thought we could put together..."

"Oh? What?" I directed the question toward Darren.

He ducked his head as he answered. "Well, I thought we could maybe do some sort of anti-bullying thing..." He ended his suggestion with a shrug.

Ben slowly grinned. "That's a great idea!"

Darren lifted his head to look at Ben. "Really?"

"Yeah! But what would we do?"

"We could do a benefit and raise money for a charity," Connie suggested.

"Yes! Perfect. This weekend. Saturday."

"Whoa, slow down," I cautioned Ben. "That's pretty short notice."

"We can still do it. You know the coffee shop that just opened up? I got to know the guy who owns it when I stopped in one day. He has live music every Saturday evening, and I'm sure he'd let us play and make it a charity event. People already come to those so we wouldn't have to gather a bunch of people. Come on, you know we're never going to be able to get everyone together after graduation for something like this. This Saturday is our only chance."

"I guess... Ok, if you can set it up, we'll be there."

Ben's grin widened. "Then it's all set. I'll let you know the details when I find them out."

"I'll get the word out on social media," Jill announced to no one's surprise.

The prospect of putting together several songs that everyone would agree on in just a day and a half was a daunting and unwelcoming thought, but Ben had enough optimism for all of us twice over. It wasn't often he was this excited, but when he was, it was exhausting for anyone around him. Though I loved him, I was glad when he and the rest of my friends went home. I finished my homework, studied for the upcoming end-of-the-year exams, and was completely brain-dead by the time I snuggled under my blankets just after midnight.

Chapter 52: Ben

There was a larger turnout at the coffee shop than I had been expecting. Jill's social media prowess proved very helpful, and we'd raised quite a bit of money before the Underdogs had even gone on stage. The event officially started at seven o'clock and was supposed to last until eleven o'clock. The breaks those of us on stage took became more frequent and longer-lasting as the night dragged on, everyone getting tired.

It was during one of these breaks that I spotted my dad. Whether he had wandered into the coffee shop on accident or come here because he somehow knew I'd be here I wasn't quite sure, but I assumed the latter as his eyes immediately landed on me as he stood just inside the door. Not wanting anyone to be aware of his presence, I excused myself from the stage and weaved through the crowd until I came to him. Not two seconds of standing near him were needed for me to know he was drunk. I pulled him outside into the darkened street, an easy task as he was of no mind to fight me.

The light cast from the nearby streetlamp produced an eerie shadow over his face, but I had enough light to see him clearly: the stubble on his chin; his unruly, graying hair, though it still held much of its dark color; his tight-clenched jaw; and even his brown eyes, sparking in the dull light.

"What are you doing here?" I questioned, crossing my arms over my chest.

"I found out you'd be here and figured I'd stop by," he slurred.

"Yeah, I guessed that." There was nothing welcoming or kind in my tone. "Why? I told you to stay away."

He shoved a finger in my face, nearly falling as he shifted his weight. "Listen here, boy. I am still your father. You've no right to tell me what I can or can't do." He leaned back against the coffee shop, looking as relaxed as he could, though he most likely needed the building for support. "I'm not here for you anyway."

"What are you talking about?"

"I'm taking Joey with me."

I stared at him for a moment, having no response to this. *How could he even think of taking Joey away?* Anger rose within me the more I thought about it. He was choosing Joey over the rest of us. It was true that ever since Mom died, he'd favored his biological children over my adopted siblings, but now he was placing Joey over even his other biological kids, though I wouldn't have wanted to be near him anyway.

"You can't be serious. What makes you think I'd let you take Joey or that he'd even want to go with you? You've hardly been around since he was born. He doesn't even know you!"

"He's young. He'll get used to me quickly."

My fists clenched at my sides as I spoke through gritted teeth. "You'll never get him. I won't let you. If you want to be a father, sober up and be a father to all of us."

HERE'S TO THE UNDERDOGS!

I turned from him, planning to end the conversation there and re-enter the coffee shop with the satisfaction that I had gotten in the last word. My plans were spoiled as I felt a jerk on my arm, turning me to face my father just in time to see a fist fly toward me. This wasn't the first punch I'd ever taken, even from my dad, but it was so unexpected that I fell back, bracing my fall with a hand. The pain that shot through my wrist told me that was a mistake.

Careful of my throbbing wrist, I pushed myself to my feet, ready now for anymore punches my dad might throw. What I would do if he did try to hit me again I wasn't sure of though. I didn't want to get into a fistfight with him, not because I thought I'd lose, but because, despite all his downfalls and flaws, he was right: he was still my father.

"You don't walk away from me!" he shouted.

It probably would have been best to just keep my mouth shut, but since when was I ever smart enough to stay quiet?

"Just following your example," I retorted harshly.

That comment would have resulted in a slap had I not backed up before his hand met my cheek. His being drunk was helpful to me as it resulted in my reflexes being quicker than his fist.

"Just get out of here!" I yelled, not thinking about the chance that those inside could possibly hear us; though, as none had come out yet, they most likely couldn't over the sound of the band.

"You don't learn quickly, do you? I'll do what I want. You're *my* son. You listen to *me*. And I'll take Joey if I want. Who's gonna stop me?"

"Me." I squared my shoulders and crossed my arms, standing directly in front of him.

It was a mistake to cross my arms. I may have thought it looked impressive and intimidating, but it proved to be a hindrance. My father sneered and swung at me again. I wasn't prepared and couldn't disentangle my arms soon enough to stop the punch, and his fist connected with my jaw this time.

Licking my lip brought the taste of blood to my tongue, but that wasn't enough to make me back down. I'd always been one to stand up to bullies when the opportunity arose, and now was no different. I was even debating fighting him, but the choice was taken from me as I heard Colette behind me.

HERE'S TO THE UNDERDOGS!

Chapter 53: Colette

I had not expected the anti-bullying event to go as well as it did with such short notice. The coffee shop was filling up before we'd even set up, and those who came gave generously. The owner of the shop did well, too, with many people staying long enough to buy a coffee or baked good. He'd probably never seen this much business in one night. And the band was amazing. I knew they were getting tired, but they pushed through and kept bringing people in with their talent. Darren, of course, stayed in the background, but Maggie did manage to get him on stage when she announced that the whole evening had been his idea. I had to snicker at his appearance: he turned red faster than I'd ever seen, looking about as uncomfortable as a dolphin in the desert.

The band went on break shortly after Darren's moment of embarrassment. I managed to start a conversation with Luca, still a difficult task, but our friendship was beginning to grow, mostly because I was too stubborn to give up.

I'd been talking with — mostly *to* — Luca for some time when something he said reminded me of a question I had for Ben. I looked around, but couldn't spot him, which was rather unusual. He was generally easy to see or hear, often with Joanna, but now I saw her alone and c ouldn't find Ben anywhere in the shop. I excused myself from my conversation with Luca and went in search of my best friend.

After scouring the coffee shop with still no sign of him, I began to ask around if anyone had seen where he'd gone. Maggie was the one to inform me that he'd gone outside with a man about in his late forties. Having a good idea who the man could be, I thanked Maggie then found my dad on the chance that I was right and things didn't go well. He hurriedly followed me, and we exited the shop just in time to witness Ben's dad hit him. Ben looked like he might fight back, and I ran toward them in an attempt to stop a full-on fist fight.

"Hey! Leave him alone!"

This got their attention, though Ben's dad looked past me and at my father who was approaching more calmly, a stern look set in his eyes. I faced Ben, hands going to his blackening eye and swelling lip. My endeavor to lead Ben inside and clean him up was greatly opposed as he insisted on staying to see what happened between our fathers.

"I invite you to accompany me to the sheriff's office down the road if you please," my father offered much more kindly than I would have.

"What for?" came the slurred retort.

"I think he'll have much to say about your abusing your son who is a minor no less."

Mr. Connley took a few steps back. "I'm not goin' anywhere with you. I just came for my son."

"Your *other* son," Ben mumbled.

"That doesn't explain your treatment of Benjamin."

Ben's dad scoffed and muttered something incomprehensible as he turned to leave, apparently assuming the conversation was over. Not sharing this notion, my father stepped forward, grabbing Mr. Connley by the arm.

"This way."

He began pulling him down the street, Mr. Connley protesting every step. A look from my dad informed me that getting Ben inside would be best.

"Come on, Ben," I urged, tugging gently on his arm.

He seemed reluctant to follow, but did so just the same. He walked through the coffee shop with me, head down to hide the marks on his face. Avoiding our nosier friends, I led him to the back and into the kitchen.

"Why didn't you come get me?" I asked, patting his lip with a rag.

He shrugged in response. "I didn't want anyone to know he was here. I figured I could get him to go away on my own." He laughed dryly. "I guess that didn't work."

I dropped the rag into the sink. "I'm sorry, Ben..."

"Don't be. At least something will be done about him now."

My head took on a puzzled tilt. "I thought you didn't want the law involved?"

"That was before he threatened to take Joey a second time."

Having no words that would help, I only nodded.

"Wanna go back out?"

"That's for you to decide. Are you up to it?"

A small smile lit his face. "Of course." He exited the kitchen, and I followed.

The mishap involving his father proved beneficial to our cause, people giving even more towards the charity after learning what had happened. Ben bounced back to his usual self quickly, though I noticed his frequent glances at the door. At last, my dad returned. Ben and I both hurried to him, spouting questions concerning what had happened. He took us into the kitchen before speaking a word.

Once the door was shut, he spoke. "Nothing is definite yet, but I wouldn't be surprised if your father were incarcerated within a few weeks."

"He's going to prison?"

"He'll most likely be jailed for no more than a month, but his parental rights will be restricted."

Ben nodded slowly, staring at the wall as he processed this. "But...he won't bother us anymore?"

"Not so long as the courts and I are around to prevent that." My father stepped forward, laying a reassuring hand on Ben's shoulder. "It's over now, son."

Ben smiled gratefully at my father, and I saw in Ben's eyes that he wanted to hug him. My father must have seen this too for he pulled Ben closer to hug him. Grinning, I took the opportunity to hug them both. Dad laughed, but only allowed this for a moment before disentangling himself.

"How much longer is this event supposed to go on?"

"About an hour more," Ben answered my father.

"Alright." Dad turned to address me. "I'll take your siblings home with me now. I expect you home within an hour and a half unless I hear otherwise from you."

"Of course, Daddy."

My father nodded and exited back into the main shop, Ben and I following soon after. I saw Dad and my siblings leave as Ben took the stage again with the rest of the band. I'd gotten out of singing all night, but as there were only a few songs left, Ben apparently thought I should have to sing. Had it just been him asking me, I could have refused, but once he had rallied the entire coffee shop, there was nothing to do but join him in singing. I'd be sure to get him back for this at some point.

The last hour passed quickly, and it was a struggle to get everyone to leave. Once the shop had been cleared out, the few of us left helped clean up before saying goodbye to each other and heading home. My parents had left the porch light on, but the rest of the house was dark as I silently made my way to my room. Snuggling down under my blankets, I took a few minutes to reflect upon the day as well as look ahead on what the next week held before falling asleep.

… HERE'S TO THE UNDERDOGS!

Chapter 54: Colette

Graduation neared, and the school turned into a madhouse, everyone preparing either for college or summer vacation. Most who weren't going to college were at least getting summer jobs or continuing their current jobs, only working more hours.

It was the last day of school— a day of testing. As much as everyone relished the end of the school year, the last day was dreaded by all. Those of us who had prepared were mostly just excited, but the shirkers did everything they could to avoid finals: calling in sick, skipping school, claiming they couldn't write or didn't have time to study— all they were doing was delaying the inevitable.

"You ready to ace this, Ben?" I asked as we walked into history class. "Ha! That'd take a miracle. But I think I'll do alright."

"I want confidence!"

Ben's eyes turned terrified. "Ok! I'll do great!" He hurried to take his seat while I smirked at him from across the room. After our tests had been passed out, I mouthed 'good luck' before starting mine.

HERE'S TO THE UNDERDOGS!

At the end of the school day, Ben and I met up at our favorite frozen yogurt shop with all of our friends in celebration of the end of the school year. As can be imagined, everyone was giddy and excited. Jill rambled on about her plans of going into cosmetology, Nate informed us of his plan to start a band over the summer, Darren surprised everyone by saying he had been accepted into college, and Ben and Walter geeked out talking about their respective colleges and majors. When the conversation rolled around to me, I tried to divert everyone's interests to something else, but it was no use. I'd been avoiding their questions about my future for months now, and Jill would settle for nothing less than the truth...or at least what I led her to believe was the truth. After all, how could I reveal my true intent of joining the CIA? Other than my parents, Ben was the only person who knew I'd been pursuing this, and now that I'd been accepted, I certainly couldn't tell anyone else.

I avoided the truth by convincing Jill that I was going to spend the year traveling and working on my photography. It was clear she was skeptical of this, and for good reason, as I was not one to waste time simply finding myself or traveling with no plans concerning my long-term future. Thankfully though, she pressed the matter no further.

We spent the rest of the afternoon and evening together, going to Roy Rogers for dinner rather than returning home, then journeying to the park and eventually the beach. With no school the next day, and graduation scheduled not till the day after that, there was no reason to go home and get to bed at a reasonable hour...or at all. We stayed up on the beach all night, sitting around a small fire and recalling fond memories from the school year just past. I couldn't have asked for a better final night with all of my friends together.

HERE'S TO THE UNDERDOGS!

* * *

After setting up for the party the next day, my dad insisted on some father-daughter time on Friday, to which I didn't object. Our first stop was the shooting range in town, then lunch at the cafe, and then we simply drove around the backroads, talking all the while. I was going to miss these times with my dad. He was my very best friend, and I'd be leaving for training in less than a month. After that, who knew where I'd end up or when I'd get the chance to come home. I glanced over at him from the driver's seat, his merry smile and bright eyes bringing tears to my eyes as I thought of how much I'd miss him.

"Eyes on the road, Sweet Potato," Dad cautioned softly. "What's on your mind anyway?"

I knew I couldn't lie to my dad and shrug this off like I could with others. "Just thinking that I'll miss you."

"You won't miss me quite so much if you remember to call me," Dad chided teasingly, referring to the summer I'd spent with my aunt in Texas. After just one week, calling my dad had sunk low on my list of priorities, though I still cried every now and again for missing him.

"I'll certainly call. And if I forget..." I paused, meeting his eyes once again, "remind me?"

"Always, Jellybean."

And thus was another cherished memory created on Friday, the 17th of June, 2016.

* * *

Graduation day had arrived. I was treated to a delicious breakfast of sausage gravy and biscuits, after which I showered, got dressed, and drove myself to school early enough to have sufficient time to get ready and spend every moment I could with my friends. There were five of us Underdogs who were graduating, along with scores of other students who we would never know as well as we had come to know each other. Tears filled every eye, smiles brightening each beautiful face. A final round of hugs were given before we took our seats alongside our fellow classmates, eagerly awaiting our names to be called.

A cheer and boisterous clapping followed each name. Proud family members and friends rose to their feet in support of their graduate. A moving speech was given, though none were too attentive as they longed for the end. And finally, ten simple words were spoken: 'Congratulations to the Westbrooke High graduating class of 2016!'

I'll not say much of the chaos that followed. Cheering, shouting, tossed caps falling to the ground as the owners rushed to collect them back, pictures with family and friends— those were the highlights. Some left the school grounds moments after the ceremony ended, and others I'm sure stayed later than was appreciated by the faculty, but my family and friends rushed to my house for the graduation party that would take place.

Mom and I had put together a playlist for the party and had set up in the backyard a few speakers borrowed from our church. What food we didn't provide was brought by the graduates attending. Lights and flowers lined the driveway and decorated the backyard. I took a moment to privately thank God for the sunshine on this day.

The afternoon zipped by, filled with games, laughter, singing, dancing, and friends treasuring this final time of being together. As the day wore on, guests left at their leisure until all but Luca, Joanna, and Ben had left. My mother was certainly grateful for their volunteering to help clean up, and no more than an hour and a half was needed to get the yard looking as spotless as it had looked just two days prior.

The four of us made our final goodbyes, Ben and Joanna looking as though they never wanted to leave the other's side. Ben turned his fedora over in his hands, staring at the grass as he appeared to be trying to find some particular words that he wished to say to Joanna. At last, she broke the silence.

"Just hurry up and ask me out already."

Ben turned red as his head shot up, eyes meeting hers. A grin spread across his face, but it seemed he was still at a loss for words as he simply nodded and offered her his arm, a gesture she gladly accepted. It didn't take long for him to warm back up to his usual goofy self, for, as they were walking away, Ben planted a kiss on Joanna's cheek and took off running. She stood stunned for a few seconds before running after him, yelling. Having to calm my laughter, I held Luca back as they disappeared down the street. I feared what he might do to Ben if he had the chance to catch them.

Once he stopped glaring after them, Luca allowed me a final hug, and we agreed to spend as much time together as we could over the next three weeks. It was hard to watch him go. Now that Ben and Joanna had finally admitted their feelings for each other, I knew much of Ben's time would be taken up with her. Jill left for college in less than a week. That left Luca as my last best friend, and I didn't want to lose him. At times I wondered if the two of us could possibly have a

future together, were it not for my vow to not get involved in another relationship for a few years. By then I was sure someone would have been lucky enough to snatch him up. So, for the foreseeable future, a close friendship was all we would have, and I was content with that.

HERE'S TO THE UNDERDOGS!

I myself left the house, walking to the covered bridge and watching the water beneath from the edge of the bulwark. I reflected privately on the events of the past year. It would always be a year to remember, a lifetime of memories made over a period of months. I had gained friends, brothers and sisters in Christ, valuable life lessons, and memories to reflect upon for years to come.

As I sat alone, a cool breeze further loosening the curls I'd spent long, tedious minutes on many hours before, I breathed a toast for my friends that was to be heard by my ears alone.

"Here's to us — the unnamed and unknown — and to those who are just like us, struggling to get by, to stay alive, to thrive. Here's to the Underdogs!"

The End

Epilogue

Ben fiddled with the small object in his fingers as he waited for Joanna by the river. He'd been waiting to give her this treasure ever since he'd finished it on the flights to and from RIST when he'd visited during the school year. A smile played at his lips as he imagined her reaction when he gave it to her. Then he frowned slightly, fearing that her reaction wouldn't be as joyous as he hoped. What if she didn't like it? Or what if it scared her away? It was a rather large gesture, hence why he'd put it off until now. As he would be leaving for college the next day though, he couldn't delay presenting the gift any longer.

At last, Joanna arrived. When she called to Ben, he nearly dropped the object in the river but tightened his fist around it just in time. He put his hand behind his back as he turned to face Joanna and was struck by her beauty, as often he was. She always looked the same — chestnut hair in a long braid, hazel eyes sparkling, a perfect smile brightening her face — but Ben was always dumbstruck when he saw her. Today, however, she didn't smile and her eyes didn't sparkle. Instead, there was a sadness to them, her lips pulled down in a frown.

"Well?" she spoke, tossing her braid over her shoulder. "Why did you ask me to meet you here?"

"Uh…" Ben cleared his throat as he continued, "I have something for you." Swallowing his nerves, he slowly brought his hand from behind his back and opened it to reveal what he had almost lost at the airport all those months ago when he and Colette had been fooling around.

Joanna smiled faintly. "It's beautiful, Ben."

"You like it?" Ben grinned, relieved that his work had not been in vain.

Joanna nodded, then spoke again, hand outstretched, when Ben continued to simply stand in silence. "Put it on, silly."

"Oh. Right." Ben fumbled with the ring, but finally slid it onto her right ring finger. "It fits."

"Perfectly," Joanna whispered, feeling tears brimming in her eyes.

Feeling the same sinking in his heart that his girlfriend felt, Ben pulled her to him and wrapped her in a tight bearhug. For months he'd been excited about going off to college, wishing the day to arrive sooner, but now he wanted the opposite. All he wanted was to stay with his girlfriend. *Gosh, I love calling her that,* he'd thought many times since they'd become official. Joanna still had a year of school left, so she couldn't come with him and stow away in his dorm room. So, for the past few weeks, they'd spent as much time together as possible, hardly leaving each other's side.

Ben squeezed Joanna tighter, whispering against her ear, "I'll miss you. I'll call every day. I'll write you sappy love letters like the old days. I'll send you songs and gifts. I'll text you every minute of every day."

Joanna pulled back from the hug enough to look at Ben. "You'd better not text me when you're in class."

There was a long pause, then a drawn out, "Of course not…" from Ben.

HERE'S TO THE UNDERDOGS!

Ben would, of course, do just that and pay more attention to Joanna than his classes though she'd be miles away. He would also write songs for her and record them with the help of his dorm mate, Laufy. Ben would play guitar and sing, Laufy sitting behind a drum set, and, after Ben gave some long, sappy intro, they would play as though Joanna were right there with them. He also kept his promise and wrote Joanna frequent love letters. He thought of her nearly every waking moment of the day. Eventually, he caught on to his friends' hints that they were sick of hearing about his girlfriend, though he still forgot often enough and raved about how amazing and beautiful and funny and cute she was. And when Joanna visited him, they found out just how right he was. All of Ben's college friends loved her and agreed that she and Ben were meant to be.

Joana lived for Ben's letters. School was…school with highs and lows, but his letters always brightened her week. She kept them tucked away in her nightstand, and when she especially missed Ben, she'd lie in bed, snuggling the teddy bear he'd sent her, and read every letter over again. A few of them were tearstained, and the words in the creases of the papers were becoming harder to read, but Joanna didn't need to guess what they said. She had the letters practically memorized.

Wanting to surprise Joanna, Ben didn't warn her that he'd be present at her graduation. Instead, he sneaked in after everyone had been seated then hopped up on his chair and cheered as loudly as he could when Joanna went to receive her diploma. She nearly cried there on the stage and ran to him as soon as she'd shaken Principal Jones's hand. The reunion was so touching and sweet and pure that no one had any doubt from that day forward that, if anyone could survive, together, the ups and downs of life, it was Ben and Joanna.

HERE'S TO THE UNDERDOGS!

A Very Special Thanks to...

Mr. Mark Hodgson

Though I've loved creative writing since 2nd grade, it wasn't until high school that I even thought of pursuing my writing as a career, and I have my high school teacher, Mr. Hodgson, to thank. He was the first person to encourage me to turn writing into more than a hobby, and not just through his words. He pushed me to enter a poetry contest, would settle for nothing less than my best work on school papers, and even introduced me to a wonderful online writing group and urged me to at least sign up for a trial month. That turned out to be one of the best decisions I ever made for my writing. Through that group, my writing and my courage to share my writing has blossomed. Had it not been for Mr. Hodgson's encouragement though, none of this would have happened, at least not this soon. Thanks to my high school teacher, I was brave enough to pursue my dream and am now a published author at the age of nineteen.

Saige Ross

If it weren't for my good friend Saige Ross, this book would never have been written. It was Saige who inspired me to give Ben his own story (fun fact: he was originally a side-character for a book that had no real storyline), and she was the main influence that kept me writing even when I wanted to give up and move on. Often I would complain to her that there was no point, that I was stuck, that I simply didn't want to write Underdogs anymore (in true procrastinator form); Saige always encouraged me and kept me going. I truly owe this whole book to her.

A Special Thanks to my Launch Team

Mom & Dad (ADA and Robin Aardsma)

My siblings: Autumn Aardsma <3, Zach Aardsma, and Megan K. McEndarfer and her husband Benjamin McEndarfer

Saige Ross

Mark Hodgson

Melissa Hodgson

Chloe Hodgson

Margaret B.

Abigail Hodgson

Ashley Chris

JonnyMac

HERE'S TO THE UNDERDOGS!

Josiah Vincent

Carina Hight

Chloë Mali

Naomi Johns

Brooke Haines

Tatia Aussant

Holly Ciampi

Alexandra Willows

For more by Shannon Aardsma, visit her website at https://www.shannonaardsma.com/

Made in the USA
Columbia, SC
20 December 2019